LocoThology
Tales of Fantasy and Science Fiction
2012

Loconeal Publishing
Amherst

LocoThology
Tales of Fantasy and Science Fiction
2012

Arranged & Edited by Gary Wedlumd
Cover design © by Nathanial Stewart

Loconeal books may be ordered through booksellers or by contacting:
www.loconeal.com
216-772-8380

Loconeal Publishing can bring authors to your live event. Contact Loconeal Publishing at 216-772-8380.

Published by Loconeal Publishing, LLC
Printed in the United States of America
First Loconeal Publishing edition: August, 2012
Visit our website: www.loconeal.com

ISBN: 978-0-9850817-4-4 (Trade Paperback)

Table of Contents

Hot Encounter
by J. M. Odell

The place was pitch-black, warm, and wet. It stank like a cesspool. It also gurgled, expanding and contracting in a slow, steady rhythm. And it rolled, a long, slow undulation.

Alison groaned and pushed herself up on an elbow. She felt like she'd been hit by a freight train. Sweat slicked her flight suit to her body. Reaching over her shoulder, she found the neatly severed cords of her chute. Her auxiliary pack was still on her back, though, and felt fine. Maybe that mattered; maybe not.

She pushed herself to her hands and knees. The ground was soft and uneven. It felt like trying to maneuver in a bouncy castle. "Okay, I said I was up for a new adventure. This isn't what I had in mind. Is it someone's idea of a joke?"

The gravelly voice came from the darkness. "What do you recollect?"

Alison jumped. She squinted into the gloom, but couldn't see anyone. Nor did she recognize the voice. "I jumped, following my student. I'm a skydiving instructor, and it was his first solo. He was doing well. Then there was a hot blast above me, and, well, that's all I remember." She coughed. "I can't see a thing." Unzipping her suit, she rooted around in a pocket. "I have a lighter here somewhere."

"Hang on, I have a lamp." A pale, bluish globe flickered, illuminating a lean man with a dark beard. He was dressed in khakis and a jacket that looked to be made of pockets. "I've been conserving the battery while I waited for my matches to dry. Don't strike that lighter quite yet."

Alison frowned, but her attention was caught by her surroundings. The small, round cavity looked just like it felt, full of pillow-like mounds and bumpy protuberances. "Are the walls pink, really?" She pulled off a glove, and reached out. The side was firm, but her fingers came away sticky. "Yuck."

"Yeah. You're . . . inside a dragon."

Alison froze, and blinked. "Excuse me?"

The fellow held up his hands. "I know, but that's where you are. You were lucky. When it swallowed you, your parachute cords wrapped around its teeth. You'd have gone down its gullet, were it not for that. I cut you loose, dragged you here. This little spot is safe enough, but we can't go far." He pointed. "The gullet's down that way, nostrils are up there, and the gas chamber is further back."

"Right." Alison shook herself, and tried to make sense of his words. "Did you see anyone else?" Worry knotted her throat, and her voice broke. "Seventy-three jumps, and I've never lost a student—until now." It was the only job that had ever really suited her, the only one she felt she did well. This, however, looked like a colossal screw-up. Even if she could get out, how was she ever going to explain it?

"Here. This might help you feel better." The fellow passed her a metal flask. "My friends call me Sean."

"Alison." She unscrewed the lid and took a sniff, but in the general miasma, didn't smell anything new.

Sean's tone was gentle. "You said your student jumped first, right? Well, your parachute was roasted, but you weren't, and he'd be well below you. I'm sure he's fine, just a long way behind us. Dragons travel fast."

That was some comfort. Still, from what she could see, this made Ahab's time in the whale look like a minor setback. Lifting the cask, Alison took a big swig. It tasted vile and burned all the way down. She erupted into coughs. Fumbling, she screwed the top back on and passed the flask over. Her voice rasped. "What is that?"

"Home-brewed scotch. Rather young, I'm afraid. Life's too short to wait around." Sean held the flask out again. "Like another?"

She raised a palm and choked out, "No, thanks."

"Maybe later, then. How much fuel is in that lighter?"

Alison reclaimed her breath before she answered. "It should be full." She straightened and looked around. "Wait, you said something about a gas chamber. You aren't thinking to ignite it, are you? I'd love to get out of here, but there must be another way." She wondered which would be worse, being blown apart, or digested.

"Have another drink." He passed her the flask. "Let me tell you a story about a friend of mine, Stubborn Pete."

Alison took a careful sip and passed it back. The liquid still burned, but was more manageable. Maybe her throat had gone numb. "Shouldn't we be planning our escape?"

"Not just yet. Sit back, relax."

Alison pursed her lips, but leaned back against the wall of the chamber. Her stomach was still in knots. Waiting didn't sound like a good idea, but she didn't have a better plan.

Sean gave her an approving nod. "That's it. I'm going to turn out the light." With a soft click, the darkness returned. His voice turned chatty. "Now, Pete had brains enough to share with a friend, but not a lick of common sense. A hard worker, though. He'd put in twice the effort of most men just to avoid an honest day of labor."

Alison snorted. "He sounds like a real gem."

"Funny you should say that. Pete and I were sitting in the pub one day when we overheard a conversation. Turns out, one of the lads had a line on some gemstones, small stuff, easy to fence. Pete decided to get in on that."

"You mean, steal them?"

Sean chuckled. "Liberate, is what Pete would say. He tracked the lad back to a wholesaler. The building was tall and skinny, a real firetrap, only one door, and no windows until you got up high. It didn't look like much, but they'd invested in security. They were canny, too. Eventually, the other fellow gave up. Pete tried near everything, couldn't get in."

Alison coughed, and fanned her face. "Is the smell getting

stronger?"

"Here." Again, Sean placed the flask in her hand. "Take another sip."

"What if the gas gets worse and we can't breathe?"

"It won't come to that. Trust me. I've been in here a full day, and I've been studying these beasts for over a year."

Alison raised her eyebrows, though she knew he couldn't see. "You've been studying dragons? I thought they were a myth. How did you find them?"

"It's not easy. They avoid people. A dragon is a picky eater, except for a female getting ready to mate. Then she'll gulp down most anything. You happened to be in her flight path."

"And you? You said you know these creatures. How did you end up in here?"

Sean chuckled. "I was net fishing, hip-deep, when she swooped down for a drink. Dragons are amazing, can skim right over the surface. I couldn't get out of the way in time. Got caught in the backwash. I managed to grab a tooth, held on, and then crawled my way back here."

"Oh." Alison licked dry lips. She'd been swallowed by a dragon, only to find someone who sounded an even bigger misfit than she was. Wasn't life grand? She shook her head. At least his story was interesting.

"Anyhow, Pete just about gave up, but he came by the name 'Stubborn' honestly. He noticed an old cannon standing in a park, not far away. It pointed toward a window in that building. Pete got an idea. Worked out all the trajectories, but, well, I was concerned. Talked him into a different approach."

"What did he want to do?"

Sean sniffed the air. "We're getting close, I think. It takes her a while to replenish the gas. But I'll finish my story. I've moved around a bit. There's lots to see in this world. Anyway, I'd spent time with a circus, and still had contacts. I convinced Pete to join up, so he could learn how the human cannonballs did it without getting hurt. He did, stayed over a year, until he was ready."

Alison held up a hand. "Hold on. Are you telling me he planned to shoot himself through that window?"

"Of course, he didn't use the cannon. Even so, his plan worked a bit too well. Pete smashed right through, hit an interior wall. Good thing he was wearing a helmet. Sent gems flying everywhere, knocked him cold. The owners found him when they got in, called the cops, had him arrested."

"All that, and he failed?" Alison snorted.

"Well, not quite." Sean chortled. "Turns out, he wasn't unconscious the entire time. Pete realized he could get in but not out, not without help. So he built some clever hiding places into that helmet, and he used them. When he was searched, they didn't find anything. And they could see he hadn't moved much, hadn't tossed anything out the windows. The cameras would've shown. Pete was charged with trespass, but that was all. He played dumb, pleaded guilty right off, paid the fine. The police returned his belongings, including his helmet, and let him go."

"So, he got away with it. They didn't even know they'd been robbed. But, they must have been suspicious. Didn't they recognize him from his previous attempts?"

"I'm sure they did. Once they cleaned the mess up, they probably figured it out, but by then, I'd helped Pete disappear, in return for a cut. I bought a plane ticket and supplies, and I've been studying dragons ever since."

The air quality had gotten worse. Alison's lungs labored. She wondered about the tale, and why Sean had told it. "Are you suggesting we do like Pete did, and shoot out of here? Is that your plan?"

"I've been considering it. See, she usually expels the gas first. There's a tinder-tooth right under her nostrils. It ignites the stuff on the way out. If we fire her up in here instead, her mouth will act like the cannon. Most of the gas will be ahead of us. We'll have to pass through the tail end of the flame, but that's all. And that's where my plan ends, I'm afraid. We'll be in freefall."

"Can't we wait until she's on the ground?"

Loco-Thology

Sean turned his lamp back on. "Even if we landed somewhere safe, it would be like falling two or three stories, probably onto rock. By my calculations, she's over the ocean right now. Her route should hold, right over the major shipping lanes, and they're busy this time of year. Shouldn't be hard to find a ship. We'll have a good vantage, at least."

Alison touched the straps on her chest. She chewed on her lip, and considered the problem. "My suit is flame retardant, and I have a secondary chute." Unclipping her pack, she checked it over. It seemed all right. "No extra harness or drogue chute, though. You'll have to hold on, wrap your arms through my straps. I might be able to shield you and get us down. Without knowing how far up we are, or what the conditions might be, I can't be sure. It'll be dicey."

"It's still our best shot. Do you have your lighter handy?" Sean pushed himself to his feet, and led her forward, under the uvula. "I think we'll need to stand here."

Alison swallowed, but moved to join him.

The dragon's tongue quivered. Her teeth were like stalagmites. Milky-white, they came to mid-hip, and tapered to a point. Alison eyed them. They were the grab-and-swallow kind, not meant for chewing.

"Get ready to create a flame." Pressing himself close, Sean wrapped his arms through her harness. In the somewhat fresher air, she could smell the booze on his breath.

She wondered if he was combustible, too, but suppressed her snort. It was an idle thought, born of nerves. Alison had always expected an adventurer's death, but this was ridiculous.

Squaring her shoulders, she flicked the lighter. The flame caught. With a whoosh from the fireball, they shot forward. The dragon's maw was wrenched wide. Sunlight made Alison squint as they blasted out, into the air.

Sean wrapped his legs around hers. His weight unbalanced her, dragging her down.

They tumbled.

The cold stole her breath. Wind scraped at her seared skin.

Alison peered through streaming eyes. All she saw was blue and gray, featureless sky and ocean. Without landmarks, it was impossible to gauge distance. She fought panic.

Then, in the distance, she noticed a small plume of smoke. Alison squeezed her hand between herself and Sean. Closing her eyes, she pulled the cord, and hoped the chute would hold.

The weather was good. It gave her hope.

The chute flew open. It dragged them back. Sean was jarred loose.

Alison grabbed his arms before he could fall.

"Thanks." He tightened his grip around her.

Alison nodded. The chute held. She was gentle with the cords, but maneuvered them down.

The ship grew closer.

Her eyes skimmed the decks. She closed in to drop Sean on the aft deck.

Alison was now much lighter. A draft caught her. She flew sideways. Stretching, she caught one foot around the rail.

Sean grabbed her and pulled her down. "That was close." He steadied her.

A sailor skidded to a halt beside them, looking confused. "Where did you come from?"

Alison released the catches on her chute. It flew off.

Sean grinned at the sailor and pointed into the sky. "From up there. Emergency landing."

Shielding her eyes, Alison followed his finger. From this distance, the dragon was little more than a speck. It resembled a bird, winging away.

"Thanks for the delivery." Ignoring the sailor, Sean flashed a cheeky grin and offered her his hand. "So, for our second date, would you care to see what they look like on the outside?"

Maybe there was something to be said for misfits. They weren't dull, that's for sure. And, chances were, her days as an instructor were numbered. No review board was going to believe this. Alison laughed and took his hand. "This gig was getting old,

Loco-Thology

anyway. I think I really am ready for a new adventure."

About the author:

After wrapping up a career in Information Technology, J. M. Odell discovered a new obsession—writing. Her short fiction has appeared online in *Triangulation: Last Contact*, and in *Golden Visions*. When not scribbling, she battles weeds, weather, and wildlife for control of her garden.

The Sunmistress's Mending

by James Beamon

I cried out from nightmares and delirium as I woke. The yell was a hoarse, desperate voice that I did not recognize as my own. My body burned in pain. Later, I would realize that the smothering darkness oppressing me were the linen dressings that swathed my body and covered my face. Right now, I warred against the abyss, the searing hot black.

Gentle hands touched me, told me to ease back down. I listened.

"You are safe here, Sunmistress," a familiar voice soothed. It belonged to Various; I could almost see his concerned look as he comforted me with hands and words. He was right by my side, as he had ever been since I had taken up the Yellow Mantle.

I tried to talk, to say his name, to describe to him my pain so he could relieve it. Words came out as groans.

"Shhh," he said. "Do not rush speech. The battle is over. Rest now."

The battle . . . my nightmares had been real. It did not seem possible. How could one man wield so much power? How could anyone, much less one of the unwashed and godless, defeat the Children of the Lifecolors?

I could feel my hand in Various's. It was under this aegis of protection that I rested and healed.

Images of the battle plagued my dreams. Our armies amassed in the valley, our weapons gleaming in the light and warmth of Lord Sun. Their army, the undeserving, gathered atop the hill behind that old man.

To think, we laughed at the sight of him. A bony and ancient man with weathered skin as black as onyx, he looked as if he would fall at the first strong gust. His intense eyes were sunk into his skull while a disheveled mess of white hair erupted from it. Was this their leader or a jest meant to distract us?

Earthwarden began the charge at the head of his ranks. His invocations to the Earth Mother enveloped him and his followers in the brown shield of her protection. Earthwarden yelled her praises and a tremor of angry ground shot out ahead of them as a wave to crush the heathens.

The old man simply pushed. He pushed at nothing but air with his two gaunt hands and the powerful wave turned back. The tremor smashed into Earthwarden and his followers, breaking their ranks, crushing their bodies.

We all fell silent, sharing the absurdity and obscenity as we looked at the devastation that had only taken a second to reap.

Firetender, by his nature the quickest of us to anger, sounded his assault at the sight. His ranks glowed crimson. He called for blood. He summoned fire from the bowels of the earth.

The old man smacked the ground. Our men fell into the earth and dissolved in a lake of fire.

Just like that, the Lifecolors of Brown and Red were extinguished.

Blue and Green came alive in concert. They were the oldest of the mantle bearers, the most seasoned. The Green Mother called forth a legion of barbed angry vines from her ranks. Father Sea summoned a dominating wave of water from his.

The old man crossed his arms. Barbs turned and buried themselves into the faces of Father Sea and his men. The wall of water thundered down onto the Green Mother.

That left myself and Stormcaller. I saw him falter with a look of anguish and disbelief. But he set his face, and the gray glow emanated throughout his ranks.

I silenced Stormcaller. I had already seen too many of us destroyed. Despite tradition, I was going to call on my Lord, Overseer of all life, Master of the Lifecolors.

I alone glowed yellow. My Lord did not need an army of men

to commune with Him. I was the devoted maiden. The chaste one; I was enough.

I beseeched my master. Empower me, your mistress. Avenge those colors under you that fell. Burn the godless, those that would scorn the Lifegiver's gift.

I do not know what the old man did. But the world went dark, as if Lord Sun was eclipsed. We all looked to the heavens, but Lord Sun was naught. I feared He abandoned me.

Then I was surrounded by His warmth and light. Only I, His mistress, had His blessing, and I put my mind to turning the golden rays into the old man's ruin.

But the rays would not move. They turned hotter, brighter.

I called out to my Lord as my skin blistered. He was deaf to me. I screamed as the men around me disappeared behind the wall of white light, and my skin melted.

The scream followed me into the waking world. Various' hands and words found me again. They were my companions until I found sleep again.

Time passed in this manner, in ways I could not chart. The battle would haunt me countless times. Various was always there. He gave me water. He fed me cooled lentil soup through blistered lips. And I healed.

"Ever the watchful attendant," I told him one day. "You must get restless just watching me sleep." My energy was growing; I was spending more time in the waking world.

"Watching you rest is restful, mistress," he said. I imagined his smile behind my bandages. "It is watching you war in sleep that is not."

I could ask for no better companion.

Various told me three weeks had passed since the battle. Surely the new mantle bearers chosen to succeed the fallen were done learning the inner Mysteries. I feared that I would not be ready to march with them against the godless, but my nurse attendants told me I would be free of the bandages within another week.

"Do not fear, Sunmistress," Various said. "The indoctrination is taking longer than usual. They are initiating alternate mantle bearers for each Lifecolor."

This had only been done once before, during the Grave Plague. Alternates contradict the gods' promise of protection to the mantle. "What of our Lord Sun?" I asked.

"Soon there will be another Sunmistress junior to you."

I fell silent. Were we to break all of our covenants with the Lifecolors in our pursuit to bring the godless to the light?

The day arrived for me to shed my dressings. I became anxious. First the nurse attendants would cut my bandages and then bathe me in aloe milk. I would soak in that wonderful, warm tub of aloe milk until it turned cold.

I bade Various stay while the nurse attendants cut. I had no need for modesty with him; he had seen every part of me when I ritually bathed in the life-giving warmth of Lord Sun, as sacrament. I wanted him to be the first person I saw after so long in darkness.

The time it took to cut away the bandages was torturous. The light of Lord Sun got brighter for each layer they removed. And then I was free.

Oh Sun! His light was ever bright to my unaccustomed eyes. I held my hand up to shield them. Soon, my vision came. I saw Various and my heart fell.

The smile on his face was not that radiant smile I had imagined so many times in the darkness. His smile did not reach his eyes. I had never seen that look. It was pain and revulsion, as if it sickened him to look at me.

I demanded a looking glass from a nurse attendant. I gasped as I saw myself in the hand glass.

"You call this healed?" I screamed at her. She tried to explain things I cared not to hear. There was no explanation for this. "Your medicines were as prayers from the godless. Look at me!"

Various was looking. His look was one for lepers and mange-ridden strays.

"Leave me."

"Sunmistress . . . ."

"Out!"

He withdrew. I dismissed the nurse attendants as well. And I was left alone with the looking glass.

My skin was an abomination, a landscape of red angry sores and leaking blisters. My nose was a pocked and lumpy bulge. Where there had once been a vibrant field of golden locks there were now only errant, sickly wisps of yellow that clung wetly to my skull. I no longer had eyebrows.

I no longer had the strength to stand. I sank to the ground and wept into my marred, leathery hands.

After my tears had run their course, the nurse attendants showed me to the tub of aloe milk. They bathed me in silence while I stared at my own obscene reflection wavering in the milky surface. They let the air dry me because towels would rob my skin of the milk. Then they clothed me in a softened linen robe and led me back to bed.

The elders would come seeking council at any time and even in this condition I dared not defy their wishes.

Various led them in, as if he wanted to shield them from the sight of me until he no longer could. All three of them, the Warrior King, the Heart of the People, and the Voice of the Lifecolors stared at me for long, painful moments.

"Lord Sun shine on you all," I greeted them.

"Receive his rays as well," they intoned.

The Heart of the People ignored the chairs the nurse attendants had arranged for the elders and sat beside me on the edge of my bed. "How do you fare?" he asked.

"I live. I strengthen."

"Yes. I'm sure," he said with a smile that bled sympathy and sincerity.

The Warrior King and the Voice of the Lifecolors sat in the chairs. Various took up his position to my right. His face was emotionless.

"You look far from strong," the Warrior King said. "And I am loath to wait for your recovery, Sunmistress. The enemy breeds a better defense with each passing sun."

"I am stronger than I look, Warrior King. I will be ready when you sound the horn for battle."

"With your information, our armies will be ready in a week. Will you be ready as well, Sunmistress?"

"I shall. But I do not understand. What information can I give to you?" I expected the Warrior King to enlighten me, but the Voice of the Lifecolors rose from his seat instead.

"The key to destroying these godless black people."

"What key, Voice?"

"You alone survived the touch of that old necrow's corruption. You know what color it is."

"What he did . . . it had no color."

"Madness!" the Voice spat. "Mortal hands cannot turn aside gods and goddesses. He has the favor of a Lifecolor, a color we have not yet recognized. A Lifecolor who is angry because we do not exalt him. What did you see?"

I shook my head. "No color came from the necrow. They are ever godless."

The Voice made no effort to disguise the disgust on his face. He turned to face the Warrior King as he spoke.

"Then it is as I said before. These heathens draw their power not from a Lifecolor, but on the Deathcolor itself."

"Nothing living beseeches Black," the Heart said from my bedside. "To do so is to die."

"The proof is there, Heart," the Voice said. "It is etched into the very skin of these people."

"The plan holds," the Warrior King said. "We employ all of Life together to banish Death. Is there any other matter before we make tactics?"

"Just one more matter, Warrior King," the Voice said. He turned and faced me. "Ajinu," he spat the name, my name, something that was never said once a maiden became Sunmistress. "You are now junior to the new Sunmistress."

"What? Why?" His words were a stranglehold.

"You are supposed to be a reflection of our Lord Sun. Now the very sight of you taints His perfection. It is a blasphemy for you to be His mistress, just as surely as if a man had defiled you."

"But . . . but He still blesses me!"

"As He blesses us all, Ajinu. Consider yourself favored to remain in His sight and as the next nearest hopeful to becoming His mistress."

I could not find the words for protest. Even if the words came, how could anything I utter sway the decision of an elder? They were the living embodiment of the Will, Word, and Warmth of the gods.

The Voice addressed Various. "Follow me to the Sunmistress. I must inform her of her ascension."

Various hesitated for a moment as he looked at me. It was a moment curtailed by a brisk nod of his head as he walked out behind the others.

I was left alone.

* * * * *

The nights leading up to the march, I slept restlessly. The old necrow came to me in my dreams. I knew his visit was something more than my own making.

"Why have you come to me?" I asked him. "Are you to finish what you began on the battlefield? I am yours to murder. Or have you traveled through dream to laugh at my scars? Your laughter drowns in the ranks of thousands."

His voice was gravel. "I have spared you to change you. The ways of your people are a dungeon, your own arrogance a warden. Now the warden is dead. Walk free of your prison."

"I'll see you burn for what you've done!" I screamed. But I screamed into the void, as he had gone from me.

The days of that week were a listless existence. My only companions were the occasional shuffle of nurse attendants as they went through the daily routine of their occupation and the sound of my own mouth as I chewed food.

The old man came to me again, this time with a question.

"Why do you seek to subjugate us?"

"You refuse to prostrate yourself before Lord Sun and His children. The Gods of the Lifecolors cannot tolerate such blasphemy. The godless will be made to heel."

The old man smiled. "All who cannot show you their god's color are godless. Child, do you think that neither the sun shines down upon our faces, nor that the rain blesses our crops as it does yours?"

Waking up, I instinctively looked for Various. Then I remembered he was not here because I was no longer his duty. And I laughed at myself for all the foolish fantasies I had ever entertained, girlish notions impossible for one whose body was reserved for Lord Sun.

Restless now, I lay in the dark, thinking things I never had before. I wondered why Lord Sun, whose power had filled me so many times in the past, chose to share His light and warmth with those that would scorn His greatness.

The old man came again the night before the march. He brought with him a cache of many colored chalks and papers.

"Show me the color of your lord sun."

I picked up the yellow chalk. He presented me a sheet of white paper.

"Draw for me his symbol so that I may see it."

I drew the circle, His everlasting presence. Then I crossed the lines through the circle from east to west and north to south. His presence radiates to all corners.

The old man crumpled the paper without so much as a glance. He presented me another sheet of paper, this time yellow in color.

"Draw for me his symbol so that I may see it."

I tried but the yellow chalk would not show beyond the yellow of the paper.

"How can I when everything is the same?"

But the old man was gone.

That morning I awoke to a blonde wig at the foot of my bed.

There was only one person who thought enough of me to defend me from the jeering stares of others. The hair was vivid yellow, every bit fitting for the Sunmistress I no longer was.

I loved and thanked him a hundred times over.

Thus I began my second trip to the heathen lands, this time in a supply wagon instead of the carriage reserved for mantle bearers. I did not let the heat of Lord Sun nor strangers' stares break my demeanor.

The Warrior King himself led our men. The first night we made camp he called to his tent all the mantle bearers and successors.

"I am taking no chances on suppressing these heathens," he told us. "When I give word, all of you will call to your Lifecolor. Alternates as well, not just the mantle bearers."

It was blasphemy of the highest order. Everyone's protest was sharp.

"The Lifecolors are gods. And we have already defied their wishes by initiating alternates. You cannot break the covenant to sate your whims," Green said.

"One chosen bears the mantle. One chosen communes with the god," Brown recited.

"I am not interested in the teachings, mantles," the Warrior King said. "I am interested in success. Their will done. I am an elder, the Warrior King, the Living Testament, the Judgment of the Heathen! Who are any of you to question my decree?"

The Voice of the Lifecolors and the Heart of the People had not come with us. The Warrior King's word was absolute.

"This could be a good thing," Stormcaller told everyone. "The black man's power is great."

"Hmph! No power is greater than our Lord Sun," said the new Sunmistress. She cut her eye at me and continued. "At least not when His blessings are fully bestowed. I do not like your plan, Warrior King, but I heed and follow."

Brazen heifer! Her mind was wet from the ink of the teachings, her foot a virgin to the battlefield. She had not seen what

Stormcaller and I had.

It was all madness. We were to heed and follow a chain of blasphemies from the Will of the Gods to punish the godless for their blasphemies.

When we were within a day's march of their border, the old necrow came to me in dreams again.

"You have not stopped your army. Have you learned nothing? They will be destroyed, down to the last."

He spoke bereft of arrogance, all of it matter of fact for him. We would be destroyed if we continued. But of equal fact for him was the idea that I could stop it.

"What can I do?" I asked him.

"Once you have learned, teach."

I woke up certain that, between his power and our own blasphemies, we were marching to our doom.

I tried to make sense of all he had shown me in that last day's march. What was the source of his power? One god? Many? Was it truly the Deathcolor... and did death overrule all life?

I saw the hill in the distance with its tiny camp and many specks that were getting bigger every step. I thought of how Lord Sun had been shining on them this whole morning and how He would continue to shine on them long after we had perished.

At the base of the hill, with our armies amassed and at the ready, I looked up at the old man. He had not changed, but he seemed so much stronger than the last time we'd met here. He kept his eyes fixed on me, and the sadness in them was unmistakable.

The Warrior King drew up to the front and faced his army.

"Mantle bearers! Alternates! Commune with the gods. Unleash their fury on my command."

Our men became a rainbow of colors, a landscape of blues, greens, reds, grays and browns. The Sunmistress glowed yellow. I closed my eyes and saw a piece of yellow paper.

I felt Lord Sun blessing me with the full measure of His power, even though I was no longer Sunmistress. I no longer thrilled at the feeling. I no longer could. What happened to 'one chosen bears the mantle, one chosen communes with the god'? Where had everything sacred gone?

I pushed beyond the power I once rejoiced in.

I saw the sun for what it was. Unfeeling. Impartial. Deaf to us.

I felt the oceans and earth, fire and rains as well. I could feel the undercurrent, a moving force behind all the hollow colors we prayed to. The moving force washed over me.

It was so alive, so immense and so, so beautiful. I had never known such joy.

The old man was there. He smiled.

"You have learned. Now you must teach."

From without, I heard the Warrior King.

"Now mantles, now!"

I felt their streams go up, the waters and fires, lightning and sunburst. I took my hand and grabbed them, choking them out.

When I opened my eyes they were wet with tears, my closed fist still outstretched. All of my people were looking at me with awe and wonder.

"We must change ourselves," I shouted to them all. "We are better than the forces we pray to. We are capable of more than the harm we do for their sake. Lower your weapons."

"Who are you that we should listen?" the Warrior King asked. He looked to the Sunmistress.

I felt her reach to the sun from the undercurrent. I turned the beam on the Warrior King and turned him into dust.

"I am Ajinu," I told my people, "the one who has seen the death of our gods."

Everyone stared in mute shock, as if the world had frozen into ice. I had violated the inviolate. No mantle had power over the Warrior King, the living embodiment of the will of the gods.

And I had used what we held as the lord of the gods to unmake him.

"You have seen with your own eyes," I said into the silence. "Our ways are wrong. They must end. And you are the ones who must kill them. To do this you need to be braver than being ready to raise your weapons and die. You must be ready to lower your weapons and change."

"Lies! She speaks lies!" the Sunmistress yelled from across the field, her face screwed in rage. "Her falsehoods come wrapped in the garment of Lord Sun's light, but she is tainted, corrupted by the necrow. Do not falter before the gods. Gather to me, Children of the Lifecolors."

Various left the Sunmistress' side. He came over to me, kneeled down and took my fingers in his. His smile reached his eyes. I squeezed his hand.

Firetender went to kneel before the Sunmistress. Stormcaller came to me. His alternate chose the old ways.

The Sunmistress and I looked out over our people. They cast their gazes back and forth between her and me, their former enemies upon the hill all but forgotten. They fought a different battle now, much different than the one they had come here for.

And to those who were brave enough, I would be there. I had much to show them. I had much to teach.

About the author:

James Beamon writes because he has to . . . and he can't find anything worth watching on TV. But he doesn't need TV when his wife is a muse and his son is amused by the stuff he makes up. And the cat—well, the cat's not a fan of speculative fiction but has learned to attack on command. James calls Virginia home but his IT work takes him all over the globe. A quick peek into his mind and latest projects can be found at http://fictigristle.wordpress.com.

Dolls are for Kids

by Carrie Ryman

"In my day, we didn't need all that science. We girls were perfectly happy playing with our Barbie and Ken dolls."

My Aunt Miranda just didn't get it. She was a middle-aged technophobe. Why would anyone want to play with dolls that couldn't move on their own? Plastic dolls that couldn't talk and dance and laugh? My shipment of SimClone materials had just arrived in our airshoot, and I was eager to get started on building my first community. I was too old to play with dolls anyway. The SimClone kit was my 14th birthday present from my Uncle Max.

"Dolls are for kids, Aunt Miranda. And this isn't for fun; it's for school. Remember we get extra credit in Science, Psychology and Sociology. And we get double credit in Economics if we build a successful neighborhood."

"Yes, Audrey, I know that, but… it just seems wrong. Have you thought about how the Simpsons feel?"

"SimClones!"

"SimClones. They're made out of flesh and blood, just like you and me!" My aunt was almost shaking, and she slammed down the coffee pot for emphasis. I loved her, but I was glad she was only related by marriage. Clearly, I got my mellow personality from Uncle Max. My parents disappeared shortly after I was born. We think they were abducted. Anyway, Uncle Max and Aunt Miranda are the only parents I ever knew, so I try not to think about it too much or let it bum me out.

"But they're not humans," I continued. "They are partially synthetic humanoids. And, unlike humans, they have limited ability for complex reasoning–that's what Mr. Peterson says. Years of technology and genetic research went into designing them so they could be used for scientific research without the moral issues you'd have with real humans." I sighed. Sometimes Aunt Miranda was such a downer.

"Well, research or not, it's just not right playing with any living thing that way. Promise you'll be gentle with them, treat them with respect. I didn't raise you to be cruel. Audrey?"

I turned away and mouthed a profanity. I might have to re-think some of the challenging scenarios I had been planning for my SimClones.

"Promise?"

"Okay, Auntie. Okay. I promise not to cause them physical harm." I grabbed the circular parcel and turned away from her, mimicking her silently. Making faces always made me feel a little less slavish. Obedience didn't come naturally for me. Of course, I wouldn't physically hurt them. What did she think I was planning–a SimClones torture chamber? Psychological trauma and heart-wrenching misery were much more interesting.

I made sure my bedroom door was locked before getting started. All I needed was Aunt Miranda nosing in to disrupt my creative flow. I was intrigued by the human condition and planned on going into psychotherapy or better yet, working in a psych lab, conducting behavioral experiments. I knew that SimClone research would look good on my resume and make me into a real scientist.

With the SimClones, I could create a neighborhood of very distinct individuals, all with physical and mental traits of my choosing and watch them respond and interact and create progeny. Then I could really have fun by adding conflict and challenges and observe how they respond. And when the SimClones grew too old or the relationships stale and predictable, I could void them and start over with new ones. At least that's what the online manual said. I wasn't sure if I could do that, terminate one. But I reminded myself that, despite Aunt Miranda's panic-struck concern, SimClones were not human beings. I planned to record everything and attach a copy of my SimClone research journal with all my college applications. I had the whole summer ahead of me with plenty of time to create, study and record.

I grabbed my mp5 tune-pads and stuck them to my earlobes. The urban beat of the Magic Pumpheads filled my ears and got me into creation mode. I extracted the contents of the SimClone kit to make sure it was all there. Instruction CD, a DNA seed drive for my computer, sterilized face masks, one pair of tweezers, six clone tissue molds, six DNA seeds, growth formula, growth lamp, disposable gloves and alcohol swabs. Perfect. The instruction CD was unnecessary. As soon as Uncle Max started dropping hints about my big birthday present, I found the instructions online and read the whole thing several times.

The first step was infusing my SimClone seeds with the personality and physical trait data that I wanted. I had been planning a database of traits for weeks so downloading the data into the seeds only took a few minutes. I took great care in labeling each seed so I knew which traits went into which clone. I used a simple nomenclature of A-D, with matching names to help me remember them. There would be Alexandria, Brandon, Cassie and Derek.

I decided to use only four of the kit's tissue molds to start, keeping two as backups in case I lost any. All four would begin life as young adults in peak physical condition. I donned a facemask and gloves and swabbed the cranial cavity of the first clone mold. Each pre-filled tissue mold was about 8 inches long, shaped in the human form and set within a blue metal box. They consisted of an opaque, white gelatin substance, but were firm to the touch. I carefully lifted one of my four programmed seeds with a pair of tweezers and tucked it inside the cavity. I labeled that one SimClone A. I chose the female gender, although cross-gender was also an option.

SimClone A or "Alexandria" would be the Athletic Aggressor, the outgoing leader. The association of SimClone A with its type A personality would make it easy to remember. Alexandria would have long, ash blonde hair and aqua eyes.

I proceeded to implant seeds into the others.

SimClone B or "Brandon" would be the bashful male who

appreciates and thrives on beauty. Brandon would have a passive temperament, with a fine-boned body, blonde hair, blue eyes and artistic skills.

SimClone C or "Cassie" would be the comedienne. She would be confident and sassy. Cassie would have shoulder-length carrot red hair and impish green eyes.

And then there was SimClone D or "Derek". He would be the dashing hero with a debonair, flirtatious nature. His demeanor would be impeccable. Derek's eyes and hair would be the color of dark chocolate. I designed him a lot like the hero in one of Aunt Miranda's romantic e-novels.

They would all begin life with equal intelligence. I wanted them to start off on a relatively similar playing field.

The last step was adding a few drops of growth solution. Then I lined up each mold, side by side, to rest beneath the lamp and flicked it on. 4:12 p.m. I recorded the time in my journal. The online instructions said: "You can almost set your i-band by it." Within 24 hours, I would have my first group of living, breathing SimClones. My chest felt tight with excitement.

I printed out a sign that said, "Do not enter. Scientific Experiment In Progress." After fishing around in my desk for a magnet, I stuck it to the outside of my bedroom door. The big bold letters on white onion paper looked official and serious against the silvery steel surface. Hopefully, Aunt Miranda would take heed and stay away. I didn't have to worry about Uncle Max. He respected my privacy and treated me like an adult, at least when Auntie wasn't around.

That evening and into the next morning, my level of anticipation grew. Each hour that passed seemed like an entire day. Luckily, Uncle Max had chores for me to do. Sweeping out the greenhouse and watering and fertilizing the plants took me most of the next day. Uncle Max, a brilliant horticulturalist, was a quiet sort, and I enjoyed helping him out there. I was sorry for the other kids at school who had to eat synthetic produce, and I sometimes shared my lunch with them. Real food tasted so much better, and anyway, manufactured plants were a real crapshoot in terms of chemicals and other crud.

Uncle Max lifted off his plaid cap and brushed a handkerchief across his forehead. Well into his sixties, he was still robust and his skin was brown. He reminded me of the antique furniture I had seen in a shop window, the kind that was made of real wood from trees. While most people wouldn't think of venturing outdoors without spraying on at least 400 spf sunscreen, Uncle Max went out brave and bare-faced.

I almost dropped a crate of tomatoes when my i-band announced the time. It was 4 p.m. Almost birthday time! "I gotta go, Uncle Max."

"Time for the unveiling, huh? Go on, I'll finish up here."

"Thanks!"

"Hey, Pavlov."

I turned to look back at him. "Yeah?"

"Good luck!"

"Thanks!"

I raced into the bedroom and lifted the lid of each SimClone tissue mold and watched them, notepad in hand. The sound of Aunt Miranda whistling in the hallway sent me back to the door to lock it. Back at my station, I heard a clicking sound. It grew louder. The molds were shaking.

"Damn." It was only my knee knocking nervously against the bottom of the desk. I took a deep breath and tried to calm down. "Act like a real scientist, stupid." I looked at my i-band. It was 4:13 p.m. "Damn." It was a favorite word, used often in the privacy of my own room. I jotted down notes:

June 18, 2136. 4:13 p.m. Lamp temperature is normal. No change in color or texture of specimens. Residual growth solution is present and stable. No indication of movement or sound from SimClones A, B, C or D. As long as I'm not wiggling the desk with my knees, I thought.

There was a rap at the door, and I jumped. "Do you have any laundry for me? Audrey!"

"NO! Go away!" I shouted, throwing my bedroom door a look that could warp the metal. Aunt Miranda had the worst timing. When I looked back at my desk, all four molds were bathed in a glow of intense blue light. It was so bright, I could no longer see the gelatin forms beneath it. Then a high-pitched wail rose from my work area. I plugged my ears and hopped up and down. It was happening!

"Audrey!" I could barely hear my aunt's hysterical voice amid the shrill screams coming from the vicinity of the molds. "Audrey! What are you doing to them? Open this door right now!"

I rushed to the door. The last thing I needed was her in my room, disrupting things. I opened the door and stepped outside, closing it behind me. "Auntie. That sound is perfectly normal. It's not them. They're not even alive yet." I placed my hands on her shoulders. "Will you stop worrying?"

"I'll stop worrying when you're done with this awful experiment. It gives me the heebie-jeebies just thinking about this going on in my own house." She put her hands to her face. "Oh! That sound. They must be in pain!"

"No. It's not them, Aunt Miranda. It's just the life essence you're hearing. It's a chemical reaction that is rejuvenating the DNA. They're not even alive yet. Now I have to go!"

"Audrey, this is making me sick, I tell you. Please, please don't go through with this." What a state she was in. Aunt Miranda's hair was sticking to her sweaty brow, and she pulled at the neckline of her jumpsuit with both hands.

"It's too late. I can't stop it now. Don't worry!" I closed the door and re-locked it.

The blue light had faded and the room was silent. I peered down at the clone trays. Four pairs of eyes blinked up at me.

It's alive! I thought, triumphantly, remembering a really old horror movie that Uncle Max and I once watched.

I quickly made notes, writing only a word or two at a time. My eyes darted back and forth between my journal and SimClones A through D. I didn't want to miss another second.

June 18, 2136. Approx. 4:16 p.m. Happy Birthday, SimClones. All four specimens are showing signs of consciousness. Pupils are reactive and functioning. I'd learned that one from a video on Med-U-tube. I turned off the lamp and moved a small penlight above them. I poised the tweezers above each one, waving them tantalizingly. Each SimClone reached up with tiny, milk-white arms to grasp the tweezers. Motor function appears to be normal. Skin tone is pale, but unblemished. Physical characteristics of SimClone A, B, C and D are as programmed.

"What in the blazes am I doing here?"

The first vocalizations came from SimClone A, as I'd expected. And as expected, there was a haughty indignation to her tone. Alexandria was the first to step out of the tray and stood, teetering on the edge of my desk. She looked to be just under eight inches tall so very little settling had occurred. Alexandria was a bit shaky from the ordeal of birth. I carefully picked her up around the waist, holding my other hand beneath her in case I slipped, and carried her to a plastic box that waited on the other side of my desk.

"Let me go! How dare you? And where are my clothes?" I felt a new emotion, hearing her little voice laced with fear, but partially disguised by words of bravado. Perhaps I was feeling maternal or maybe it was just pride of accomplishment. I wasn't sure which. I lowered her slowly to the bottom of the box until her feet touched down. The walls of the box were 22" high, a good three times their height, making it impossible for them to escape. Alexandria stood there, hands on her waist. And then she began to shake. I nudged her gently toward the back corner of the box where a pile of miniature clothing lay. She quickly dressed in the skimpiest outfit there, which made me giggle when I remembered her mock modesty just a few minutes before.

I decided to keep communication with the SimClones to a minimum, to speak to them only when absolutely necessary. I wanted their focus to be on each other and not me. This would enable a more realistic behavior study.

A faint rustling sound came from the area of the trays, and I looked back. The other SimClones were climbing out of the trays. Derek was helping Cassie out of her mold, gripping her delicate waist. Her red hair fell over his bare back as he lifted her up and out.

"There you go, madam," said Derek.

"Oh! Well, aren't you a charmer?" Cassie winked at him, then realized she was naked and covered her chest and nether regions.

Brandon stared in awe at everything around him, but took no notice of Cassie, who was fully nude and mere inches away. He touched the sides of the shining metal mold. He spoke in a very soft voice. "Oh. Look at this. And look at this! Oh!" And then he spotted Derek and he turned red from head to toe. Too bad that heterosexuality wasn't a programmable trait for SimClones. I comforted myself with another look at Derek who was a dark-haired Adonis. He would probably make anyone blush.

I was elated to hear that their communication skills were just as the manufacturer had promised. SimClones came into the world fully functional and with a firm grasp of whatever language one chose. I, of course, chose American English.

I transferred the rest of them gently into the box and leaned in closer to introduce myself. "Hello. I'm Audrey."

"Oh!" The girls made faces and squeezed their noses, and the boys waved their hands in front of their faces. "Someone forgot to brush her teeth this morning!" That was Alexandria. "And you don't have to shout, you big goon!" Yep, she was type A alright.

Derek doubled over, laughing, still unconcerned about his nudity.

Brandon and Cassie moved off into the corner of the box and grew busy rifling through the pile of clothing. Brandon was being particularly selective about his ensemble. Perhaps I made him too effeminate. Would he mate?

I covered my mouth and moved a little farther away. "Sorry," I said. "Well, I just wanted to say that you are all safe here and will be very happy and well taken care of, I promise. Now don't mind me, just go about your business."

They responded instantly by replacing my company with that of their own, which I liked and also didn't like. But at least it freed me up to start recording their behavior in my journal.

Over the next few weeks, I had few conversations with them, and they didn't seem to notice me much, if at all. Once in a while, I'd see Alexandria glancing up at me as she whispered into Brandon's ear or Derek would flash a brilliant smile up at me. He perpetually wore an expression that was part hammy actor and part politician. I guess it's hard to tell the difference.

I kept my promise to Aunt Miranda and didn't harm them. And they seemed happy enough. What was there not to be happy about? I provided them plenty of food and beverages and a warm place to sleep. I gave them everything they asked for, except for access to porn on my cell phone. I shut off that function after I discovered Derek engaged in a shuddering, sweaty display next to my phone one afternoon. It was disgusting.

Uncle Max built a proper house for them to live in a few weeks after they were born. It was similar to the box in that it was only open at the top, but it was sturdier with soft carpeting and had glass windows so they had more sunlight. I marveled at his handiwork, and the SimClones raced around excitedly the minute I lifted them into it.

"Now this is more like it! It's about time we got some classy digs," said Alexandria, eyeing one bedroom and bouncing on the bed.

"Thank you, Audrey! Oh, thank you!" said Brandon. He kneeled on the carpet and ran his hands over the soft texture. Then he rushed to the window and gazed out ecstatically. It was lined up with a vase of orange lilies that Aunt Miranda put on my desk. Brandon grabbed a miniature tablet of paper that Uncle Max had made for him, and he began drawing the flowers. Brandon was quite the artist.

The house was fully furnished with split sections for their privacy. I was particularly interested in how their sleeping quarters would be decided among them, as I provided only two double beds.

Surprisingly, Cassie and Derek took the first bedroom.

"What? No waterbed? Well, I guess we can make do!" said Cassie as she pulled Derek into her arms and fell down onto their bed. Then she jumped up and pummeled him without mercy with one pillow.

"Hey, watch the extremities, missus. You might be needing that one someday."

"I might be needing it sooner than you think," said Cassie with another wallop.

I didn't understand all of their grown-up talk, but I laughed and recorded as much as I could of it. They were engaged in a full-blown pillow fight. Cassie was winning. When their game progressed into a more sweaty affair, I turned away, feeling unnerved. It was still daylight, for God's sakes. I heard them exchange a long wet kiss. Yuck. My SimClones definitely had all their hormones functioning properly.

Alexandria claimed the other bedroom, and Brandon slept on the couch in the living room. I felt sorry for him, but I didn't interfere. Alexandria, with her quickness of temper, was not one to be crossed. And I guessed that Brandon, though he didn't seem afraid of her, didn't want to push her buttons either.

That night, I slipped out of bed and silently tiptoed over to the edge of their house. The feverish squeals of their pleasure, though muffled a bit by the wooden walls, were unmistakable. One peek through the window confirmed that Cassie and Derek were, indeed, getting it on. Their limbs were intertwined and pale in the moonlight. It was mesmerizing and also a bit embarrassing.

I pried myself away and headed to the bathroom, grabbing my notebook along the way. I sat on the toilet, jotting down notes of my observation.

A few weeks later, and it was a done deal. Cassie was puking into the toilet.

I brimmed over with the news at breakfast. "They're going to have a baby, Uncle Max. Did you hear, Aunt Miranda? Isn't that great?" She was still only lukewarm about the idea of my

SimClones experiment. But that was several notches higher than her initial reception. I often found signs of her presence in my room, like the vase of flowers, and I hoped she was not interacting with them in my absence. I asked her not to.

"No, that's not great," she said, dropping her fork onto her plate with a clatter. Great, here comes another lecture, I thought. "How are you going to give her proper pre-natal care? And what happens when it's time for the baby to come? Which one is it, then? The pregnant one? I hope it's not that sassy redhead. But then the stern blonde isn't much nicer. Why did you make the girls so snarky?"

"It's Cassie, the red-haired one. Derek is the father. Aunt Miranda . . . you're not talking to them when I'm gone, are you?"

"No. I told you I wouldn't, and I haven't. But I do go in there to clean from time to time, and I do have eyes and ears, you know. I don't see how it would hurt to talk to them anyway, Miss Smarty Pants."

"It would interfere with my experiment. So don't do it." I'd sounded a bit more commanding than I'd intended.

Uncle Max gave me a stern look and kicked me under the table.

I forced a pleasant smile and added, "Please, Aunt Miranda."

"Give me your word you'll stop this soon. It's just not right. Tell her Max."

Uncle Max looked at me, then back at Aunt Miranda, then at the door. I could tell he just wanted to escape. He hated confrontation of any sort.

"Well, yes," Uncle Max attempted to sound serious and upstanding for Aunt Miranda's sake. "You should think about it very carefully." That's what he always said when he was put on the spot or forced to go into parental mode.

"You remember I told you about Katrina's cousin, Denise? She's the one who gave me all her used SimClone clothes and home furnishings. Well, she got into Stanford because of her SimClone research." I tried to calm down, but I could feel my cheeks getting red with indignation. "Anyway, I'm just beginning my project. It would be a waste to stop now."

I threw my napkin down and left the dining room. Back in my bedroom, I slammed the door shut then re-opened it softly. I could hear my aunt and uncle talking out in the kitchen. Aunt Miranda's voice was raised in that shrill way when she was especially irked. More frightening to me was the hushed tone to Uncle Max's voice. I prayed that she wouldn't convince him to make me stop. How could she ask me that? I'd just started my research.

I decided it was time to change things up, rock the boat a bit. Adding stimuli was part of the process, after all. I brought out the old box and relocated Brandon and Cassie into it, along with the bed that Alexandria had been using, as well as a few other bits of furniture. At first, no one was happy about the change. Deprived of his art supplies, Brandon sulked in one corner of the box and slept on a chair. Deprived of Derek, Cassie stayed in bed and talked to her rounded tummy instead. Alexandria cursed up at me for stealing her nice bed. And Derek tore apart the living room in a fit of rage. He also glanced sideways at Alexandria to see her reaction to his bare-chested physique in action. I noted this, with delight, in my journal.

I was hypothesized that SimClones, who were designed without the complex morals of real humans, would follow their most animal instincts if removed from all rules of society, especially those that determined proper social behavior and rules of etiquette. In other words, I believed that Alexandria and Derek would soon be getting it on, and Cassie would be completely forgotten. I was also interested in seeing how the relationship between Brandon and Cassie developed.

A kiss! There it was. No more than three days passed, and Derek was already making the moves on Alexandria. I scribbled down notes of my observation. I knew she had been attracted to Derek. She never failed to twirl her blonde tresses when he was looking her way. And she was always especially nasty to Cassie. That was another clue. Girlfriends, they were not.

"What are you looking at, girlie?" Alexandria yelled up at me. "Why don't you get a life, you big giant?" She pulled Derek into another room and slammed the door. It didn't keep me from seeing them. But I always respected their requests for privacy, or at least tried to be less obvious when they voiced their objections. I always had my video recordings to rely on if my direct observation wasn't welcome.

Eventually, they forgot all about me again, and I went back to my overhead vigil by the desk. From there I could see into both the house and the box.

In the box, Brandon still kept to himself. He was eating very little. It seemed that he was as socially inept as they could come, satisfied only with a tablet of paper and a view of something beautiful. Unfortunately, that did not include women. Back in the drab surroundings of the box, all his passion for life was gone. I made notes and waited. I was disappointed that he still had not shown any interest in females, though I had caught him smiling suggestively at Derek once or twice.

I resigned myself to the fact that Brandon would never mate or reproduce. The idea of voiding him was tempting. SimClones weren't human, after all. They were lab-bred synthetic humanoids. It was no different than working with laboratory mice. But still... I knew I couldn't do it. The very idea filled me with nausea. I felt like a failure. A real scientist wouldn't let morals get in the way of important research. That way of thinking was so 21st century.

After a few weeks, Cassie's belly was significantly larger. She was waddling back and forth in the box with her hand on her lower back. The gestation period of SimClones was much shorter than human beings. Cassie continued to rub her belly and talk to it. She never raised her voice above a whisper so I couldn't hear what she was saying, but it didn't have her usual upbeat tone. I missed her entertaining sense of humor and sass. Maybe that's just what motherhood did to women. I'd have to read up on that and see if it was normal, an anomaly or just a SimClone thing.

My journal entries were especially important the next day.

July 24, 2136. 11:35 a.m. Cassie is showing symptoms of psychosis. She has responded to her isolation from her mate with increased repetitive movement and prolonged emotional detachment. She does not respond when spoken to by Brandon or me. She appears to be in the third trimester of her pregnancy, and has been increasingly sedentary.

Brandon is disinterested in his surroundings and has only made half-hearted attempts to communicate with Cassie. He has stopped bathing and is eating less each day. A large canvas and paints have been provided, but he has declined to use them.

Derek and Alexandria have been arguing on a daily basis. Alexandria has been observed slapping him on three occasions. Derek has responded by laughing and walking away. Their initial romantic connection appears to be completely severed, but I did not observe the impetus for this conflict.

July 24, 2136. 8:47 p.m. Cassie has gone into labor. She seems to be in a lot of pain. I have given her a carefully measured dose of anti-inflammatories, but they do not seem to alleviate her pain. Derek has responded to Cassie's screams by demanding a reunion with her. Alexandria has, surprisingly, also voiced some concern for Cassie and offered to help her deliver the baby. Brandon is in an emotional frenzy, urinating on the floor and showing signs of extreme emotional trauma. I have refused all their demands in an effort to push their emotions to a heightened state of arousal. This will garner the most interesting observations into the humanoid psyche.

Just after midnight, I relented to their demands. In an effort to provide more social support, I decided to relocate Alexandria and Derek to the old box. "It's about time, you stupid idiot!" said Alexandria as she and Derek climbed into my hand.

I lowered them both into the box, and Derek jumped out of my hand before I was even close to the bottom. Alexandria started to step off then stopped. She shot an angry sneer up toward me and ground her high heel into my palm of my hand. She forgot all about me once she saw Cassie in the bed. They both ran to Cassie's side and sat by her bed, sobbing.

Cassie delivered her baby at 2:13 a.m. The baby was still-born, unfortunately. Everyone was crying. Derek sat next to the bed, sobbing over and holding the dead baby. Alexandria sat on the bed next to Cassie, patting her hand. Brandon was as far from the scene as he could be, but he brandished a paper clip. It must have fallen into the box from my desk. He pressed one sharp end of it against his throat, threatened to commit suicide if I didn't get him out of the box soon.

"I'll do it. I swear," he croaked. "Get me outta this dark hell hole. I need light!"

I didn't want to move Cassie so soon for fear of more bleeding, but I promised him I'd move them all back to the house in the morning. I didn't want to separate anyone again, at least for a while. After giving Cassie some time to heal, I planned to start a second study, this time on the effects of sleep deprivation.

Speaking of sleep, I needed to get some myself. I reached into the box to extract the dead baby. It was half the size of my pinky finger. Cassie stared straight ahead. Derek fought to hold onto the child and kicked my hand a few times, but I had to remove the baby due to the foul smell. I stepped into my personal bathroom and dropped the baby into the toilet, then pressed the vacuum button. The fleshy red speck disappeared in a swirl of air.

I noticed that the bedroom was unusually bright. How much time had passed? It was much too early for dawn. I stared out my bedroom window. It was still night outside. But the room was bright like a white light had been turned on overhead. It was eerie.

Something jarred me, and I lost my balance, stumbling to one side. The whole room and everything in it began to shake. Was it an earthquake? We hadn't had one since the tectonic plates were fused. My shelves crashed down to the floor, ebook discs flying off. I fell down to my knees, grabbing the fibers of carpet between my fingers to hold on. It felt like the whole room was turning upside down.

I heard a roaring sound and then a horrible screech and looked up. The ceiling of my room was gone. I was frozen with fear when I saw what was there. It was incomprehensible and horrible, the most horrible thing I have ever seen.

A big giant's face stared down at me. His voice was deafening, and I cried out, covering my ears against the blast of his roar.

"Make a note that specimen 0002A, known as Audrey, has continued to demonstrate a lack of compassion and exhibits little respect or concern for the welfare of her wards. The specimen shows a marked disregard for anyone, including her family, in an effort to seek knowledge. Indeed, the desire for knowledge seems to be prevalent in all humanoid forms, no matter their size."

About the Author:

Carrie Ryman lives in Mukwonago, Wisconsin. She attended Kent State University. Carrie has had her work published in *The Gateway Press, The Binnacle, The Awakenings Review* and www.bestnewpoems.com. Carrie has participated in CVNRA's Nature Writers' Workshop and AllWriters' Workshop. She has also provided poetry and fiction reviews for the *Sotto Voce* magazine.

Sleeping with the Fish

by Diane Arrelle

She pulled another pair of pants from the never-ending pile of laundry. Swiping her arm across her forehead, she inwardly cursed her stepmother, the king and her life. Between the hot black iron and the fireplace, it was stifling. No wait, she decided, it was more than stifling; it was hellish.

The only relief was the small breeze that occasionally drifted into the window overlooking the distant waves.

Oh well, she shrugged in resignation; she only had to iron clothes endlessly until she died. Mortality did have its perks . . . . It gave her something to hope for.

She picked the heavy, black iron out of the coals, and her arm started moving methodically once again, just as it always did, always had too. She glanced out the window at the greenish-blue swells and fantasized about a forbidden swim. She used to love to swim, back when her father had been alive.

Sweat mixing with tears dripped off her chin onto the trousers she was ironing and created little puffs of steam. Suddenly the iron stopped at a bump in the pocket. She felt like smashing the lump, but a small voice told her not to do it.

She looked around and found the source of the voice in the fireplace. She heaved the black iron at it.

The small fairy quickly dodged it and yelped. "Hey, is that any way to treat your fairy godmother?"

The girl snapped. "Some fairy godmother! You disappear while I'm at the damned ball and leave me there in rags. My stinking stepmother gets me trapped here for life by promising that dumb, inbred prince that I could spin straw into gold, so now because you went off on some vacation, I'm stuck ironing mountains of clothes for the rest of my days. I could have used a little help somewhere along the way!"

"That's right, always blame the little guy!" the small fairy snapped. "Look I'm sorry. You were my first gig, and, frankly," The wee lady with fluttering wings blushed a deep red. "I didn't go on vacation. I was . . . was . . . damn it, I was recalled and sent back for training."

The girl started laughing, "That figures. My life has been one disaster after another. First Dad croaks and leaves me with that witch and her ugly daughters, and they make me spend my days cooking and cleaning. The only pleasure I ever had was swimming in the waves over there, but now that's been taken away, replaced by even worse hard labor. And now I discover that my fairy godmother is a washout!"

The glow around the tiny fairy dimmed a bit. "Look, I'm sorry. But they've put me back and now I'm here to help you."

The girl sighed. "Fine! Grab an iron."

"Look, I really have come to help. Just take that wad out of the pocket you're about to press, and appreciate all the help you get. Not every girl gets a fairy godmother. Consider yourself lucky!" the fairy snapped, and with a tiny puff of jeweled dust, poofed out of the locked room.

The girl reached in the pocket and found a handkerchief full of beans. She studied them for a moment than groaned. "Yeah, what's this, a nutritious snack? Heck, I'd rather have a chocolate bar." She threw the beans out the window and leaned out to watch them fall the three stories to the ground below. She briefly thought about jumping out the window and enjoying a little free fall before the end, but wiped the sweat from her face and returned to her drudgery instead.

A rustling sound from outside startled her. She turned toward the window and gasped. There, close enough to touch, was a giant beanstalk. Without a moment's hesitation, she stepped onto the sill and hopped onto the stalk and started climbing up. She knew what would happen if she climbed down. They'd catch her and put her back. She gave one glance to the ocean waves crashing in the distance and thought, *if only I could escape to the water, I'd sail away and be free.*

She climbed upward effortlessly, her arms strong from the continuous ironing, and after a while she reached the fluffy white clouds and ascended through them. Finally, she reached the top and found herself outside a castle.

It was giant-sized. She walked up to it and went inside.

Then immediately turned around. It was filthy, and she knew that if she stayed she'd get captured and have to spend the rest of her days cleaning enormous messes. She started back toward the beanstalk when a boy rushed up behind her, pushed her down and screamed "Outta my way! It's coming!"

She landed hard in a sitting position and watched the boy run as he struggled to hold a golden treasure and a chicken. "How rude!" she yelled after him and then felt the clouds shake as giant footsteps approached.

She jumped up, ran to the edge and grabbed the stalk. Climbing down as fast as she could, she felt it suddenly began to rhythmically vibrate and sway. She gasped because someone below was chopping the base.

"Just great!" she mumbled and decided to take fate in her own hands. Pushing off from the beanstalk she leapt away from it and all the earthly restraints that trapped her. As she plummeted through the clouds she saw the ocean below her and steeled herself for the fatal impact. Even the one thing she loved, the sea, would betray her.

Just as she hit the water, it shimmered, grew soft and she glided into it. She continued her downward momentum, wondering why her lungs didn't burst.

The tiny fairy godmother appeared before her. "Got it right this time!" she sang and twinkled away.

The girl suddenly realized that she didn't have legs anymore as she flicked her tail and headed to the other mermaids swimming toward her. Maybe her fairy godmother had finally gotten it right this time after all.

About the author:

Diane Arrelle, the pen name of Dina Leacock, sold more than 150 short stories and 2 books. When not writing she is a senior citizen center director. She resides with her husband, her younger son and her cat on the edge of the Pine Barrens in Southern New Jersey (home of the Jersey Devil).

The Love Spell

by Gary Wedlund

My mauve toenails poked out from under the quilt. I wiggled them, but it didn't improve the look. Dancing under the moonlight during spring solstice had not been kind to my feet. I wondered what I had in my handbag. If mother didn't give me time to fix it, I'd have to wear the good Mary Janes I'd been saving, the ones with the soles that didn't flop.

At the bottom of the loft, Mother busily poked at a lizard, trying to keep it down in the caldron. The yellow ones were difficult. They tended to float after filling their lungs with air.

"Ummmm, smells good." I wrinkled my nose when she glanced away.

"You're late." She pressed my books and a burnt ladyfinger into my arms. "Take the trash bag to the creek on the way down the holler, you lazy wench."

I toed into my shoes and blew a kiss over my shoulder toward mother. As I started to leap through the door, she kicked it, bouncing me off the step and my feet into the mud puddle that mom said helped encourage the encyclopedia or Fuller Brush salesmen to go around back. Not that any were desperate enough to come our way without a compulsion spell.

"Don't forget it's your first day past solstice after your first moon time. Magic's mandatory, or the Lord will strike you dead!" Mother shouted without bothering to open the door. "And bring a plump one home, if you know what's good for you, you hear? Time you earned your keep!"

She meant . . . well, she had high hopes for me.

The burlap bag only had a little in it, thank the Goddess. I dumped corn husks, bark chips, assorted candle spoilings and a gnawed femur off the side of our tiny footbridge near the gravel road and left the bag hanging from a post, to pick up on the way back home.

I crossed then went back, throwing the ladyfinger over. It had a mauve nail. Coincidence? Hummm . . . I managed to forget most of our rituals in clouds of wine, but the revelation about the finger color matching my chipped toenails gave my stomach a flip.

And, I never ate ladyfingers, or anything with meat in it, else mother would win. I'd eat some onions on the way to school; they were everywhere.

On the four-mile walk, I had plenty of occasions to wash the mud off the patchwork hem of my supposedly virgin-white dress by visiting the creek whenever it crossed over the lane.

All my dresses were pale because mother said, "Better to see if you've cavorted with the Dark Lord."

This she hoped for, but I'd consecrated with the Lady of Light alone, and had no desire whatsoever to play with the Dark Lord half of the equation; under blankets, or clouds of wine or anything. No matter what mother and Aunt Hilda say about me being such a disappointment.

Maybe, when I graduated, a handsome and polite boy would like me and buy me a house, so I was saving myself, no matter how bad it got.

I had plenty of time before school. My mother had just wanted me out of the cottage. Someday I was going to make a sundial and she'd not get away with kicking me out without my knowing the time before I got to school. Electricity hadn't made it up our holler, so a clock was out of the question. I might have dawdled and even found some parsley leaves to freshen the baking soda I fingered over my teeth.

I painted my toes red on the front wooden steps, under the little steeple with the rope leading to the bulbous brass bell. I had a tiny corked bottle of house paint I'd borrowed from a big pail in back of the town's firehouse during our communal firehouse restoration, and used a stick with cat hairs glued to it. It took an hour to dry, but no one had shown up yet.

Way too soon, Emily Sue did. I bent between my knees and started blowing on my feet, real fast, getting lightheaded.

"What's the matter with you? Don't you even wear socks?"

She stepped out of her father's brand new Edsel. She'd said that from way over there, probably so her father could still hear how rude she could get. He smiled at her back as she walked my way, toting a brand-new—only-one-year-old briefcase for her books and fancy lunch of sandwiches and store-bought potato chips.

"I'm letting my toenails dry," I said. *Stupid, stupid, stupid; it will only encourage her.*

"I do that at home. You know, a place with walls and a roof, not aluminum and likely to blow away, along with the outhouse, in a tornado."

"If there was someone else here, would you be talking to me?"

"No." She sat on the grade-schooler swing, in her blue dress and socks, black and white saddle shoes and blonde, hot-curling-machine hairdo, gawking at my legs. The willow tree blew behind her, and for a moment she looked pretty.

"I want to be friends." My stomach churned. Sometimes I yearned to be the Dark Lord's and not the Lady's. That way I wouldn't feel compelled to say things that made me appear idiotic.

All of this reminded me that I was supposed to take my final leap as a full witch and do a serious spell today, as the day-after part of the ritual of the first solstice, post my first moon time. Oh, I'd done little things, but the rites brought great power, so I needed to do something, "particularly ugly," as my final test of post-pubescent maturity.

Turning Emily Sue into a frog seemed a good idea, but it wasn't the Lady's handiwork, and besides, there'd be hell to pay if I borrowed mother's crock without explaining. Then, once I'd explained, she'd gloat, want in on it and . . . well . . . thanks, but no thanks. I'd have to think of something else to do in order to prove I'd made the final jump into fullness.

And besides, who knew if I wouldn't screw the frog spell up and turn her into a pretty collie instead. Then I'd have turned to the dark side for nothing, having made her something everyone wanted to pet, or maybe even something that wanted to follow me home.

Aunt Hilda said I was the most powerful she'd ever taught, but I also screwed everything up because, "She isn't balanced by the darker male half!" Then she told this belief to everyone in the family.

Just about all the women in the coven had occasion to laugh about it; even while dancing sky clad under the moon, which is so embarrassing even Emily Sue's worst seemed silly. Nobody likes being laughed at, in certain situations more than others. I put my shoes back on, not too worried if I smeared or even stuck.

A few more kids came and huddled with Emily Sue, putting me out of my misery.

Miss Einsteed was having a frizzy hair day. It was all the static from the lingering solstice, but I didn't tell her that because she was Baptist. I knew a spell for her hair, though Miss Einsteed wouldn't have appreciated it and I didn't even bother with it for myself.

She didn't mind telling us about her beliefs all the time. I knew some witches who were Baptist, and I tried to understand it as a form of passion. Passion is blessed and a gift from the Goddess, so it's hard to fault.

Miss Einsteed always wore an enormous silver cross and held it in a bloodless-white fist while giving morning prayers. During these prayers it felt like she was looking right at me through her venous eyelids. She said her devotions with her eyes pressed so tight her eyelashes vanished. Everyone else shut their eyes too. I felt very weird watching and even weirder when Emily Sue peeked and caught me.

The prayers came right after we were made to stand, put our hands over our hearts and pledge our souls to the United States of America. It's how I learned my left from my right. During this I mumbled, "For witches stand," but only pretended to say the rest of it.

It seemed like everyone wanted a piece of my allegiance, but there was only so much left to go around. I was hemmed in by Miss Einsteed's Baptist God, the Dark Lord and the United States of America. Sometimes I think they were all the same.

That's why I like the Goddess. She's just good and unpresuming, unlike everybody else who wants something.

* * * * *

Afternoon break is my favorite time. Miss Einsteed lets the eighth grades through seniors out of the room so she can focus on the grade-schoolers. Usually everyone goes out front and mingles or kicks the liver ball. I used that time to run out back to the trashcan and see if there was anything good left from lunch before they burned it.

The bumblebees were pretty thick, but I untied my grey wool belt, did a swirl and caught their attention with my dancing. They flew into a swarm to match my body movements.

I pointed.

The bees chased each other over to the honeysuckle.

Emily Sue had left half a cheese sandwich, and George had only taken one bite out of his apple. That was plenty of food. I didn't need much and could forage on the way home, starting with whatever dripped from that beehive, dabbing it up with some of the honeysuckle tops they could do without.

"Trash picker, trash picker!" George stood at the corner of the schoolhouse with both fists on his hips. He smiled like he'd found buried treasure.

"I am not." I put the half-eaten sandwich behind me and wiped the apple juice off my mouth with a shoulder. "I was just looking for something I lost."

"What you got worth losing?" His smile broadened, and he motioned to those in front. Soon everyone came around to look at me, all twenty-three of them.

I dropped the sandwich back into the trash without turning around to see if I missed, then showed my hands. "I don't have anything. I was just looking for something."

"She's a trash picker," George said.

"Trash picker, trash picker." Everybody picked up the chant. "Trash picker, trash picker."

Emily Sue added, "She's just poor white trash, so it suits her. My mother says to stay away from poor white trash; they'll give you lice."

"Ohhh, I don't want her lice," Janice, Emily Sue's best friend, though only an eighth grader, said.

Everyone backed up like they were being careful, in case I chased them, giving them lice. They all went around front.

My heart sank. Next time I saw them it was just going to be worse. When I looked back at the sandwich lying on top of the trash, I realized I wasn't hungry anymore.

* * * * *

The last hour was a math test. I filled mine out fast, not caring much if I passed it, but wanting to finish first so I could run to the woods and get away from everyone's stares and taunts. Then what? Everyone would go home, and I'd not have made my final leap and proven to the Lady—so she would love me—and the Lord—so he'd leave me alone—that I was a witch.

Pulling one of Emily Sue's hairs on the trip up to hand in my paper proved irresistible. She slapped her head and said, "Hey!"

"Sorry."

I walked by George. He wore one of those new flattops, but I made my fingernails into tweezers and swiped one of his as well. "Get away from me, white trash," he hissed.

"Sorry."

"What's going on?" Miss Einsteed asked, having looked up from her work with an elementary student.

I handed her my paper. "I'm done."

She glared at the paper and then me. "Poorly, I assume. Were you hitting fellow students, Miss Browning?"

"She pulled my hair," Emily Sue said.

"Just one. Accidentally. I said I was sorry," I said.

"Maybe we should stay after school and help clean up after

everyone is released and enjoying the rest of the day?"

I asked, "Why do you phrase things like a question when you don't mean to?" I was genuinely curious.

Some of the younger children snickered.

"Do you want to make it two days, Miss Browning?"

"No ma'am," I said, though I really didn't mind. Cleaning up might prove helpful, in fact, and the longer you did it, the later you delayed going home.

When everyone left, I started sweeping.

"Make sure to move all the tables and get underneath."

"Yes ma'am." I moved tables and swept while she graded papers. "May I ask you something, Miss Einsteed?"

She looked up. I could tell by her eyes that she didn't like me.

I bent over and swept the day up into the dustpan. "Where do you think unkindness comes from?"

She looked back at her papers and answered, "Evil, pure and simple. There is either a love for the Lord, or a love for Satan. One cannot serve two masters."

I sorted through the dirt, carefully picked out all the hairs and put them into my dress pocket. "I think so too."

"What do you mean, Miss Browning?" She put down her pencil.

"I've seen things. Bad things. Enough bad things to not like bad things very much. And in school, nobody is kind to me. I don't know; maybe it's because I'm different. People don't understand people who are different, but I kind of like that part. It makes me feel better about the things I've seen."

"What have you seen?" She stood and gave me her full attention.

"Oh . . . things; nothing special."

"I see." She paused and adjusted her glasses while squinting at the door. "Do the other children taunt you, Miss Browning?"

"All the time, but I can fix it."

Miss Einsteed shook her head. "That will be enough for today. You should go home before your mother starts worrying. And try to not get into trouble tomorrow."

* * * * *

I walked past the county gas pump to the soda shop and mercantile, finding the third and final booth in back. There in the dark, I lit a tiny candle in the ashtray and made a circle around it in salt. I took three red leaves out of my bag to set them in a triangle. A dab of chrysanthemum oil sanctified each leaf. By the wandering glow of the candle, I wove the hairs into thread pulled loose from my ball of yarn.

Halfway through, Mister Simpson asked me if I wanted anything more than water. I said, "A bowl of vanilla ice cream."

He glared at my candle, but took my week's nickel and walked off to get my ice cream. I chanted, "Red leaves, from earth. Birth to death. Keep the Dark Lord's evil away. Goddess love to me. Love to me."

Someone put the new Elvis song I liked on the jukebox: "Love Me Tender", though "Don't Be Cruel" was closer to what I had in mind.

When I had three new strings, I wove them into a braided ring.

Mister Simpson came with the ice cream and said, "You can't burn a candle in here," like he'd been thinking about it for a while.

I kissed the ring and blew the candle out. "It's just a little one and safe in the ashtray."

"What's that all about, anyway? The candle, I mean? You over here in the corner of my shop, doing whatever you're doing?" He scratched a day-old beard under a screwed up face, looking like he was thinking I might be up to no good.

"I can't see what I'm weaving without a little light from the side. All the threads are tiny," I said, while I brushed my candle and leaves back into my handbag. "It's just a little light," I repeated while setting my ball of yarn in there as well.

"Just you watch what you do in here. I can't have you burning a hole in my table. If I knew you were up to something stupid, I'd kick you out."

Up at the counter, two girls from school were glancing and

snickering. One hid a Camel cigarette between her legs, maybe burning another hole near her hem, but I could see and smell the smoke and the nearby ashtray had new ashes in it.

Mister Simpson walked behind his counter.

I kissed the ring two more times, and said, "Let it be, let it be, let it be."

* * * * *

It was twilight when I passed by our little movie theater. George spotted me and came right up, making me cringe. He grabbed my arm, said, "I'm sorry for what I said today," and bought me a ticket to *Invasion of the Body Snatchers*. I couldn't put my head back because he held his arm around my neck and kept rubbing my shoulder.

His sister, Betty, shared her popcorn without my asking.

When it got scary and everyone started shrieking, I took a sip of her Coke because she was hiding her face in Billy's chest. But when she caught me she didn't seem to care and went out in the lobby to buy me one of my own.

* * * * *

It was really dark all the way home. I couldn't even see my feet. It was still a full moon, but a cold rain drizzled it out of sight. I used a borrowed newspaper for a hat, but the hat was limp as an old tissue by the time I tossed it in the raging creek on my way across our rickety bridge.

"Did the Dark Lord kill you for not doing a spell?" Mother asked.

"Uh-uh," I said before grabbing a potato out of the larder and sitting by the lantern to read the family grimoire.

Mother came closer, knelt on the floor and stabbed me with an eye. "What did you do? Tell me, tell me, tell me."

I showed her my ring finger while taking a bite of the raw potato. The yarn was mostly the color of blood. "I spelled them with their hair."

"Ah, haaa, haa, ha." She stood and turned, clapping. She nudged the curtain aside, looking out, as if expecting that I'd dragged home a meal. "What kind of nastiness did you make them do?"

"Something they won't like," I said.

Her clapping slowed, and she took a step away from the window pane. "I smell a fish. What's that mean?"

"It was a big spell; that's all that matters."

She put her hands on her hips and rolled her eyes. "What did you do, you useless worm?"

"I made them love me."

* * * * *

My red toenails were smeared and crusty in the morning sunbeam, and paint was hard to get off, so I didn't dare think about it. I leapt off the last rung of the loft ladder. My thighs ached from the bruises where mother had whipped me with the broom handle.

During my trip to the door, she held up the gleaming butcher knife. "If they love you so much, no doubt you'll be bringing one home, like I told you to yesterday. Don't forget to take them around back so it's tidy."

After running to the bridge, I vomited clear yuck over the rail. From the gravel roadway, I heard her screaming all the way across the holler, "Even if you don't want them to, I'm pretty sure one will be following the likes of you home."

I couldn't imagine it. My home wasn't fit for children. It wouldn't be fit, even if my mother didn't find them tasty and irresistible and worthy sacrifices to the Dark Lord. I tried to think of a solution, all the way to school, but nothing came to mind.

I arrived early, but so too did everyone else.

Emily Sue brought me a sack lunch with a peanut butter sandwich, bag of New Era potato chips and an orange.

Everyone put money in a jar. Billy handed it to me. "We took up a collection, knowing how you don't have anything decent."

Miss Einsteed asked me if I wanted to say the morning prayer. I was afraid that anything I said might cause something more to happen. I said, "Help us be good, stay away evil, and thank you for the presents," and left it simple, being careful not to say anything three times in a row all day long.

Everyone talked to me, but I didn't know what to say back. When the day was done—finally—I asked Miss Einsteed if I could stay over and help her clean, "Because I only got a D on my pre-algebra."

"Oh, that's no problem, dear. I'll give you some tutoring."

"No thank you. I'll figure it out and do better next time. All I want to do is help you sweep up."

The other children hesitated, but left because their mothers kept track of them. Several waited by the steps anyway. When I finished, Billy and Emily Sue waylaid me like bookends. We rode in the new-smelling Edsel all the way to the soda shop where it was their treat.

"I have to light my candle and do something," I said, getting it out and putting three red leaves around the ashtray.

"What are you doing?" Emily Sue asked.

"I'm making three strings and a new ring with it."

"What's the candle for?" George leaned a second straw toward me from his soda and kissed my cheek.

"Ummm. Well, when I wave the new string over it, it makes the string harder."

"Oh, like what my pa does with the ends of his shoestrings," George said.

"Uh-huh."

"You doing that again?" Mister Simpson ambushed us.

"She's just making a ring. We'll be careful," Emily Sue said.

George nodded.

"Well, keep it in the ashtray." Mister Simpson left napkins and walked away.

"Love Me Tender", played on the jukebox.

"Those words aren't right," I said.

"Oh, I love this song." Emily Sue swooned with her head and shoulders, side to side, while looking at me dreamily.

"It's almost right." I put the new ring on. "But for my ring it should go like this: Love yourself tenderly. Love yourself sweetly.

Never let yourself go completely. And always love you so. Make it so, make it so, make it so."

George sat back with a zombie stare.

Emily Sue stopped blowing bubbles through her straw and set her 7-Up on the table. She appeared as if she were about to drool.

"Well?" I let the word slip like a whimper.

"That's lovely," Emily Sue said, picking her 7-Up back up and taking a sip.

"You should consider being a poet." George smiled.

Emily Sue looked at the bubbles surfacing on her drink and said, "I don't know what they put in this stuff, but I feel wonderful."

"My head is like, whew!" George jerked.

Emily Sue laughed.

George slapped the table, making me jump. "You know what it is? We've stopped picking on Mary." He patted my arm and beamed.

"That's it. You're right, George," Emily said. "What was the point in all that?"

"We were such idiots. Mary's great fun. And a poet. She can keep us entertained." George bent over and hit his head on the table like he meant to punish himself by smashing the front of his flattop. When he came back up, he said, "I think the way I acted was all about me. You know, home and homework. Miss Einsteed droning all day, blah, blah, blah. Not that any of that is a decent excuse." He patted me on the hand again.

"Oh, I'm sorry too. But you would not believe my father. He is always in my face about everything. It makes me irritable." Emily Sue rolled her eyes. She put the back of her hand up against her mouth and whispered, "He called me a prostitute yesterday, just because I went to the movies. I just need to learn to cope and not take it personally."

I sighed, and thought of the only thing that came to mind. "That's terrible."

"Oh yeah," George said. "You wouldn't believe what some

parents do to kids. Hers isn't the worst story by a long shot."

I nodded toward George and hummed, "Um-huh."

* * * * *

I hopped up the three tall steps of the Trailways bus that came at seven o'clock every Thursday. It only took half the money in my jar to pay for a ticket all the way to Louisville. From there I went to the police station and told them I was an abandoned orphan of parents who beat me. They didn't believe a word until I showed them the bruises. I said, "I don't even have a birth certificate with a last name on it, but all my friends call me Mary."

They had to put me somewhere safe after that.

And regardless of where I ended up, one thing remained constant: I adored myself. You see, some of the hairs in that ring were mine.

Not only that, but Emily Sue gave me the most divine new pink for my toes as an unbeknownst goodbye gift. You would just love how they look in the early morning sun.

About the author:

Gary Wedlund is the author of *Abi Shaman Within, Search for the Queen, The Condotte's Daughter, Zombies in Our Hometown* and *Atomic Zombies*. He is a member of the Ohio Writers and North Columbus Fantasy/SciFi write groups and the Columbus Writing Workshop and contributes toward the improvement of writing, right here at Loconeal Press.

Penra's Folly

by Angie Hodapp

Castle Osidria's south wall rose high above the Penra Canal. My great-grandfather, King Clydus IV, cut the canal through the mountains to connect the harbor west of the capital with the Gillogavi Sea to the east. He imagined he would stand atop the wall and watch the crimson sails of the merchant ships pass below. He imagined he would fatten his treasury by charging the ships tolls and taxing their wares.

My great-grandfather was an idiot.

To begin, he failed to cut the canal wide enough to accommodate the reach of even the smallest ship's oars. That aside, he ignored the Yano ambassador who explained that in Yanoi, *Gillogavi* means *ship breaker.*

Osidrian merchants who traded with the Yano Islanders laughed at both the canal and its architect. Even if they could sail it, why bother? Why risk the Gillogavi Sea only to be tolled and taxed for the privilege of passing into the harbor when they could ride the trade winds south, sail up Osidria's western shore, and spend their hard-earned gold dropping anchor in every port town's brothel?

I am yet a young woman, a virgin queen, but even I understand that simple men make simple choices.

The merchants called the canal Penra's Folly. I imagine my great-grandmother reels in her crypt whenever her namesake is uttered thus. Yet to this day, seafarers swear by it to call the winds to their sails or calm tumbling seas.

Odd they should consider something so cursed a thing of good fortune.

I jumped off the wall into the Folly once, and not long ago. Gedeon's idea, not mine. I was fourteen and as in love with him as I knew how to be. I suppose I would have followed him through the Nine hells and back, or stayed there, had he asked me to.

I suppose I still would.

* * * * *

Three days before Gedeon and I jumped off the wall, my younger brother, Stiv, Osidria's crown prince, turned ten. Uncle Relliam took the day from sitting court beside our father to join us at the Folly. He spread his cloak on the rocky ground and sat, his back against a lichen-covered boulder.

Stiv delighted to have our favorite uncle in audience, but, ever anxious to join his friend, dove immediately into the cool water. I, however, took time removing my slippers and overskirts and did my best to appear indifferent as I looked for Gedeon among those already in the water.

My heart sank. He was not in the water, but sitting on the far bank of the canal beside Polly the tanner's daughter. I slipped into the water, then under it, and stayed there until my lungs burned for breath.

When I emerged, I heard Stiv call, "Watch me!" He swam to the base of the wall and began to climb. Water streamed off his skinny shoulders as he grabbed the first knobby stone, and then the next, and the next.

"I'm watching!" Relliam shouted. To me he said, "What is that?"

I squinted into the sun to see where he pointed. "A branch."

"That it is a branch is clear, Theanna. Why is it lodged in the wall?"

"It marks the highest climb. Whoever reaches it next will pull it free and lodge higher."

Relliam fell silent. He hooked a finger over his lips and gazed at the branch, nearly two-thirds of the way to the top of the wall.

Still far below it, Stiv overtook our cousin Colliver. Perhaps because it was Stiv's birthday, or perhaps because Stiv would be king, the older boy shrieked gamely and fell back into the water. Stiv laughed and continued to climb.

"How long has it been in its current position?" said Relliam.

"Since Summersdawn Eve."

"And who put it there?"

I glanced across the canal at Gedeon. His black hair hung wet to his sun-darkened shoulders. The sight of him lounging in the grass beside Polly Tanner clawed at my heart. As I watched, he whispered in Polly's ear. She turned her freckled face to the sun and laughed.

"That boy? How old is he?"

"Sixteen. Only just."

"A man, then, and not high born, I'd venture. Has he obligation to land or livestock?"

"Neither."

"Then what is his trade?"

I wondered at my uncle's sudden interest in Gedeon, but knowing my place, I answered simply. "He has none, Uncle, unless scriptor is a trade."

I had hoped this would impress him. Surely an apprentice in a Marestian scriptorium was more pious, more devoted to the will of the Nine than those who labored under some blacksmith or cobbler.

"Scriptor?" Relliam laughed. "No, scriptor is not a trade. A trade puts muscle on a man's bones, food on a man's table. By the Nine, he was handed a quill and put to work. Was he orphaned or abandoned?"

By the Nine? Stunned, I faltered and nearly slipped under. Outside the walls of the cathedral, it was profane to swear by the Nine. We Osidrians lived and died by the will of the Nine, who loved the motherless and unwanted as much as they loved the daughter of a king. It was written. Why should I not be free to love as the Nine loved, regardless of trade or station?

"Don't look so addled, Theanna. He was one or the other or the Nine take my tongue. Which is it?"

Again he had cursed. He had never spoken so freely to me, nor, as far as I knew, to any child of the court. Perhaps he no longer thought of me as a child. "Abandoned," I replied. "Left at the gate of the cloisters when he was newly born."

He crossed his arms and gazed past me. "Some children raised by Marestian charity speak the vows, but that one . . . ." He shook his head. "No, scriptor he may be, but he must swear freely. Mark me, Theanna. He will be forced to choose a life, and soon."

My heart weighed like a stone in my chest. It had not occurred to me that Gedeon might swear his life and loyalty to the Order. His love as well. The Marestians did not marry. If Gedeon took the vows, he would be lost to me forever.

"What if he chooses not to swear?"

"Then he will leave the city."

The stone dropped into my stomach. The water turned cold. "But why?"

"He is not Osidrian. Look at him. Who in the capital would give him work?" Relliam narrowed his eyes at Gedeon and tilted his head first one way and then the other, the way a butcher appraises an ox just before he scores its throat. "He has the look of the Yano about him. Tall, dark skin, wide at the shoulders."

"His eyes are green," I said. "As green as an Osidrian's. As green as the sea."

My uncle leaned forward and rested his elbows on his knees. "Theanna, what do you think? That you are free to choose a life with a motherless half-blood? You are the sole daughter of House Carvarick. You're fourteen. Your marriage will be a matter of diplomacy, and if your father has his way, it will be soon. In fact," He paused, and when he spoke again, his voice was low. "you should have it that King Ruiard of Kethedrus has sent your father letters on behalf of his son."

For a moment, I forgot to breathe. Why would my father wed me to that spoiled Kethedrian? What purpose would such an alliance serve? Osidria and Kethedrus had signed a treaty three generations before my birth. As far as I knew, the keeping of that peace had never required a marriage.

I tested the sharper edge of my tongue. "What malady prevents Prince Victasch from writing his own letters? Has he no hands? Or has he a simple mind? Please deliver my thanks to my father, Uncle, but no. I prefer a man who knows how to handle his quill."

A smile tugged at the corners of Relliam's mouth. I had not meant to be funny, only to declare my position. By the time he made to speak, a shout and a splash stopped him. We turned, saw Stiv surface and shake water from his hair.

"Did you see, Uncle Relliam? Did you see? I nearly made it to the branch!"

Relliam laughed and waved. "I saw you, Stiv! You're as strong and clever as our future king should be. But for Osidria's sake, I beg you, do not let your mother see you play at such risk."

Stiv grinned. Just then, Colliver swam behind him and pushed him under.

Curse you, Colliver! I tensed. My breath caught in my throat.

Stiv emerged. He sputtered and sucked in a strangled sob.

The other children in the water froze in their games and stared. Colliver threw me a worried glance. I kicked and made to swim toward my brother.

"Leave him," Relliam said.

I paused. "He's scared. He's choking."

"If he cannot be tempered by play, how will he fare in battle?"

"He's a child."

"He's the heir. *Leave him.*"

I looked back at Stiv. He flailed and coughed, trying to tread water while he wiped tears and spittle from his face. He watched me and waited for rescue.

My limbs felt leaden. I was caught. My whole life, I had been told that Stiv was my responsibility, that should any hazard befall him, the blame would be mine. Leave him? I loved my brother—I love him still—but for the first time in my life, I saw my future unburdened by him. It was a future of shocking brilliance, of terrible beauty.

I turned my back and swam to the embankment, then pulled myself out of the water. Despite the high position of the sun, I shivered as I yanked dry skirts over wet.

Behind me, Stiv grew quiet. The silence stretched into long, empty moments, but I refused to turn. Guilt prevented me from meeting his gaze or facing the stares of the other children. They, I knew, waited hungrily to see what I would do.

Eventually, they grew tired of waiting. Their clamor returned. I breathed.

"It's for the best, Theanna," Relliam said. At first, I thought he meant my leaving Stiv to settle his own scores, but he must have considered that matter settled. "Clear your heart of that boy, that Marestian orphan. He will bring you nothing but pain."

In a hurry to be gone, I tucked my slippers under my arm and walked barefoot toward the rocky path that led to the castle gates. I stopped just short of the dappled shade beneath the trees and spared a glance over my shoulder.

Polly Tanner was in the water with the others now, playing the captured maiden in a riotous game of Yano Let Me Go. Gedeon still sat on the opposite bank. His eyes met mine.

How long had he been watching? How much had he heard?

Nothing, of course. The canal was thirty feet across. Our voices could not have carried. But if they had, would he have cared?

Go rescue the maiden, I thought. I turned and stalked up the path.

* * * * *

Stiv's birthday feast was to begin at nightfall. Five-hundred Osidrian nobles were expected at the castle to eat and drink and dance and toast the health of their future king.

I should have been excited.

All afternoon, I had tried to get my mother alone. If there was any truth to Relliam's claim that I would soon be engaged, I needed to hear her deny it. Surely Relliam had been playing a cruel lark. Mother would never allow my father to ship me off to Kethedrus for a crown. But all day the preparations had overtaken her, and I'd received no such reassurances.

At sunset, I climbed the stairs to the castle's southern wall. Far below, the canal gleamed like molten gold in the sun's last rays. Beyond it, on the opposite slope, dusk had already swallowed the trees and cloaked the path to the cloisters in purple shadows. The path Gedeon would have already taken back to his home. I shielded my eyes and found the cathedral's spires halfway up the mountainside—nine white spikes stabbing skyward above the treetops. The bells would ring soon, three peals at full dark to call the Marestians to prayer.

I leaned over the balustrade. The branch, only fifteen or twenty feet below me, was long dead and dry as brushwood. The thickest part of it was perhaps no wider than my wrist. From it jutted dozens of smaller branches. Oddly, they all pointed skyward as though they were turning phantom leaves to the fading sun. I leaned farther, balanced on the toes of my slippers. What would it be like to jump, to fall free for breathless seconds and plunge into the cool depths of the Folly? The idea set my head spiraling. So far as I knew, no one had tried.

"What are you doing?"

I spun as though I had been caught stealing apple cakes. "Stiv, you startled me. What if I had lost my balance and gone over?"

"You were thinking of it."

"Not truly. I would be too afraid, I think. Wouldn't you?"

He squared his shoulders. "I'm not afraid of anything. I'm to be king."

Perhaps you should be afraid of that.

"Someday," Stiv continued, "I'll jump. While everyone is watching. Then they'll know how brave I am."

"Perhaps I'll jump beside you."

He pouted. "You won't. You're not brave enough. Just today, you were too afraid to put Colliver to rights when he pushed me under."

"No, Stiv. I chose not to help you *because* you are to be king. No small part of bravery is knowing how to fend for yourself."

"But he's bigger than me. He made water go up my nose."

"He was playing, Stiv." Annoyance edged my tone.

He sniffed. "When I am king, no one will dare push me. Just like no one dares push Father."

I sighed. He was ten. Only a boy. Someday he would understand. But not tonight.

I smoothed imaginary wrinkles from the shoulders of his doublet. "You look handsome tonight. Did you choose the silver-and-blue yourself? A good choice, either way. It makes you look quite regal and rather grown up."

"You fuss and prattle when you're troubled. Are you cross with Uncle Relliam?"

"Why would you think so?"

"I saw you quarreling today, at the canal. What did he say to make you leave?"

"There was no quarrel, Stiv. I wanted to rest before your feast. We'll have so much fun tonight, won't we?"

"You're lying. If he troubled you, I will ban him from the king's table tonight. I will make him sit at the far end of the hall with the minstrels, where he'll be served no wine and only the toughest cuts of meat."

I stifled a laugh and tried to match the formality of his decree. "Thank you, Stiv, but Relliam spoke sincerely of matters that do not concern you. In truth, I wonder if I offended him by leaving so abruptly."

The sun slid below the horizon, turning my brother's cheek from warm amber to darkling blue. "What matters do not concern Osidria's future king?"

I raised an eyebrow. "Mind your tongue, Brother. A good king knows when his offer has been refused, and when he has said enough."

His proud expression fell. Chastened, he nodded.

"Good. Now offer me your arm. It's time for your party."

* * * * *

The king's table sat along one end of the great hall. Six long tables ran its length, each laden with platters of roasted ox and smoked eel. Candles in pewter sticks cast the guests' faces in guttering light. Garlands of white elavieve blossoms adorned the stone walls, glowing like fireflies where the candlelight could not reach.

The elavieve was my favorite flower—nine luminescent petals arranged around a blood-red center. Once picked, it lived only a day. Legend held that it knew the hearts of those who picked it, and anyone wicked turned to stone. In ancient times, villagers called it the godsflower. They marched their accused up the mountainside and forced them to pluck one. Only the innocent came back down. Some say there are still statues high in the alpine meadows, each staring surprised at the small stone flower it holds.

Or so the story goes. I have never known the elavieve blossom to turn anything to stone, human or otherwise.

How many servants had been sent this morning to pick so many? How far into the mountains had they gone? I bit back a familiar twinge of resentment. My parents spared no extravagance for their son, their heir. They never had. To the nine hells that I had been born first. I had been born a daughter, and as such, my name did not appear on the list of succession. Should my younger brother die without an heir of his own, the crown would pass to my uncle. After Relliam, Matthis, his son.

I bit into a spiced apricot but found I had no taste for it. To my left, Father laughed uproariously and held out his cup for more wine, and to my right, Relliam sat in silence, his back pressed straight against his chair.

My uncle and I had not spoken since taking our seats. Now, as the musicians struck up a rondel and the sated guests pushed tables to walls, he leaned toward me. "Your brother does not have the deportment of a king. He never will."

I glanced at father. He had not heard. "Treasonous words, Uncle," I whispered.

"Truth is often thought treason until it is seen in proper light. Your brother is kind and gentle of heart, but he does not lead. He follows. You, I believe, he would follow to the hells and back."

"He is a boy. In time, he will learn a king's bearing."

"As a fish, in time, will learn to fly? No, Theanna. Stiv must not succeed."

My cheeks flamed. "You are next in line."

"If I wanted the crown for myself, why would I conspire with the king's own daughter?"

"For Matthis, perhaps."

"My son is lazy and impudent. He's no more suited for the crown than Stiv."

"My father is lazy and impudent, and the crown suits him just fine."

The deep resonance of Relliam's laughter echoed in the hall. Before us, my brother's guests formed circles and clasped hands. Stiv stood at the center of the circle nearest us, giggling and clapping. The dancers stepped in time to the drums and pipes. The circles began to turn.

My uncle leaned closer. "Like you, I have a king for a brother. But I was not firstborn. I have no claim. You, however . . . ." He leaned closer still. "You are a quandary. The Carvaricks have not produced a firstborn girl in nine generations. Nine. A conspicuous number, wouldn't you agree? You don't know it, but the kingdom is divided over your right to the throne."

My hands dropped to my lap. The dancers turned first one way then the other. Was it my imagination, or did several steal glances my way as they spun past? "Firstborn or not, a daughter cannot succeed."

"According to current law, no. But current law is simply a mountain that you and I must move."

I snatched a tankard of mead from the tray of a passing servant and guzzled it. Most unseemly, but who was looking? *Queen of Osidria.* So. Relliam had not meant to taunt me with the news of my impending engagement. He'd meant to warn me. The surest way to void my claim to one throne was to marry me off to the heir of another.

Relliam had also warned me to put aside my affections for Gedeon. Of course. There was the purity of the Carvarick bloodline to consider. If I were made queen, my marriage would not only be a matter of diplomacy, but of producing an heir.

No! I slammed the empty tankard on the table and ran a hand across my mouth. Stiv was the rightful heir, and Relliam a traitor. Tomorrow, once my father had sobered, I would tell him everything.

I pushed away from the table and rose. The drink, the music, the dancers—the room seemed to rise and fall around me. I felt tossed about like a ship in a storm.

Relliam closed a hand around my wrist. "Think long before you speak of this, Theanna. Your kingdom swings in an uneasy balance."

The only uneasy balance I knew at that moment was my own. I stumbled back a step. Relliam's fingers released me. I found my feet and fled.

* * * * *

On the night of any royal celebration, the children of the commoners gather along the castle road, hoping to catch a glimpse of the guests in their finery. They linger in the shadows just beyond the reach of the sentry's torches and wait for the rest of us to join them. They know, as do we, that once the dancing begins, the night belongs to us.

And so it was that hours after I had taken my leave of Relliam, I found myself crawling along the stone floor beneath the king's table. I was nearly a lady and too old to play at pranks, but Colliver and Roald had challenged me in front of the others. Having by that time drunk several cups of pilfered ale and numbed myself into the belief I had imagined my uncle's words, I considered the dare rather inspired, and I intended to settle it in my favor.

The dare was simple: steal a jug of wine from the king's table and escape unseen.

Twice I was mistaken for a dog. The first time I was kicked, and the second, I was thrown a scrap of greasy meat. I swayed on hands and knees, making careful, though bleary-eyed, progress until at last I sat at my father's feet.

"A raiding party could scale it blindfolded, given a grapnel and a bit of rope," I heard Relliam say. "A one-armed archer with an unstrung bow could send a flaming arrow over the top. Build it up, Clydus. It needs more height."

My head throbbed, but the sound of my uncle's voice sobered me a bit.

Father laughed. "What raiding party? What archers?"

"Listen to me, Clydus. The children who swim in the Folly climb it for amusement. They mark the point of greatest progress with a branch, one that tonight is lodged two-third of the way to the top. Just today, I watched your son—"

"Rellium is right, Clydus," Mother said. She shifted in her seat and crossed one leg over the other. The toe of her slipper nearly caught me in the side. "Build up the wall. Our son will be king. Would you not see him protected?"

"From what? Osidria has no enemies. I have made it so."

"Your father's father made it so," said Mother.

"All kingdoms have enemies," said Relliam. "All kings too. If not from over the mountains or across the sea, then in the heavens looking down."

"The gods?" Father laughed. "By the Nine, Brother, it was the gods who made me king."

"Then mind you say it was the gods who made it so," Mother said.

Father made a low sound in his throat, a growl meant to dismiss the unwanted counsel, to signal the end of the exchange. It was a sound I knew well.

"You endanger your people," Relliam pressed. "No man is more defenseless than he who falls under the protection of a friendless king who thinks himself well loved."

Father slammed his fist on the table. I jolted like a skittish mare and nearly knocked my cheek against his knee. His feet came down hard on the floor beside me, and he tensed as though preparing to rise, to strike.

At the other end of the great hall, the pipers struck up a branle, and the dancers cheered. A woman's voice, thick with drink, shouted, "To the center, Stiv! Our prince must dance!"

I sensed Father relax. "Fifty benneks," he said. "No more. I have better things to do with my gold than squander it on walls." Something heavy rapped against the table. "More wine!"

I scuttled away unseen and made my way through the kitchens, then through the door into the side yard.

"No wine," Colliver said.

Roald grinned. "You disappoint."

A lie. They had hoped I'd fail. Neither of my cousins, nor the scores of our friends gawping bright-eyed at me from behind them, craved the wine so much as the delight of watching me settle my debt.

Colliver took me by one arm and Roald the other. Solemn as executioners, they marched me through the castle gates and into the night. The rest—twenty of them, maybe thirty—trotted at our heels down the harbor road and sang crude taunts full of words we, at the time, only thought we understood. The cool air brought me closer to my senses, though my cheeks burned, and my head still spun. Inside, I felt numb.

My father was a foolish king. I thought of all the times I had seen him hold court, Relliam whispering in his right ear, Mother whispering in his left. Just as it had been tonight. Just as it had always been. Father was king by order of birth, but his brother and his queen ruled the kingdom. Relliam knew far more about what was good for Osidria than I had ever imagined.

And Relliam wanted to make me queen. What did he see in me that I did not see in myself?

The farther down the road we went, the harder my cousins' fingers dug into my arms. They expected I would lose my nerve and break free, dash away. And I could have. I was the king's daughter. No one dared make me do anything beyond my will. But I understood keeping true to my word and what it would mean to the others if I refused to pay my debt. So I plodded along between my cousins, placing one foot before the other.

The harbor came into view. Moonlight lay on the black water, a path that stretched from shore to horizon. The silhouettes of merchant ships rose and fell on the night tides like hulking, breathing beasts.

We came to the harbormaster's door. Colliver raised a fist to knock, but lowered it when a dark shape separated itself from the shadows where the side of the house met the wharf. Doremy, the harbormaster's simpleton son, stepped out into the light of the moon. A length of knotted rope hung from his calloused hands. Fearless, he regarded our strange assembly.

My cousins pushed me toward him, out onto the wharf. The others chanted their taunts and pressed closer to block my retreat.

I seized the front of Doremy's shirt and drew myself onto my toes. I kissed him long and well and did not stop until the jeers behind me dissolved into astonished silence.

Doremy neither resisted my kiss nor returned it, but I'm certain he tasted the salt of my tears. I had learned some things that night. That my father was a pitiable king. That Relliam was the wiser. That were acumen and not order of birth the standard by which rulers came to rule, my uncle would have the throne.

I would have the throne.

I pressed my lips harder to Doremy's and cried.

Would Stiv become wise and well loved? Would he still rely on my counsel, my rescue, once he became king? Or would he dismiss me as my father so often dismissed Relliam, marry me off to some lesser nobleman and have done with me?

I kissed Doremy's cheeks, one and then the other. I took his hands in mine and kissed the rough, work-worn skin that covered his palms. Were it not for the smell of his hands—fish and hemp, cold iron and the salty sea—I might have succeeded in imagining he was Gedeon. I pressed his hands to the sides of my face, then balanced on my toes and kissed him again.

At last I drew away. His hands still softly cradling my face, Doremy tipped his head as though he were waiting. Listening.

"I want to be queen," I whispered so that only he could hear.

The corner of his mouth twitched. The shadow of a half smile, nothing more. But his thumb tenderly brushed my cheek, and in that slight touch, that brief moment, I swear his silvery eyes held not the dullness of a simpleton, but the glint of understanding. No, it was more than that. It was *sympathy*.

The moment passed. Doremy stepped back into the shadows. He looped the rope around his forearm and glanced past me at the others. Then, without a word, he slipped inside the house and closed the door so gently I did not even hear the latch.

* * * * *

By morning, the story of the kiss had become legend.

There was the version in which I had also kissed the harbormaster himself. Another version included the Lymerian merchant who had dropped anchor earlier that day. Yet another version, every man aboard his ship. In the taverns, it was said with raised glasses that the ship's hands had worn out their oars rowing ship to shore for the pleasure of kissing the king's daughter.

The more pious among the gossips favored the account in which my kiss had cured Doremy of his affliction, and that in the three days since, he had not only been overheard reciting passages from the eight sacred texts of the Marestian holy canon, but had also written a well-structured treatise on the whereabouts of the fabled ninth. I liked this version and admit I was disappointed when I spied Doremy sitting with his back against the side of his father's house, working knots into his rope and staring idly at the sea.

Relliam was furious. Whether by his edict or my mother's, I was restricted to my rooms. My confinement, however, merely prevented me from going down the stairs.

Going up was another matter.

For two days I stood, elbows propped atop the wall, and watched the others swim in the canal below me. Stiv, Colliver and Roald, Polly Tanner. Dozens more. And Gedeon. Always Gedeon, sitting on the far bank, his sun-darkened face turned to the sky, his eyes on mine.

What did he think of me, now that he most certainly knew I

had kissed Doremy? Was he angry? Or was he indifferent? My heart ran a painful gauntlet as each speculation attacked from a different side. If he was angry, I was angry too. Didn't he understand about paying for a failed dare? Perhaps he was disappointed I'd accepted the dare in the first place. By the Nine, I was disappointed enough with myself.

Or maybe he simply didn't care. That was the most heartbreaking possibility of all.

By the third day of my confinement, my lonely postulations had nearly driven me mad. I'd received no word about when I might be released. Furthermore, I was left to suppose that Relliam was so cross over my behavior that any plans he had to place me on the throne were forgotten. But such thoughts only set me to thinking again about Gedeon. If I was not to be the queen, perhaps there still existed the chance, however slight, that I could choose him. If he wanted me.

If he wanted me.

Did Gedeon know, did he *care*, that when he kissed me on Summersdawn Eve, his lips had been the first to touch mine? Or that I had only kissed Doremy with such abandon because I had made believe he was Gedeon?

On that third day, I almost kept to my rooms. Let Gedeon wonder why I didn't come, I thought. But as the sun sank below the horizon, my resolve sank with it. I pushed open my door and dashed up the winding stone stairway to the top of the wall.

I didn't hear the soft footfalls behind me. I didn't see the shape that trailed in my wake.

Thinking myself quite alone, I leaned breathless over the balustrade. The canal was empty. Everyone had gone home. Tears stung my eyes. All the frustration and doubt, the longing and loneliness I had endured since the night I had kissed Doremy welled up inside me and broke free. Then, through my tears, I saw the branch.

Elavieve blossoms, hundreds of them, twisted around it. They glimmered in the near dark like stars. Someone had traveled high into the mountains to pick my favorite flower. And so many! Someone had twined each stem one to the next. Someone had left them where he knew I would see. Only one person could climb that high. My pulse leapt.

At that moment, Gedeon stepped out of the shadows on the far side of the canal. My breath caught in my throat. He held up a hand, a quick gesture that meant *stay there*. Then he dove into the canal, swam across, and began to scale the wall.

I leaned forward to watch him. My heart thumped inside my chest, a caged thing longing to be free. He loved me. Surely he loved me. Could I dare to hope it was true? He did not stop at the branch but climbed higher and higher still until he pulled himself over the balustrade and stood beside me. Water dripped from his dark hair and sodden clothes to puddle at his feet.

"The branch," I said. I could think of nothing else to say. "How did you—"

"Do you like it?"

"No. I mean, yes. Of course I do. What I meant was, you climbed *past* it. Why haven't you lodged it higher?"

"Why do you think?"

I stared at him in silence. All along, he was able to climb this wall. Why not stake the branch atop the wall for all to see and claim what was rightfully his? I couldn't imagine—not at first. But then I knew. Had he done so, the game would be over. The others would have nothing to strive for, no mark to surpass. No hope. Gedeon understood something I had not yet learned—that hope was no one's right to take.

I opened my mouth to tell him I understood, and maybe that I loved him, and that I'd give up everything—who I was, who I would become—to be with him, if only he'd ask. But Gedeon spoke first.

"I'm taking the vows."

A terrible chill trilled through my body. "When?"

"Tomorrow."

"But why?"

He took my hand in both of his and kissed the backs of my fingers. The touch of his lips left a bright spot of warmth on my skin. "Why do you think?" he said again. "If I don't, they'll send me away. And your uncle is right. No one in Osidria will give me work. If I do," He nodded to where the cathedral's spires rose high above the trees on the opposite side of the valley. "I'll always be near you."

"You'll be a priest." Tears pricked the backs of my eyes. "A priest cannot marry."

"And you'll be a queen. A queen cannot marry *me.*"

I stared at him. *A queen.* How did he know of Relliam's intention?

Gedeon answered my unspoken question. "Your uncle acts on behalf of the Order. Check the accounts of the Carvarick bloodline. A firstborn girl comes along every nine generations, but she never succeeds. She dies young, or she joins the Sisters of Maresti. But dig deeper, and you'll see that the deaths are suspicious, the vows forced. After the last queen was born, the king's council changed the law. They hoped eight generations would be enough to erase memories of old treaties forged between gods and men. Enough to silence the Marestians the next time a girl was born first."

"Me," I said.

"You."

A night breeze brushed my hair off my shoulders and ruffled the hem of my skirts. I shivered. "What treaties? Why should the Order care who wears the crown?"

"The Marestians are the keepers of the old ways. According to the ninth text of the holy canon—"

"There is no such text." Since I was old enough to sit still and listen, I'd been made to suffer through holy lessons. It was known that the gods never granted us a ninth. They left the cannon unfinished so that we would constantly strive to live in accordance with divine law. Only acts of goodness and faith would incite the gods to someday bestow upon us the final text. Not unlike dangling a scrap of meat in front of a dog, I'd always thought, to make him dance.

Gedeon smiled. "There is. I myself have made twenty-seven replicas of the ninth text since I joined the scriptorium."

My head swam. I fought the urge to lean against the balustrade. Whatever was coming, whatever I was about to hear, I felt I should receive it standing of my own accord. "What does it say?"

"The gods promised that every nine generations, only during the reign of a firstborn queen, they would venture from the heavens to walk among us. Miracles would occur. Faith in the divine would be restored, and the people of Osidria would be rewarded with eight more generations of peace and prosperity."

I shook my head. *One divine promise for another.* "Why would my ancestors have wanted to prevent such things?"

"Because, dear one, the only way to establish one's own authority is to discredit the authority of others. Even the authority of the gods."

Gedeon still held my hand. Warmth spread from his fingers to mine, but the rest of me felt as cold as the winter sea. If my ancestors killed their firstborn daughters to assert the primacy of their authority over Osidria, what would the Marestians do to assert theirs? I bit the inside of my cheek until I tasted blood. "What will happen to Stiv?"

"The Order knows you are fond of him, but they are angry with your family for betraying the Nine."

"They cannot hurt him. *They will not.*"

"If your father and his council stand in your way, do not doubt that your brother will be . . . removed."

Dizzying eddies of fear whirled through my head. I glanced over the balustrade. "And if he dies, it will be thought an accident."

"Yes."

"So I must choose. My brother's life or my own."

Below me, the canal rolled slowly past the base of the wall, a ribbon of black in the purpling dusk. The narrow canal, the inadequate wall—both were monuments to the folly of my ancestors. As I watched, the canal seemed to undulate like a snake, a cunning and patient predator.

"It would not kill you," Gedeon said.

"What?"

"A jump from this height."

"I know," I said, though in truth I was not sure.

"Then what is there to fear?" He shifted his grip on my hand so that we stood side by side, facing the balustrade.

My blood turned to fire. Flames pulsed through my veins. Jump? This was a dare of an entirely different sort, but a dare nonetheless. I recalled Relliam's command that I not go to Stiv's aid, that I not swim to his side and hold his head above water while he cried and gasped for air or admonish Colliver for playing too roughly. That was Stiv's trial as surely as this was mine. Only I would not fail.

My fingers tightened around Gedeon's. Tomorrow, he would take his vows. *Tomorrow—not today.* In this moment, he was offering me all he had to give. A leap beyond the reach of fear. Swift passage from our old lives to our new.

I kicked off my slippers and gathered my skirts in my hand, then climbed onto the balustrade and crouched there. Fearless, Gedeon leapt up beside me and stood. He offered me his hand, but I refused and rose to my feet alone. Another breeze blew across the top of the wall—no more forceful than the last, I'm sure, but it felt like a gale intent on pitching me over the edge. My knees quaked. I blinked down at the elavieve blossoms. They glittered like tiny jewels on the spindly fingers of the branch. The branch looked different somehow. Smooth and perfect. No less dead and dry than it had always been, but . . . strange. It was beautiful, really, in the ghostly glow of the godsflowers.

I inched sideways until I was clear of the branch. Gedeon did the same so that he stood to the other side of it. Both together and alone.

"Are you ready?" he asked.

I looked into his eyes. "I'm ready."

My toe found the edge. The hem of my skirt fanned out before me, fluttering like doves' wings on the cool night air. I held my breath and stepped forward into the void. In one dizzying moment, I felt my body tip beyond the clutch of my own volition.

"Theanna!"

Stiv? The voice called out from behind me, then above me. I was falling.

"Theanna, wait for me!"

Wind rushed past my ears. Down I plunged, both weightless and leaden. *I'm not afraid of anything,* my brother had said. *I'm to be king.*

You, I believe, he would follow to the hells and back.

"Stiv! No!" I screamed into the wind.

I hit the water kicking. Frantically, I tumbled in the cold, the sudden silence of the Folly. My skirts swirled around me, twisted about my arms and legs, bound me to the deep. Which way was up? I thrashed and fought for the surface. My lungs burned for air.

I knew, once Gedeon had assured me, that I would survive the jump. But would Stiv?

At last, I broke free. Blood thrummed in my ears. I beat the water with my arms. It splashed it into my eyes, my nose and mouth. I strained for breath. Gedeon swam hard in my direction, shouting words my mind could not decipher. All around me, black water rippled in the moonlight, the scales of a giant beast. I turned frantic circles, looking for my brother.

I could not see him. "Where is he?" I cried. "Is he under? Find him!"

Gedeon reached me. His shouts were garbled. Incomprehensible. He threw an arm across my chest and tried to drag me toward the far bank.

I coughed and sputtered and clawed at his arm until I broke free. "Stiv! Stiv!" Where had he gone in? Where had the surface been broken?

"Don't look." Gedeon had moved behind me. He hooked his arms beneath mine and tried a second time to drag me toward the bank. "I'm sorry, Theanna. I'm so sorry. I thought it was only a story! I didn't know what they could do. I swear I didn't know."

Didn't know what? I understood his words and the sorrow they held, but nothing more.

"The flowers were for you. A gift. On my life, I had no hand in this. Oh, Gods, Theanna, don't look up."

I stopped fighting, stopped breathing. *Up.*

I turned my face to the sky.

My brother lay across the branch, his small, still body faintly illuminated by the godsflowers. His arms were thrown wide to the sky. One jagged limb of the branch had pierced his chest. Another, his belly. A third, his thigh.

Even as the scream ripped from my throat, my mind refused to make sense of what I saw. Surely the gruesome tableau was staged. A farce. How could such a thing be possible? The branch was too thin, too dry and brittle. It should have broken under the weight of anything heavier than a bird's nest. Heavier than the rains in spring.

Heavier than a garland of elavieve blossoms.

* * * * *

Two years have passed since I leapt into the Folly. My father died not long after Stiv, of grief, it was believed. When Relliam refused the throne in favor of a seat at the council table, the council had little choice but to give it to me. The Marestians and their consorts can be quite persuasive.

In the months after my coronation, the people of Osidria claimed all manner of divine encounters. A mysterious stranger given lodging and a night's meal paid his penniless host a chest of ten-thousand gold benneks. Surely this was Elihu, the spider god. A merchant ship tossed about for hours on the Gillogavi Sea was inexplicably pushed against the winds and tides, away from the rocky shore. The ship's hands reported having seen a woman on board, a blue-haired maiden dressed in ribbons of kelp. They insisted it was Kiersa, the water goddess. A noblewoman who had died in childbirth, whose body had already been prepared for burial, sat up and tore the grave clothes from her limbs after a man unfamiliar to the family arrived and insisted the father lay the baby on the woman's breast. Vaari, the snake god.

Soon, miracles became nothing more than fortunate events. Thorny fields produced wheat. Sick oxen recovered. Creditors forgave debts. Mutes spoke.

Now, even that type of talk has ceased.

I once disguised myself and stole down to the wharf to see if such fortune had befallen Doremy. I found him sitting, as always, against his house, working knots in his rope and watching the sea. I stood far away and well in shadow, my face obscured by the hood of my cloak. Even still, he paused in his handiwork and for the briefest of moments looked into my eyes. He might have smiled. Then he turned back to the sea. Waited. Listened.

Fortune has no place in the hearts of such men. Doremy is among the lucky ones.

My first act as queen was to order the damming of Penra's Folly. Relliam insisted my treasury would not bear the expense. I ordered the castle's south wall built up. Again, my uncle denied me. My reign, he said, was blessed by the Nine. A wall of any height would make no difference.

Relliam suggested instead that I order the branch chiseled from the wall. I have little power and have accepted that I am the Marestians' puppet. But that I will not allow. Every generation must leave its folly. The branch is mine.

Every day, I have questioned the circumstances of my brother's death. Did he jump of his own will, or did someone—my uncle, I often suspect—goad him? Did Relliam throw him over?

I no longer know what I believe.

Gedeon is troubled as well. He wears the crimson robes of his Order and sits on my council. But he questions the very canon he spent his youth replicating and tells his confessor nothing.

Oftentimes I lie awake and recall how strange Gedeon's branch looked the night we jumped. How beautiful in the godsflowers' glow. Unyielding in the wind. Smooth as stone.

About the author:

Angie Hodapp holds an MA in English from Colorado State University and is a 2002 graduate of the Denver Publishing Institute. When she's not writing or reading, she's probably watching movies, hanging out at the dog park with her Norwegian Elkhound, or hunting for the perfect latte.

Unparalleled

by Susan W. Peters

Everythings's just a bit off
 in the perpendicular universe.

Lovers collide at right angles,
hunters aim at the sky,

crows lose their sense of direction,
shortcuts are longer.

Museums hang Jackson Pollock
top facing west,

explosions, quiet intakes of breath,
swallow silence.

About the author:

Susan Whitley Peters, a member of Kansas City Writers Group, teaches English at a local community college. Her work has been published in *Light* and *Kansas City Voices* as well as online journals, and has appeared in several anthologies.

For Lileas

by Gary Pattinson

Stars fled past the generation ship at near relativistic speeds. Mag-boots gripping the outer hull, Rorrie MacDougal heaved on the meter-long wrench until the airlock jammed. Father's cronies wouldn't be pursuing him out of Habitat Alpha now.

Across an expanse of hard vacuum, the vast cylinder of Habitat Beta, the ship's other living module, rotated on its axis. Rorrie's gaze caressed the greenhouse dome. There, nine Earth months before, he'd secretly wed Lileas, his forbidden love. Today, if he won out, he'd hold Lileas once more and kiss their wee babe.

The radio crackled.

"Rorrie, I'll not let ye unite the clans with that whore."

Father viewed everything through a political lens.

"Lileas and I will fight our way to each other's side if we must," Rorrie said. "I'm gonna claim them, Lileas and your new grand-daughter, blast you. Next generation makes planet-fall on New Scotland. The feud between habitats Alpha and Beta ends now."

A pause before Father replied. "Son, I see your mind is set—very well, the clan Beta bastards hold the port passageways, but my Alpha lads hold the starboard. Come and we'll let ye cross," his father said.

"Thank you, Father. I'm sliding the stairs to level nine. Headed your way," Rorrie said, giving lie for lie.

The clans always guarded the passages between Alpha and Beta, but no one ever considered the airlocks. Who'd be crazy enough to cross raw, empty space? Rorrie grinned, and with a flourish, he secured the massive wrench across his back like an ancestral claymore ready for battle.

His helmet tracked a reticle on Beta's distant hull. He signaled his 'puter.

In his mind's eye, Rorrie saw Lileas and himself, surrounded by children, running and leaping the hills of New Scotland as its three moons rode the skies like ancient gods.

Beta's distant airlock rose into view across just 300 meters of interstellar space. Just.

"Rorrie son, where are ye?"

The 'puter released his mag-boots.

Rorrie leapt.

For Lileas, their wee babe, and New Scotland that would be hers.

About the author:

"Weaned on fairy tales and hero adventures, Gary Pattinson read his first space opera at age nine. A Liberty Hall Writers denizen, his work has appeared in *The Drabblecast, Ray Gun Revival, Horizon, and Everyday Fiction*, among others. His blog resides at strangetidings.wordpress.com"

Butcherman

by James A. Ford

A tentative knock on the front door of the shop stirred Butcherman from his work. He took off his apron and washed his hands in the small sink next to his table.

"Yes?" he inquired before opening the door.

"It's Marshal Finn," came the deep voiced answer from the other side.

"Oh Yes, of course." Butcherman opened the door only halfway and slipped outside before shutting the door behind himself. The heat struck at once. It was not yet 11 am but already the sky seemed to blaze like an oven. Butcherman remembered stories his mother told him of another world, a world long ago when this far north the land was covered half the year in something cold called snow. She spoke of other animals, not just man, hundreds of types, some of which man ate. So hard to believe, like a fairy tale.

Marshal Finn had the glum face of a mourner. He was dressed in the elegant uniform of a military general. Tall, he had at least eight inches on Butcherman, but for some reason he seemed to be overshadowed by the shorter man.

"I just wanted to make sure that everything was alright?" Finn said.

"Everything is fine."

"She . . . was my daughter you know."

"Yes, of course I know. It will all be over soon. Don't worry," Butcherman said.

"She was sick quite awhile," Finn continued.

"I know, but there is no problem."

"I just wanted to check."

"I understand. Goodbye Marshal Finn."

"Goodbye."

As he watched Finn shuffle away it was hard to believe the man commanded the military troops for the town and several other towns as well. A man of decisive action, Finn had put down the Lacarnaro revolt in less than 48 hours. To see him now, though, one would never guess.

After another moment in the heat, Butcherman turned and went back inside to work at his stained table.

He was only the second Butcherman for this town. The first had served a long time and died while still in office, collapsing of a heart attack one afternoon on the very table at which this Butcherman now toiled.

Twenty-five years ago Butcherman had attended the special school in the capital city; had later honed his skills though the apprenticeship system, and finally received a Butcherman position in his home town, after his elder mentor's death from the heart attack.

That was his first job. The meat had been tough and disagreeable, but that had been expected, given its age. Tradition decreed that he, the new Butcherman, should share the meat with the whole town. That had only been possible after he'd minced it into a fine ground beef.

He had worked on it all day: chopping the choice cuts, then grinding them in the big old-fashioned grinder, mixing in onion and garlic; pepper and salt. Although it had been his first job, the results had made Butcherman proud.

These days he usually worked only a few days a week. Some weeks, if things were slow, he would still go in, tidy up and re-clean his knives and grinders. More often of late this was all he had to do. A Butcherman had a sacred duty to his own community. He could work outside of it only if given special permission.

He only worked when someone in his town died.

* * * * *

One morning a city official came to see Butcherman.

"Your new apprentice." He pointed to a large, well-muscled, young fellow.

"Hello sir." The boy tipped his cap to Butcherman.

"Hello," said Butcherman, barely giving the boy a glance. "I thought I had quite a few years left."

The official shook his head slightly and held up a hand. "Yes of course . . . it is not meant like that. We are simply instituting a new policy of earlier placement."

"Really?"

"Think of him," The official pointed at the new apprentice. "as a helper, to ease your work load. He will learn by doing, just as you did, but over a much longer period."

"But there is barely enough work for me right now," Butcherman protested.

"Don't worry, soon that may change."

"How? Do you expect everyone to suddenly start dropping dead?"

"No, of course not. Listen, just show him . . . ." The official searched for the boy's name.

"Carl," the boy provided.

"Just show Carl everything you do, and give him whatever tasks you see fit."

And with that the official turned and left.

Carl was a strange one. Butcherman decided this right away. Within days of the boy coming to work with him he found the young fellow's eagerness almost offensive. *Did I seem this way to my mentor when I first started? Probably.* Carl was almost in a hurry to learn the trade, and that was not right. There was nothing Butcherman could point his finger at and say, "Ah Ha," but there was definitely something. For instance the boy was always asking about Butcherman's long career.

"You must be very satisfied, you know, to have worked so long for this town?"

"Yes . . . Yes . . . I guess I am satisfied with the job I have done. Why?"

"Oh no reason. I just wanted to find out if, overall, you think you had a pretty good career?"

"Yes it has been fine." Butcherman found such talk tedious.

"You are probably looking forward to retiring? You are at that age, I believe."

"Somedays, perhaps." *So tiresome.* Butcherman had not really given retirement much thought, but he resented Carl reminding him of it. What would he do with himself? Perhaps dying on the job, as his mentor had, would be the best way to go. Then he could truly become part of the community.

* * * * *

One morning Butcherman couldn't find his favorite knife. He'd last seen it with Carl the day before and thought the boy may have taken it to his room and forgotten to return it to the utensil rack. It was Carl's day off so Butcherman had a look in Carl's small, dingy room at the back of the storage building.

There was no sign of the knife, but Butcherman found something else: A letter sat in one of the desk drawers. A set of instructions printed on government stationary were addressed to Carl. Butcherman read, unable to believe at first. Then he spun around as he heard a throat clear behind him.

"Carl?"

"I'm sorry but they've taken the leap. It's policy now." Carl shrugged his heavy shoulders, pointing his chin at the letter. "The same will eventually happen to me. You see, there just isn't enough quality meat out there. We have to start harvesting."

"You mean murdering."

"Culling may be more accurate."

"Murdering."

"If you wish. It was determined that we apprentices would initiate the program through the existing Butchermen." He shrugged again and looked away. "I guess they figured you guys were already part of the system."

"What is next?"

"Soon, the program will be expanded to the general population."

"Who?"

"The old mostly; anyone over sixty will be harvested."

"Murdered."

"Whatever. It will allow the rest of us to live better lives."

"Sixty isn't very old," Butcherman said.

"No, you are right." Carl nodded. "You are proof of that, but I guess they had to start at a point where there's enough product."

"Product?"

"That is exactly what . . . it is."

"What happens when the *product* runs out, lower the limit to those over fifty and then forty?"

The new apprentice shrugged his shoulders and grinned, indicating the conversation was over. Butcherman looked at him and knew that what he had said made perfect sense.

"Be quick." He shut his eyes.

* * * * *

The new Butcherman worked steadily all afternoon. It was his first job in the position, and he wanted to do well. He had his former mentor to thank for the superb recipe he was following. It was all in the proportions: just the right combination of meat ground with onion, garlic, salt and pepper.

When he was done, he wrapped a portion of the meat for each family in the town. Larger families received more, single individuals the smallest. When he finished he placed the meat in his refrigerated truck, took a deep breath and drove off to meet the town.

About the author:

James A. Ford is a writer living wth his wife and two daughters in Ottawa, Canada. He is a fairly boring person, but in an interesting way. His stories though are never boring, to date he has over forty published. James has no plans to ever stop producing more.

Down to a Sunless Sea

by Anatoly Belilovsky

I could see everyone from my seat in the corner, everyone but Old Maksimych. Yury the Weasel played *v duraka* with Fat Van'ka; he kept glancing at his cards, as if searching for something he might have overlooked earlier. Nosy Nikolai blew cigar smoke at the candles in the wall sconces. Black Nikita, long parted from the hair that gave him his nickname, drank with the same diligence that made him the second best porridge minder in the Fleet when sober: second only to Maksimych.

"Hope he didn't die up there," said Nosy Nikolai. The smoke above him was thick enough to turn pinpoint candle lights into dim orange globes.

"Nobody's *that* lucky," said Yury the Weasel. He scowled at the cards in his gnarled fingers, as if sheer force of ill-will could make them amount to something.

I rolled my eyes at the ceiling, wishing I had the money to go back upstairs. Old Maksimych was still up there, and still at whatever he was doing—which, curiously, for the last hour had not produced any creaking noises.

"He could have deserted," said Nosy Nikolai. "Down the back stairs and keep walking. California is a big place. Not enough *Okhrana* to track everyone down."

Outside the window, Lombard Street dropped down Russian Hill and snaked back up again toward the Presidio like a giant gaslit leash, slack for the moment but unbreakable nevertheless. *Svyataya Anna* was waiting for us, a black ship in the black water of the San Francisco Bay, due to steam at sunrise.

"It's simple arithmetic," Fat Van'ka said. "He's a Chief Porridge Minder. If he does not waste his money, he can afford more time with the girls." He poked a skeletal finger at the ceiling, then flicked a speck of dirt only he could see off one of his cards.

The Weasel laughed. "You don't think he's wasting his money now?"

"He could just gamble it away," said Black Nikita. "*That* would be a waste." He raised his bottle to his lips and pointed its bottom at the ceiling; his *samogon* went down with the plaintive, high-pitched splash of the next-to-last mouthful.

"He could spend it to get drunk," said Nosy Nikolai. "But then he'd be a—"

"Then he'd be me," Nikita interrupted, "and you'd all think you see double at turn-of-watch."

That got a laugh, a syllable's worth.

"I'll give you this," said the Weasel. "Maksimych hasn't steered us wrong yet, here or in Yokohama or Manila . . . ."

"Or any other port," Nosy Nikolai said. "Knows his houses of ill repute, he does."

"Of *excellent* repute," said Black Nikita. "Best girls anywhere."

"Maksimych always says to treat the girls with respect," said Fat Van'ka. "Could be we're just getting back what we've brought in." He turned to me. "What do you think, Mishka?" he asked.

I shrugged. Thinking about Charlotte always seemed to bring me to the next day, when I would sink into the bottomless dark sea while some other sailor drowned in her bottomless dark eyes. Black Nikita glanced my way, uncorked a full bottle and passed it to me. The harsh *samogon* burned down my throat; tears poured from my eyes, chasing the vision away. I passed the bottle back in Nikita's direction, closed my eyes, leaned back. The armchair's gentle pressure on my back triggered in my body other memories of touch, ones I did nothing to dispel. I practiced living in those memories.

"Not a talker, our Mishka," said Nosy Nikolai and blew another smoke ring at the ceiling.

For a time, only the seagulls' cries and the rustling of the cards bent the silence. When at last we heard a creak, it was only

Maksimych trudging down the stairs.

Old Maksimych had the porridge minder's pallor, paler even than his fellow submariners, startling in contrast with the deep-tanned merchant deckhands. He had the porridge minder's eyes, too: quick to find their target but slow to leave it.

Only one thing about Old Maksimych made him different from all the other porridge minders.

Old Maksimych was old.

"I think I'll go relieve the boy on the night-watch," Maksimych said. "The kid should have a couple of hours here before we steam. It's important, at his age."

Nikita laughed out loud, almost spilling his drink. "Important? Like food and drink and limes and fish oil? As if lack of it could bring you to a bad end?"

Maksimych said nothing.

They teach you in porridge school never to trust a quiet pot. You have to think ahead of porridge: turn down water flow if you don't like how the pressure needle is twitching, or if the bubbles look too ragged in the boiling water. Or if the glow's uneven. You have to feel it in your gut when porridge does not look quite right.

Maksimych had that look about his silence.

"I smell a story," I said, more to myself than to the others, but then the room grew still, eyes flicking from Maksimych to me and back again.

"I didn't say anything," said Maksimych. He looked around the room. His gaze fixed on me rather longer than on the others.

"Exactly," said Black Nikita. "The only story worth hearing is the one nobody wants to tell."

There were nods around the room, and an expectant silence.

"A story," Maksimych repeated. "Not much of one, I'm afraid." His eyes widened just a bit, as if he'd spied a long-lost friend in the smoky recesses of the salon. "I knew this kid on the *Svyatoy Sevastian*. A bit like you," he said, jabbing a finger at me. "Proshka and I were apprentices together in the porridge chamber. A smart kid, took to porridge like a duck to water. You would think there really isn't much to porridge minding: one eye on the pot, one on the pressure gauge, a hand on the pump clutch—"

"What about the other hand?" Fat Van'ka cut in.

"You cross yourself with that one. Or slap your face if you feel like falling asleep. Porridge can kill you faster than British guns," said Maksimych. His eyes had gone dreamy. He was off on the familiar voyage now, telling the story the way we'd always heard it. "Sometimes you don't know what got you worried—"

"We want a story," whined the Weasel. "Not a minder school lesson."

Maksimych blinked like a man pulled out of a good sleep. He sighed. "The story is about Proshka, and he had a way with porridge. He'd sit there fiddling with the clutch, and the steam would stay steady at seven atmospheres no matter if the captain ordered the submersible to full speed or slowed to steerage way. Only one thing wrong with Proshka. He never went to a brothel. Not once."

"Didn't like girls, did he?" the Weasel said, sniggering.

Old Maksimych leveled him with a dead-flat stare. "He liked one girl. A girl he grew up with, in a village outside of Vladivostok. Every port we went to, he'd volunteer to stay on the ship, minding porridge. He kept saying he half understood how it worked; that he wanted to talk to Old Man Mendeleev to ask him how he got the idea."

"God gave him the idea," Fat Van'ka muttered. "God looks out for the Tsar of the Righteous. And for his Empire."

"Amen," most of the others mumbled, some with irony, but most not.

"God or *Leshy*," Maksimych said, "Proshka didn't care. He just wanted to know."

"Nothing wrong with that," said Black Nikita.

"You'd think so, wouldn't you?" said Maksimych. "Well, he got his wish. In port one day, the Captain got an envelope with sealed orders. Nobody knew what was in them, but he burned the pages, right in his cabin, and called in our Chief porridge minder.

Nikulsky told me later: the Captain wanted to know if they could go to eight and a half atmospheres of steam, and Nikulsky told him, 'Yes, if Proshka is on the clutch.'"

"Eight and a half," Black Nikita said with a curl of the lip. "I could do eight and a half in my sleep."

"So could I," said Fat Van'ka. "In a new boat. Beaded porridge—"

"Well, I wish I'd slept through that, too," Maksimych said. "It was December. We made a long surface cruise at six, then submerged and ran at three and a half for a day or so. Then we surfaced again. I heard some splashes. Then the Captain commanded, 'Full Steam!' and Proshka took over."

Maksimych stopped; sighed. He held out his hand. Black Nikita handed him the bottle without a word.

Maksimych took a long swallow, grunted, wiped his lips.

"I don't know how Proshka did it," he said. "He'd back off the clutch a second before I'd have done it, then pump more water a lot faster than I'd have dared. He redlined at seven and just kept going. The screw went so fast it made the sub shudder. He hit eight and a half atmospheres and stopped. I swear the needle shook less than the deck under my feet; less than my hands did, that's for sure.

"We heard the first explosions maybe an hour later. They were dull, rolling like a steppe thunder. Proshka and the Captain kept it up for a day and a half before dropping to cruise power. We even stopped the turbine and listened to the hull. The sea was silent; there was no pursuit.

"We put in at Vladivostok after that, and heard the news. Turns out the Fleet had mined every harbor where the Brits and the Americans had ships of the line: Scapa, Baltimore, Boston, Sydney, San Francisco. Even a place no one ever heard of, in the Sandwich Islands. One day they had the greatest navies in the world, the next—" He made a hissing sound like steam escaping from a porridge pot. "Gone. Right up in smoke, and nothing left but a lot of flotsam in the water.

"The Captain left the ship then, and came back with the Order of Svyatoy Georgiy around his neck. He went looking for Proshka to pin a gold Medal for Zeal on him. But Proshka was nowhere to be found. Even after Captain ordered all hands to the deck—no Proshka.

"Anyone else they'd declare a deserter and set the *Okhrana* on him, but this was Proshka the hero, and we had a good Captain then. Hardly ever had anyone whipped, and never without reason; not just us porridge minders, but even the deck crew. I asked him if I could go look for Proshka.

"Brave man," said Fat Van'ka. "Bad enough to have a man desert, but to cover it up—he'd'a been court-martialed himself if word got out."

"Told you he was a good Captain," said Maksimych. "So he gave me a silver rouble and a week's liberty. 'Your tongue will get you to Kiev' he said—never a truer proverb.

"Kind people pointed the way, and I found Proshka in an *izba* on the edge of town, the cleanest *izba* you ever saw, with a girl— well, maybe not the prettiest girl there ever was, but she had something better. Where she was was where you wanted to be. I couldn't blame Proshka a bit for running off.

"The two of them stood there, heads leaning toward each other like two old trees on either side of a creek. A pot simmered on the stove, cooking up something that made my mouth water.

"I told Proshka if I could find him, the *Okhrana* could, too, and then it's dancing off the yardarm for sure. Convinced him to go to the Captain, strike his head on the floor at his feet, beg to be allowed to beach.

"He did that. And the Captain picked him up off the deck, pulled the Medal for Zeal out of his pocket, pinned it on Proshka's uniform, and shook his hand. Then he punched Proshka, right in the mouth."

Maksimych reached for the bottle again.

"That's not a *good* Captain," said Black Nikita, handing him the bottle. "That's an amazing Captain!"

Maksimych took a long gulp.

"Don't keep us in suspense," said the Weasel. "What happened next?"

Maksimych handed the bottle back. "Proshka went down," he said, "bounced two or three times, slid halfway down the deck. The Captain picked him up again, sat him in a chair, and told me to get out.

Next thing I know, Proshka is hugging me and pumping my hand, thanking me, telling me that the Captain told the two of them to get on the next ship to Ceylon. He'd write a letter to the Admiralty, make Proshka a porridge maker."

"What's in Ceylon?" Fat Vanya asked.

"That's where they dig thorium, bonehead," Black Nikita snapped at him. "Don't interrupt Maksimych."

"Right," Maksimych said. "And porridge making, well, that's a whole different game. The porridge isn't behind lead crystal; it's in an open cauldron, thorium and porridge starter all mixed together, and they stir with graphite rakes, day and night. Most of them don't live longer than hatters.

"They say old man Mendeleev fiddled with thorium for ten years before he figured out how to make porridge out of it, and he was still alive then, so some get luckier than others. But Proshka . . . ."

"Three years later we put in at Colombo and I went to see him. He was dying, bleeding out from every place you could think of. Couldn't get out of bed, though when he saw me he tried.

"The girl was with him. Older, heavier, more tired. They still leaned toward each other when they sat on the bed, and their little shack was still a place I did not want to leave.

"I did leave of course, but not before they both thanked me, again."

"You are right," the Weasel said in the dead air after Maksimych stopped talking. "This wasn't much of a story. Tell us of the great battles in the old days!"

"Not much to tell of that, either," Maksimych said. "I only saw action once after the day we mined the harbors. Off Cape Hatteras, the Captain maneuvered till we all got seasick, shot off all our ammo from the deck gun. That was the last time we had trouble with the French. Weren't any sea battles after that, not worth mentioning. All the seas are Russian now."

Until that moment I had been content to listen to my elders. Maksimych himself had taught me always to look, to listen, to search for something that does not fit, and I had many questions about his tale: about words he had said in a hushed voice, odd pauses, furtive glances. I very nearly had it—

"What of the girl?" the Weasel asked. "Proshka's widow? Is she still alive? You ever see her again?"

Maksimych chuckled. "Sure did."

That was when it clicked.

"You should have married her," I said.

They all turned to me. "What did you say?" Maksimych said, looking me straight in the eye.

"You should have married her," I said. "I think you love her."

"Love her?" Maksimych grinned. "She's my age, boy. She's old. She's . . . ."

"Upstairs," I said. "She owns this house, doesn't she?"

Maksimych nodded, walked toward me slowly. Stopped with his face inches from mine.

"How'd you guess?" he said quietly.

"It's a place I don't want to leave," I said. "And my mouth is watering. And to you, it's home."

"It wasn't fated," said Fat Van'ka.

"We make our own fate," said Black Nikita.

"Some people get straight flushes," said the Weasel. "And some get flushed straightaway."

Maksimych rose, shuffled slowly to the staircase, looked up at it, then turned around. "We've a long day ahead of us," he said. "Let's go back to the boat."

"And you?" I asked.

Maksimych didn't say anything, not a word for a long time. Fat Van'ka went out first, Nikita right behind him. The Weasel and Nosy Nikolai followed, holding on to each other for balance;

neither had good head for liquor. Maksimych and I were the last men out. Both of us stopped in the street, turned around, looked at the house.

"I wonder if I'll see it again," I said.

"Shut up, boy," Maksimych growled. "Porridge has many ways to kill you. If you don't respect it, it will kill you. If you don't understand it, it will kill you. Running out of luck will kill you the fastest." He shook his head. "It's so easy to make a mistake. You put water on a fire—it dies. Porridge just gets hotter, and at those pressures, a little more water means a lot more heat. If you forget that, you'll have a face full of steam behind shards of crystal to remind you. And porridge, right there in the open. You'd see it glow, if you still had eyes."

"I know that," I said. "Why are you—"

"Because I know that look," he said. "And I don't know if I can trust you with porridge again. I don't want to get killed because this girl is all you can think about when you stand porridge watch."

"Why don't you desert?" I said. "You won't have to think about dying any more."

"You get to be my age, you don't think about *if* you are going to die, you think of *how*," Maksimych said. "You can be brave when the porridge finally gets you—the bleeds, the squirts, the tumors. You can be a hero and go down with a leaky sub, or lose pressure and get stuck in mid-ocean. Or you can do your best to catch the pox from a working girl if that's your last chance to die like a man." He turned, grabbed me by the shoulder, pulled, not too roughly. "Let's go," he said. "The others are halfway to the boat."

We staggered toward the berth in the darkness, wet April wind whipping dust into our faces and chill into our bones. Halfway down the hill we fell, got up, fell again and again before it sank in on our sozzled senses: the noise, the screams, the jets of fire pouring from broken gas pipes, and far down the hill Black Nikita, never too drunk to walk, crawling on his hands and knees like all the rest of us. We huddled till the ground stopped heaving. I ran back up the hill, Maksimych puffing at my heels.

The sun had not yet risen, but houses burned all around us, lighting our way even while they filled the air with smoke. The house we'd left leaned like a drunk, tiles raining from its roof, but fire had not yet engulfed it. I passed a row of crying girls, some dressed, some wrapped in blankets, huddling for warmth. None of them was Charlotte. A handsome woman, not young but not what even I would have called old, stood looking at the house, her face less in sorrow than weary resignation.

"Have you seen Charlotte?" I yelled. She shook her head, slowly.

I ran around the side of the house. On the side that leaned down I found her, standing in the second story window. Pieces of wood, tile and glass fell from the wall and the roof; Charlotte was bracing herself to jump into a pile of debris. I ran to where I thought she would most likely land.

She jumped.

I saw her face come at me. It seemed to take a long time, an eternity; the flickering fires lit her face, leaving her eyes dark, yet I was sure they were fixed on mine, and I could see a smile that did not slip even as she fell into my arms.

We tumbled and rolled, she coming to rest on top. I tried to breathe, but air would not come. Not until she kissed me, and then in great, gasping, shuddering breaths, tears running down my face—my tears, I thought, till I saw hers.

I was in no hurry to rise, not with Charlotte so close, but it was she who leaped to her feet and pulled me, up and away. The house fell behind us, and the burning city disappeared in a cloud of dust. We staggered out of the cloud, coughing and choking, holding on to each other. Dust hid everyone from us; everyone but Maksimych. I went toward him.

"Mak . . ." I tried to say, but choked on the dust. Maksimych looked at Charlotte so intently she lowered her eyes. Then at me, for just a moment before craning his neck to peer behind me. I turned, but there was nothing there but dust. I turned again in time to see Maksimych's fist. It was close, and coming fast.

Then I was on the ground again, in quite a bit more pain.

Maksimych leaned over me. "Be quiet," he hissed. He took my uniform cap from my pocket and shoved it in my face. The pain exploded; he had to have broken my nose. "Stay down," he whispered and disappeared into the dust.

"Mishka's dead," I heard him say. "A roof beam took his head clean off."

"Poor bastard," said Nikita's voice.

"God rest his soul," said Vanka's.

"The boat!" Maksimych said. "We can't help Mishka, but if the earthquake damaged the boat . . . ."

I heard their voices grow indistinct as they ran, fright-sobered, down the hill.

When I could hear them no more, I let Charlotte help me to my feet. The pain stopped as soon as I felt her arms around me; the world, the dust, the conflagration receded, and when her eyes released mine, I saw the older woman standing near, her face toward me.

"I'm sorry," I said.

Her face didn't move at all. Her eyes looked through me, past me, past all this world, perhaps into the next.

"I . . . I know he wanted to stay with you," I continued. "I'm sorry."

A gust of wind brought back a word or two of Russian; it sounded like Maksimych's voice, far away. They weren't clear, these words, but none sounded a bit like an apology.

Charlotte and I stood silent, too. I spoke barroom English at best, and Charlotte but a smattering of Russian, learned in—learned in a world that ended.

We let our hearts converse, each straining at the bars of its own rib cage, each beat a leap one made toward the other, never uttering a lie and leaving nothing unsaid. I let mine talk, and listen to hers, until the sun rose on the newborn world.

About the author:

Anatoly Belilovsky is a father of 2 who learned English from Star Trek reruns and went on to become a SFWA member with stories in *Nature Futures, Ideomancer, Kasma, Flagship, Andromeda Spaceways, Immersion Book of Steampunk* and other publications. He is also a pediatrician in New York. He blogs with regrettable irregularity at belilovsky.com.

Blood Born

by Meriah L. Crawford

Most people who experiment with calling demons don't survive that tricky learning period. If you call up a demon but don't do it quite right, the demon can't come all the way through. Demons apparently find this quite annoying, so they eat you and return to where they came from—usually leaving no sign they were ever there. And when the raising is successful? Carnage.

By the time I was four blocks from the construction site that morning, I could tell that the demon raising had worked. If it hadn't, the road wouldn't be blocked off, helicopters wouldn't be hovering overhead, there wouldn't be a dozen emergency vehicles with flashing lights parked in the road and on the sidewalks, and the scent of blood and death wouldn't be hanging like a haze over the whole area.

I considered turning around and driving off, but the officer directing traffic pointed at me and gestured toward the curb. I pulled over, and he held up a finger, signaling me to give him a minute. He spoke into a radio then stood waiting, looking nervously back at the site.

My client on this job was a developer who was building a ninety-six unit apartment complex on the outskirts of town, in an area that the city was trying to revitalize. For the last couple of weeks, they'd been having trouble with vandalism at the site. At first it looked like basic bored-kid stuff: discarded cans and bottles, small fires, candles, some torn clothing. But then I found a mound of disturbed earth and, buried a couple feet down, the bodies of three ferrets and a guinea pig. The next day, one of the workers was cleaning debris from a spot where one of the fires was set, and he found symbols marked on the concrete slab. The marks were faint, but they'd actually left depressions in the surface. Not much would etch concrete like that, and certainly nothing kids should have access to.

The officer finally headed over and I lowered my window. The faint scent of blood and viscera entered the car. From that distance, all I could tell for sure was there was more than one body, and it was bad.

The officer leaned down, his right hand resting on the butt of his Glock. "You Ella Farriss?"

"Yeah."

"Detective'll be over in a minute."

"How did you—"

He put up his hand to stop me and went back to directing traffic. Typical. Dealing with the police is definitely not the most fulfilling part of my job.

Until I became a vampire two years ago, I'd been planning to get my teacher's license and become a high school English teacher. But by the time the wounds had healed and I was well enough to start back at school, I'd lost all interest. In truth, my enthusiasm had started to wane even before that, but the aggression and adrenaline surges that vampirism brought made teaching children a very bad idea. Before long, I'd started doing what my mother liked to refer to as "odd jobs." The people who hired me, finding me through word of mouth, called me a "fixer." This time, it was looking like they'd waited too long before calling me in.

After a few minutes of waiting for the detective, I pulled my cell phone out and scrolled through the photos of the symbols again. The foreman had described them in a voicemail he'd left for me that morning, a little before sunrise. I'd been sleeping "like the dead," as my roommate often joked, so I hadn't heard the phone ring. Fortunately, the foreman followed up the call with an e-mail that included pictures of the marks, so I was able to do some research before driving to the building site. I'd learned that the symbols were traditionally used in demon raising—a very bad sign—but they were drawn crudely. I had hoped that meant whoever created them either failed, or succeeded only well enough to die in the process. So much for that.

Finally, I saw the detective in charge of the scene coming toward my car, and it was good news. Alessandra Pira was a tall, powerful blonde in her thirties. We'd bumped into each other twice before on jobs I'd done, and she regarded me with some suspicion, but also treated me with respect. I'd have preferred blind trust, but she was a good cop—maybe even a great one—and I knew she'd be willing to work with me.

I climbed out of my car as she came near and started to say hi, but I didn't get far.

"Ella," she said, cutting me off, "explain to me why your number is the last one the foreman called before he died."

I grimaced. I barely knew him, but he'd seemed like a decent guy, and I knew he had kids. "Damn," I said.

"What was he to you?" she said angrily. "Why did he call?"

"OK, OK, hang on." I explained about the job and showed her the photos on my cell.

She stared at them for a bit, then shrugged and said, "They must not have really been etched into the concrete, because there aren't any marks there now. In fact, that whole area is clean."

I raised my eyebrows, and her cheeks turned pink. The photos were pretty clear, but people are quick to bring on the disbelief and denial when it suits their understanding of the world.

I shook my head and said, "If I could take a look?"

"I shouldn't let you into that area, since it's part of an active investigation."

As soon as I heard "shouldn't" I knew she would, and with just a little bit of coaxing, she did. After clearing me past the police barricades, she told me that the foreman, who had died on the scene, had apparently lived only a few minutes after sending me the images from his cell phone. The other three dead were workers who'd also arrived shortly before dawn. No one else had died since then and there was no trail of blood or destruction, so I was guessing the demon was still there, but dormant in daylight. Thank the gods for that.

As we headed around one skeletal building—a three-story framed cube with no walls yet—she asked what the symbols meant.

"Oh, I'm not exactly sure. Some kind of devil worship nonsense, I think."

She gave me a mildly suspicious look, but let it go. "Any ideas yet who's been vandalizing the site?"

"Nope. I've only been on the case for a couple of days, so I'm really still getting started. Have your people been able to gather—" and I stopped there, stopped everything, because we'd come around a corner to where one of the men had been killed.

The body had been shredded. I couldn't even tell if it was the foreman. It was just a spray of blood and flesh, with bits of clothing and half a boot mixed in. The scent of spoiling meat flooded my nose, and it smelled . . . wrong. There were parts missing. A leg and some organs, at least. I caught myself as I started to try to smell exactly which parts were gone; the cops and crime lab personnel would hardly forget the sight of a woman taking deep breaths at a crime scene, trying to figure out where the gall bladder was.

And then I realized the detective was staring at me, studying me, and that I should have expressed some horror by then. It was too late to fake it with any believability, so I shook my head and said, "It doesn't even look real."

She nodded, seeming to file my reaction away as interesting information, and we walked past, entering one of the buildings that had some sheathing up. I started to go back to my question about evidence when I smacked hard into a wall of magic, and staggered back.

Pira stared at me. "What the hell was that?"

I reached my hand out and pressed it against the wall, and it was like an angry, humming shield of energy. I pushed harder, but I simply could not pass through it. And that scared me. I moved to where Pira had entered it, and it was solid there too. "It's . . . magic."

"Uh-huh," she said. "Right. Looks like mime to me."

She reached out, grabbed my arm, and dragged me forward. I slammed into the wall, hard, yelping. Pira's eyes widened, but she tried again, more gently, to pull my arm through. No dice—and she could tell I wasn't faking it. There just wasn't any way.

Pira reached for her radio, and I said, "You sure you want to do that?"

"Why wouldn't I?"

"Because no one will believe it. Even the ones who see it with their own eyes will stop believing it in a couple of days. All they'll be left with is the memory of you telling them magic kept me out of a room."

She shook her head, pulled the radio out, and held it to her mouth before the truth of it sank in. "Damn."

"Yeah."

"So, what now?"

I stood thinking for a moment, trying to decide how much I could safely tell her. "How long will you have people here? When will you clear the scene?"

She shrugged. "We have three teams out here collecting evidence, walking the area, but it will still be hours. And it will be days before we clear the scene for construction to start up again. Wait—why can I go through but you can't?"

"No idea."

"Ella—"

"Look," I said, stepping away from the magic, which was starting to get very uncomfortable, "I'm really not positive, and it's not that important, anyway. What is important is you need to have your people out of here before dark—long before dark—and the sooner the better."

"Why?"

I just gave her a look and hoped she'd go along, but it wasn't enough. And then I tried to tell her the invisible wall was dangerous and unstable, but that wasn't quite enough either. This was her job—their job—and not mine. I didn't really have a place here at all, if you went by the book. But she'd known it wasn't that simple, even before I ran into that wall of magic.

Twenty minutes later, when she learned that one of the victims was a retired Navy Seal and another had a third-degree black belt in Judo, and that the forensic team had no idea what kind of animals shredded the men, but they were all scared witless, she finally agreed to close the scene overnight. She was far from certain that I could handle it, but she was pretty sure that she and her team weren't equipped.

Of course, they didn't simply leave and go home. Officially and in front of witnesses, she ordered me out. Quietly and alone, she asked me how much space I needed, and said she would position cars and undercover officers on foot at about a two-block radius. We picked a time, and I left to get supplies and information and to prepare.

By 5:20 p.m., when the sun was nearly touching the horizon, I was back and ready to go. My cousin, Kylie, had given me an athame—a ritual knife—that she thought would let me cut through the magic, and I had a szabla—a Ukrainian sword like a short sabre—and magical protections that I hoped would do the job. I'd fought two demons before, but they'd been easy because they were already weak. One had been wounded in a fight with another demon, and the other had simply stayed in our world too long without taking blood. This one would be fresh and boiling with energy after four kills. Not to mention, I had no idea what kind of demon I was confronting.

As I stood facing the buzzing wall, I slid the athame free of its sheath. It squealed and twisted slightly, reacting to the magic just inches away. Not for the first time, it occurred to me that I should have asked for help—from some of the mages I knew, or from the police. A mix of pride and fear of exposure had kept me silent. *Stupid*, I thought, and stabbed the wall. A wave of hot, foul air threw me off my feet onto the concrete floor.

After that, finding the demon wasn't hard. With the wall of magic down, I could see the screen he had raised to keep hidden until dark—and he knew it.

Down came the screen. Out came the demon. The battle was on.

He didn't bother with weapons. Instead, the 7-foot-tall horned green demon rushed me. He moved with an impossible speed for his size, but I moved a tiny bit faster. Still, he caught my side, ripping gashes along my ribs.

The demon stumbled past me, unprepared for my dodge, and I slashed at him with my szabla. The blade tore a deep wound in his side. Both of us were hurt, but he was losing blood far faster. The enchantment that had been worked on the sword called to blood, drawing it out in rivers.

We both moved back and sized each other up for a moment before he came at me again. It was a head-on rush that turned into a dodge left, then a dive, and he slashed at me with his feet, which also had wicked claws. I could have dodged it, but knew it was as much an opportunity as a danger. The demon connected with a glancing blow, tearing into my leg as I hacked his foot clean off.

Up until then, our fight had been all but silent, but as he collapsed with a floor-shaking thud, he let out a howl that echoed off the walls and swelled into the late afternoon air above us. I hoped Pira could keep the cavalry from rushing in. Surely the sound would be enough to argue patience.

The demon was down, but far from done, and I was bleeding heavily from my own wounds. The pain hadn't reached me yet, and wouldn't while the adrenaline coursed through me, but I knew I needed a quick victory. Getting close enough without getting killed would be the hard part.

And then I felt the nauseating, itchy sensation I get when someone's getting ready to do powerful magic, and there was no more time. To his surprise, and even a little bit to mine, I lunged, jumped, grabbed a bare ceiling joist, and launched myself at him, sword first, aiming for his neck. He slashed at me, but too quickly, missing, and the szabla sliced cleanly through his neck as I crashed to the floor beside him. His massive head tipped back and thunked to the floor as I rolled away.

A blinding, stabbing light flared explosively, filling the room, followed by a groaning-screeching-roaring noise that overwhelmed all thought. It lasted for maybe a minute, maybe two. And then, silence.

The demon and all his parts were gone. The floor was clear. The sun was setting with a red glow, and a gentle breeze rustled some trash in a pile in one corner. I felt a moment of disbelief, followed by relief, and then a sickening wash of gut-churning pain that curled me into a ball.

I'd asked Pira to give me at least three hours before she came in with her people, thinking it would be enough time for me to clean up after eliminating the demon. If she kept her promise, there was more than enough time for me to lie there and recover—and it would be a lot less painful if I could avoid moving—but I knew her better. I would never have waited, not after hearing the noise we'd made, and I didn't expect her to either. I hauled myself up, actually sobbing from the pain, staggered a block and a half away to a dank, narrow alley I thought they'd ignore, and collapsed behind a derelict trash bin.

It wasn't until maybe an hour later, after the worst of the pain was past and I'd partly healed, that I noticed the thick, blue-tinged blood on my shirt and knew I was in trouble. From that moment, my priorities changed. I listened carefully, and could hear that Pira and her people were back on the site. None were near me, so I slid out, dragged myself upright, and headed for home.

I cleaned myself up, picked the debris from my halfway-healed wounds, and stowed my weapons while sucking down a pint from the fridge. And then, I drove straight to my bank. It was past five, but I knew Miroslav would still be in his office, and he would know what to do. He always did.

Miros had been a family friend since before I was born, and a treasured adviser to my father. As a child, I'd thought of him as a *niceoldguy*, and largely dismissed him. It wasn't until a few months after I became a vampire that I discovered he was a wizard—and one of the best. Since then, Miros had become my treasured adviser, too—and sometimes a sort of counselor.

I found myself tensing as I knocked on his office door and entered at his invitation. After his warm greeting I wished we could content ourselves with the usual small talk, but I knew this wasn't a problem that I could safely ignore. After a few minutes, I asked what he could tell me about the effect of getting demon blood in wounds.

"That would be bad," he said. "Extremely bad. You'd want to avoid blood-to-blood contact with demons at all costs."

"And if it does happen?"

He let out a harsh laugh. "Trust me—you don't want to know."

"But I . . . but what if I do? I mean, what if I already have?"

Miroslav froze for a moment then he groaned. "Ella." He sighed and rubbed his face. "Ella . . . you were such a sweet child. You know, I remember when you were six, and you had this red wagon with wooden panels on the sides—do you remember it?"

"Miros?"

"Yes?"

"Demon blood? In open wounds?"

"Yes." He sighed. "Yes, OK. So. Type?"

"Type?"

"Type of *demon*." Miroslav frowned at me like an impatient school teacher.

"Hell if I know."

He rolled his eyes then walked over to a mahogany-paneled section of wall, reached right through it, and pulled out a huge leather-bound book. It still freaked me out when he did that. And then I'd think "cool," and wish I had just a hair of magical ability.

Mom was an herbal witch, and Dad was a financial wizard—in both senses. But me? So far, nothing. That owl from Hogwarts would never have brought me a letter. With two witch parents, I'd had a 93 percent chance of being born with magical ability. Instead, I was a seven percenter: not even a smidge of mage. Rare and special, that's me. Just not in a good way.

Miroslav had set the book on his oval conference table and

was flipping pages with a fierce look on his face. He found what he was looking for and waved me over. "Corporeal? Obviously." He turned a few more pages. "Winged?"

"No."

He continued turning pages, and my vision blurred. The book seemed to be vibrating, and when the pages went by, the air moved more than it should. Magical books always gave me the creeping willies. Goose bumps raised on my arms, and I edged away slightly. Miroslav, of course, noticed and frowned at me. He'd demanded a lot of me in the year and a half I'd been meeting with him, but he seemed harsher than usual, and very, very disappointed. I wanted to apologize, but I wasn't even sure why. Fighting the demon had been unavoidable—and if I hadn't made it bleed, I wouldn't still be around to talk about it.

"Height?"

"Sevenish."

He looked questioningly at me, and I said, "Feet." I still knew damn little about demons and all the rest of the mystical world I'd suddenly found myself a part of two years earlier—I'd always tried to ignore that part of my parents' lives, since I couldn't really take part myself—but I did know that a seven-inch demon could be just as deadly as a seven foot one, and I also knew they could be as tall as seven yards. Or seven stories, for that matter. Seven miles? Maybe. But I probably wouldn't have lived to talk about that.

"Horns?"

"Two." Trying to anticipate the questions, I added, "On either side of its head. Curling." I gently pressed the edges of the wounds that ran along my ribs, and wondered if I'd start growing horns myself—maybe from my side. That would be attractive.

"Fire?" Miros asked.

"Um . . . ."

"From its nose or mouth, or even its . . . ."

"Nope. No fire from any orifice."

"Huh. Boring," he said, as he flipped through more pages. "Tentacles?"

Miroslav went through almost a dozen other characteristics, including color, sounds, ooze, weapons or magical items, and magical skills, before he turned the book toward me to show me some pictures.

He was turning the pages himself because we'd discovered previously that the magical books didn't like me. The first time I touched one, it actually tried to bite me. Miros said he'd never heard of it happening before, and tested me on three other books before I refused to play that game. The first one gave me an electrical shock; the second—a thick, heavy book about potion mixing—jumped onto my foot and tried to hide under a desk; and the third screamed so loudly that the neighbors (we were at Miros' home that time) actually called the police. He'd decided the books must be reacting that way because I'm a vampire, but he hadn't had an opportunity to put it to the test with another vamp. In the meantime, I wasn't getting any closer to them than I had to.

Miros had gone through eleven pages before I spotted the demon I'd killed. It was called a Narrabeen Queller Demon, and it was the butt-ugliest thing I'd ever seen, aside only from the one I'd met in person. Bumpy, slimy, oozing skin, extra-long fingers that ended in claws, and an odd assortment of eyes on all sides of its head. I looked at the description but, naturally, I couldn't read a word.

"Looks like gibberish," I said.

"No, it's demo-mageic." At my enquiring look, he added, "A cross between demonic and an ancient mage language. No one really speaks demonic or mageic, or ever did. They're really a sort of Esperanto for each group, to allow at least basic communication. The authors used a blend of the two to make sure only demons and mages—witches—could read it. They had to do both because the demons would only cooperate with their research if they wrote it that way."

"Huh. OK." I wondered vaguely why the demons would cooperate regardless, but that was a subject for another day. "So, what does it say?"

"Well," he said, scanning the page, "there's some fairly useless stuff about the Queller's habitat, culture, dining preferences and the like. It's got only basic magical abilities, like shooting low-wattage fireballs and moving small objects. Parlor tricks, really. As demons go, it's a pretty pathetic one."

I let out a harsh laugh, and he looked up.

"That pathetic demon nearly kicked my ass."

He studied me briefly. "You look fine. A bit tired and rumpled perhaps, but—"

I took my jacket off so he could see my arms then pulled my shirt up far enough to expose the slashes over my ribcage. The deep claw marks were healing well—my vamp blood gives me amazing healing abilities—but they were still ugly and red. A norm would have bled out before an ambulance arrived. Easily.

Miros knew it, and his concern showed in his face, but all he said was, "You need training."

"Yup," I said, and nodded. "Yeah. I do." It was a topic we'd discussed often. I'd always dismissed the idea, because I could easily kick the ass of any non-magical man or woman alive, but I'd never faced anything like this before. If this was the low end of the demon ranks, I needed some serious training, and soon.

He smiled, finally looking pleased at something, then turned back to the book. After a couple minutes he said, "Ah, OK, here we go." He placed his finger on a section of the text that was written in larger, darker letters. "Oh dear. 'Warning, avoid contact with Queller Demon blood. Results are unpredictable, but usually fatal within 48 hours'."

"*Fatal*?" I glared at the wounds on my arm. "Stupid damn demon. What does it say I can do about it?"

He scanned a couple pages. "It doesn't." He shook his head. "That's all it says."

"Well, that's bloody useless."

He smiled grimly. "Yes, quite. But then, it would be anyway, wouldn't it? None of this stuff applies to vampires, my dear. You're new territory, aren't you?"

"Yay. Such an adventure. How utterly fascinating. But what do I do, then?"

"How long has it been?"

"Maybe three hours."

He closed the book rather harder than he needed to. "Why didn't you come to me immediately?"

"Well, I thought it might concern the bank employees if I strolled in covered in blood and muck, my clothes hanging off me in tatters. Not to mention, I was too weak to even get myself home for well over an hour. I had to crawl into a sagging dishwasher box in an alley to stay out of sight, and then some homeless guy tried to take it from me."

His scowl finally softened. "I'm sorry, my dear. Of course." He slipped the book back through the wall, and we both sat in big, comfy leather chairs near the windows looking out onto the park. "Are you feeling anything . . . unusual since receiving the injuries?"

I waited before answering, taking a moment to be very aware of how I felt, and what my senses could tell me. I could hear Miros' secretary on the phone, explaining to a very important client that Miros was in a meeting with auditors and simply couldn't be disturbed, but would call the instant he was free. I wondered not for the first time how much she knew, but let my senses wander further. I realized there was an odd sort of buzzing sensation around the wounds. There'd been too much pain earlier to give it much notice, but the buzzing was becoming more distinct. I could almost hear it. Almost taste it. I tried to explain, but Miros just frowned at me. Again.

"All right, let me think," he said, and he slipped into an odd meditative state that I'd learned not to interfere with. His eyes unfocused and his body stilled as he turned his whole attention inward. Miros might come up from the depths with the perfect answer in a minute or two—or an hour, or a day—but I thought it was just as likely he'd come up empty. And what then? Wait and see, probably. Never my favorite choice, but one I'd had to settle for on more than a few occasions. The interaction of vamps with magic, demons, fairies, zombies, doctors, and the criminal justice system was dangerous and unpredictable, and no matter how badly I wanted to, I couldn't know the outcome before it got here.

* * * * *

Now, sitting in Miros' office, I somehow felt safe. He might not be able to solve this, and I might even die in the end, but I was tired and sore, and I knew he would do everything in his power to protect me. So, while Miroslav pondered, I set up my laptop and got to work. If nothing else, I could report my success to my client. Twenty minutes of typing later, I finished my message to the developer, explaining in very cryptic terms that the immediate problem was resolved, but the people who caused it were still unknown and should be considered dangerous, and shut the computer down. Miros was still meditating, so I closed my eyes and, almost instantly, I slept. My dreams, as usual, were filled with chasing, fighting, magic, and the sweet-copper taste of blood.

Sometime later, I awoke to the scent of burning sage and hibiscus flowers, and was alarmed to find myself lying on the floor of Miroslav's office, surrounded by seven chanting witches wearing flowing purple robes. Miros stood beside me reading from a small green book that looked like it had fangs.

"How—" I said, but Miros glared at me, and I fell silent. Fine, but he had some serious questions to answer later—not the least of which was, how the hell do I protect myself if I don't wake up when someone picks me up and carries me across the room? I tried to shift so I could see the room better, but found I was unable to move. I recognized the feel of the magic: it was a restraint spell, and an incredibly powerful one. I couldn't even twitch a finger, though I could still turn my head and snarl.

And then, one of the witches—my Aunt Clair, in fact—added a handful of something that smelled like a cross between a swamp and a big-city subway station into the fire, which was burning in a small brazier. The witches, their backs turned to me, raised their arms together and spoke the words of what I knew was a protection spell, and I felt the instant ear-popping isolation of a tight, well-constructed circle.

Usually, the circle was meant to protect the people inside it from outside interference or danger during a ritual. But this time, after a moment of staring in confusion at the oddly wavering images of the witches surrounding me, I realized I was the only one inside the circle. They had raised it to protect themselves from *me*. I'd obviously missed some interesting conversations, yet again, and I felt the familiar petulance of my youth.

So many things went on around me that, because I wasn't magical, simply couldn't involve me. God, I hated it. And even now, when I *was* magical, when I was the center of attention, I was still left out. And it made me mad—so, so mad. Twisting with bitterness. And then their chant changed, and the pressure of their magic increased four-fold, and I felt the rage moving like a force inside me in response. It wasn't just an overgrown tantrum coming on: it was the demon's blood in me, coming to life. Fear struggled for a foothold, tried to pull me back from the abyss of fury, but it was no match for it. None at all.

The air around me bent and churned, my muscles writhed, and a scream ripped out of me. Miros and the witches flinched at the sound, swayed at the force of the energy I'd released against the circle without even trying, and I felt a vicious thrill. I could stop them all. I could brush them aside like dolls. At last. I let the rage and the power build inside, restraining it until I thought I would explode. The sounds of their chanting rose higher and higher, but their magic couldn't reach me. Not now—and not ever again.

At last, I was ready: I let loose the demon.

A wave of crimson rolled out of me and crashed against the circle, obliterating it. Miros and the witches were thrown to the ground; the windows were blown out. A cacophony of screeching and howling filled the air. It was coming from me.

Oh, oh, *the pain.* Too much. It was too much. *Escape, window, escape.* I ran to the nearest one, stumbling, clawing for the ledge. I couldn't get through. I was too big. But it was a huge window. It didn't make sense. I looked over my shoulder and saw what was catching on the window frame. *Wings*. Yes. Good.

I tucked them in, tipped through the window, and propelled myself forward, falling. The air rushed against me, and it was exquisite. I stretched my wings and arched my back, and my plummet turned into a glide. I tipped them gently, knowing somehow what to do, and swept down the street, then beat the wings, climbing higher. The air cooled them, cooled me, and the rage ebbed.

I swooped, glided, soared, feeling new muscles, new power. I could sense people below me, feel emotions bubbling from them: fear, anger, loneliness, bliss. Inside myself, I felt a calm that I hadn't known since I was a child. Born from rage, I'd finally found my peace.

And then I remembered Miros, Aunt Clair, and the other witches. I discovered I could turn almost instantly, even at high speed, and aimed myself back toward the bank. I struggled so hard to fly faster that I slowed terribly, nearly lurching into a building, before I relaxed into it again. I let my body fly, the calm returned, and I moved through the air with breathtaking speed.

When I got back to the building, I latched onto the brick outside of the shattered windows with my claws. Claws? I took a moment and made note of my red skin and the wicked two-inch talons on my fingers before peering in the window. One witch, a woman I didn't know, was leaving, supported by two of the other witches. It looked like an ankle problem, though, so they could heal her easily enough. Probably would have done it already if they'd had enough magical energy left after trying to restrain me. The thought made me smile again. It was juvenile, but at least I knew I'd be taken seriously from now on.

Most importantly, Miros seemed fine as he went around the office righting tipped chairs and collecting papers from the floor. Good. I wanted to see him, speak to him, but there was one thing I had to do first; one bit of business I needed to take care of. The men who called that demon: they still had to be stopped.

The fact that stopping them was my priority told me I was still

Ella inside, no matter what I looked like. My new attributes would just make it easier to take care of them—and much easier to find them. I just had to hope that it wasn't permanent—or at least not a full-time look. But that was a problem for another day.

Beneath the buzzing of the people, machines, animals, and buildings that I felt all around me, there was a single, singing thread linking me with the demon callers. The thread led me west toward the mountains. Moving—they were moving. Fleeing. Smart. Smart, but futile. I laughed a deep, harsh laugh and dropped away from the building, spreading my wings and gliding into a powerful, sweeping beat toward two doomed men running through the dark. The vampire that still lived in me was hungry, and she would feed well that night.

About the author:

Meriah Crawford is a writer, a professor at Virginia Commonwealth University, and a private investigator. Meriah's writing includes short stories, a variety of non-fiction work, and a poem about semi-colons. For more information, please visit www.mlcrawford.com.

Night Run

by Catherine A. Callaghan

Bill Martin nearly missed the merge sign, marking the point where the Belleporte Cutoff narrowed to a skinny road, a two-lane highway. As he started to shift lanes, he felt a sharp jolt and watched a long black four-wheeler swerve into the embankment. "God damned idiot!" he shouted.

The driver had been speeding past him on the right side, called the "suicide lane" because of the low blind spot where Bill couldn't see him in his mirrors. Bill pulled his eighteen-wheeler onto the berm ahead of the other vehicle. He struggled to keep himself under control, being only a "temp" and badly in need of his job to pay off a student loan. Unfortunately, he'd be cited for an unsafe lane change, even though the accident was the other driver's fault. Bill's employer, the Arabian Carpet Company, wouldn't enjoy the repair bills.

Bill normally looked forward to the night run to Belleporte, a small city with a Colonial theme and a rich history. The run represented a temporary leap into the past when life was simpler and more secure, but this night had begun badly. Bill was delayed leaving the Arabian warehouse in Columbus, and he was forced to "fingerprint the load", help load rolls of carpet onto his trailer at the beginning of his run. Pounding rain had blurred the white lines on the freeway, preventing him from making up time, and now this.

The storm started to lift as Bill climbed down. The old moon burst briefly through rolling clouds, and light from a vapor lamp pooled on the wet asphalt. Moist air carried the odor of fertilizer from nearby fields. Cattle were mooing in a distant enclosure. As Bill hurried back, the door to the wrecked car swung open, and the driver stepped out. He was slight of build with black hair and a thin face, vaguely Italian in appearance except for the pallor of his skin. His black hat and coat resembled Puritan clothing. He walked with some difficulty and was bleeding from a gash on his forehead. A lightning bolt creased the sky and shot to the horizon immediately behind him. Through some strange optical effect, the bolt seemed to flicker through him as it descended. He appeared undisturbed by the crash of thunder.

"How badly are you hurt?" Bill asked, resisting the impulse to lay blame.

"It's nothing, just a scratch, but my car's not drivable."

A moment's inspection proved him right. The impact had smashed his radiator and driven his left front fender into the tire. *A black Lincoln Town Car. Just my luck to wreck a rich man's four-wheeler.*

Bill concealed his frustration with difficulty. "Stay here while I go back and call the patrol on my cell phone. Do you want the emergency squad?"

The stranger flashed startling green eyes. "I said I was all right. Don't report anything. Just drive me on to Belleporte, immediately." He was moving normally as he brushed himself off, and the gash on his forehead was starting to heal. It mustn't have been as serious as Bill had thought.

The accident victim's demand took Bill by surprise. "We can't leave the scene, sir. We'll have to call a tow truck for your car. Besides, we've got to report every serious accident to the highway patrol. It's the law."

"I don't care about the law, and I want you to call me Mack, not 'sir'! I have to get to Belleporte as soon as possible." He started walking rapidly toward the truck, despite his injuries, forcing Bill to sprint after him.

The Ryder trailer glistened in the moist air, heightening the effect of the Arabian Carpet Company's official logo, a magic carpet with wings plus the slogan, "We Deliver in a Day." Bill glanced at the right side of his tractor as Mack opened the passenger door and climbed in. There was little damage, considering the state of the gentleman's car, and new dents were hardly noticeable on the old body. The fuel tank hadn't been punctured. With luck, this night's storm would obscure most of the evidence. Bill was already three hours behind schedule and was tempted to follow Mack's advice, but his conscience intervened.

He circled the tractor and pulled himself into the driver's seat. "You can wait here if you like, but I'm not going anywhere till I make a report. Your car's too expensive to abandon, and I won't risk getting fired."

Mack grabbed Bill's wrist as he reached for his phone. He was surprised at the strength of the small man's grip. "Start now. I don't want any more delays," said Mack.

"You don't understand. I could lose my license if I leave the scene without reporting this accident, especially if someone's injured."

"No, *you* don't understand. I'm not injured and I must be in Belleporte before sunrise. It's as simple as that."

"You're not going to make it. I can't get there by dawn without doing 70, and the speed limit's 55."

Mack's eyes bored into Bill's. "Then do 70. If you get me to Belleporte in time, I'll make it worth your while. If not . . . ." His smile exposed strong white teeth.

Bill's stomach tightened. He was about to object that this stretch was a speed trap, but decided to keep quiet. He brought his eighteen-wheeler back onto the highway and stole a sideways glance at Mack, who was resisting the jerky movements of the old truck, which lacked air ride suspension. It was hard to believe that such a slight man could be so intimidating. Bill was nearly five feet ten and muscular, but Mack's air of self-confidence made Bill feel he'd be no match for the gentleman in a fight. For all he knew, Mack might be armed, although his expensive black suit gave no hint of a concealed weapon. At any rate, Bill decided against further argument.

The cutoff widened again into a four-lane highway and turned toward the coast. The storm had broken, and the moon shone through mottled clouds, picking out an abandoned farm house, a broken fence, a grotesque stand of trees. Bill accelerated and started to relax. He felt the power of 315 horses coming to life in his in-line six engine and remembered why he continued to drive a truck for a living during the summer, even after enrolling as a graduate student at Ohio State University. On the road, he was king and usually set his own pace.

Tonight, a stranger was setting Bill's pace for him. What did he know about the man? If Mack was a criminal on the run, Bill risked becoming an accessory to any crime the man committed, a more serious charge than leaving the scene of an accident. It would be hard to argue that he'd been forced to transport such a small man in the absence of a weapon. He could only hope to reach Belleporte without incident and plead ignorance if anything happened later.

His CB radio crackled to life with the voice of a fellow trucker. "Eastbound, look out for bears! There's one by the pickle park ahead on your side."

"I copy that. Thanks." Bill braked as he shot past the rest area, but he was too late. He heard the wail of a siren behind him.

"Outrun him," Mack commanded.

"I can't. He can accelerate faster than I can. He'll pass me and head me off." Bill again pulled onto the berm. The patrolman's motorcycle stopped just behind the truck, and the officer walked up slowly. His uniform was wrinkled. He had a pinched face and needed a shave. Bill knew he'd seen him before.

"I clocked you doing sixty-eight," he said as Bill rolled down the window. "Give me your driver's license."

Bill complied, and the officer started filling out a form. He frowned halfway through and looked up. Recognition passed between them. Bill remembered the man as Jim Ferguson, a cocky young kid he'd once trained to operate a fork lift for Arabian. He couldn't believe this misfit had found a job with the highway patrol. Meanwhile, Ferguson was taking his time making out the rest of the citation.

"Tell him to hurry it along, "came a harsh whisper on Bill's right.

Bill leaned out the window. "Jim, I'd appreciate it if you'd get this over with as soon as possible. I've been delayed three hours already."

Ferguson's gaze hardened. "Bill Martin, why should I do anything for an ass-licker like you?"

Bill winced. "You're still sore over losing your job at Arabian, aren't you? You came to work drunk that night. I couldn't let you operate the fork lift. You might've killed someone."

"You could've covered for me, ass-hole! That's what I'd have done for a buddy."

"I'd already covered for you twice and given you a warning."

The officer leaned against the door of the truck. "Tell'ya what—for a consideration, I'll do the same for you. I'll reduce this citation to a warning and let you go now."

Some things never changed. Ferguson had tried to bribe Bill not to report him to the boss the night he was drunk. Yet Bill was tempted this time. He always carried extra cash for emergencies, and all he wanted right now was to get out of this predicament as quickly as possible. If the officer hadn't been enjoying the situation, Bill might have paid the bastard off.

"Go to hell!" he finally said.

Mack spoke up: "Officer, this man was kind enough to give me a ride. I must get to Belleporte as soon as possible. It's an emergency."

Ferguson's gaze focused on Mack. "Since when is it Arabian's policy to pick up hitchhikers?"

"I'm not a hitchhiker. Mr. Martin wrecked my car, and I had no time to wait for a tow truck."

Ferguson's lips drew back in a slow smile as Bill clenched his teeth. He wasn't a violent man, but at that moment, he could have strangled Mack.

"That wouldn't be the black Lincoln Town Car about fifty miles back, would it?" Ferguson asked. "The dispatcher said there hadn't been a report. Bill, I suppose you know the penalty for leaving the scene." He knew only too well, a heavy fine and a possible jail sentence plus the certain loss of his job with Arabian.

"Let's see, now. Wrecking a car, leaving the scene, and excessive speed. That's three serious violations, Bill. I'm afraid I can't let you off with a warning, even though you're an old buddy. It wouldn't be right, would it?" Ferguson licked his lips, as if savoring every moment.

He then glanced at Mack, who was speaking in his even, commanding voice. "Let us go now." Bill looked sideways. Mack was trying to trap the officer in his gaze, but Ferguson kept looking away. There were advantages to being shifty-eyed.

"Not till I've made a full report," said Ferguson. He started walking back to his motorcycle.

The passenger door slammed, and Bill turned to find Mack gone. He heard sounds of an argument, then a scuffle, and jumped down to investigate. As he rounded the truck, he came upon a tableau. Mack had wrestled the officer to a kneeling position, and the two were locked in what looked like an embrace. A moment later, Ferguson slumped onto the berm with Mack on top of him as if he were trying to kill him.

"Stop it, for God's sake!" Bill ran over and grabbed Mack's shoulders. Mack looked up, black hat askew. A drop of blood was flowing down his jaw. His tongue flicked out and caught it, then brought it slowly to his lips. His green eyes flickered with pleasure. "What did you do? Slit Jim's throat?" Bill asked.

"Suppose I did? He'd only be getting what he deserved."

"And you'd be a murderer!"

Mack clucked his tongue and straightened his hat. "Such a conscience you labor under, Mr. Martin. When you've been around as long as I have, you'll think differently. But never mind. This poor excuse for an officer will come to in a bit. It's rarely necessary to kill."

Bill pushed Mack away and examined Ferguson, who looked a bit pale but otherwise normal except for a long mark on his throat. His eyelids fluttered, and he started to sit up.

Mack yanked Bill to his feet. "Get going! Now!"

Again, the look in Mack's eyes made Bill feel he had no choice but to comply. As he eased onto the highway, he watched the officer in his rearview mirror, expecting fury and instant pursuit. Instead, Ferguson slowly got to his feet and staggered back to the motorcycle. He made no effort to follow when Bill accelerated to seventy.

"We're in deep trouble," said Bill.

"I doubt it."

"As soon as Ferguson radios in what happened, we'll be stopped and arrested."

"Are you suggesting I should have killed that man when I had the chance?"

Bill didn't deem the question worthy of a reply. Mack had by now adjusted to the motion of the truck, riding it like a spirited horse, but he kept looking at his watch. Relaxation was impossible for Bill. If Rich Man Mack had special connections which made him immune from prosecution, Bill did not. At any moment, he expected a squadron of patrolmen to descend on the two of them, sirens blaring.

The miles rolled on. Despite his anxiety, Bill felt suddenly hungry and brought out two cold cheeseburgers. He offered one to Mack.

"No, thanks. I've already snacked." A flush was spreading across his cheeks and down his neck.

"Suit yourself." Bill proceeded to devour both of them while they traveled eastward. At least his problems hadn't destroyed his appetite. Mack sat in silence, again the image of a slight, harmless man.

Bill couldn't believe what had happened. He'd left the scene twice and helped a stranger escape after assaulting an officer. Mack's long black car and expensive clothes came to mind. For all Bill knew, he might now be transporting a mob boss to a drug payoff or some similar operation. He could think of no other plausible explanation for Mack's determination to reach Belleporte at a specified time, no matter what, although his precise speech and mannerisms didn't suggest a mobster.

Then Bill remembered the cold strength of Mack's hand and Mack's sensual pleasure when he'd brought Ferguson's blood to his lips. He realized there was an even more sinister possibility. Among the superstitious, Belleporte had been famous since Colonial times as a haven for the undead, and everyone in and around the city knew vampire lore. Although the Belleporte Chamber of Commerce exploited this fact with tours and costume parties, intellectuals at Belleporte University pooh-poohed the idea of vampires along with Salem witches. He'd half-believed the legends as a boy visiting the city, although he'd long since outgrown them. He'd once spent a night alone in the Colonial section of the cemetery to prove his mettle, and been terrified when a figure in black brushed past the shrubbery where he was hiding. The police later exposed a vampire cult whose members met by the graves, exchanged blood, and sometimes assaulted pedestrians. Bill much preferred Mack the mobster to Mack the cult member.

"Watch it!" yelled Mack. Bill's inattention had allowed the truck to drift over the yellow line. He jerked the steering wheel sharply to the right and narrowly missed an oncoming car. As it careened past, he looked into his rearview mirror and froze. A halogen lamp by the roadside lit up the passenger seat. It appeared empty, yet when he glanced out of the corner of his eye, Mack still sat there.

Cold terror crept through Bill. The stranger was neither an ordinary criminal nor member of a cult. No cult ritual could erase a person's reflection. He checked the mirror again, and the passenger seat still seemed vacant. The old legends were true. There were such things as vampires, whatever that entailed, and Mack was one of them. It explained his hypnotic power as well as his need to return home before sunrise, but whether Bill delivered him in time or not, he calculated his own chances of survival as slim. At this point, he would have welcomed pursuit by the highway patrol, even his arrest.

"You don't have to worry about your buddy, Ferguson," said Mack, as if reading Bill's mind. "He won't come charging up the highway to take you in, not after I threatened to report him to the state ethics committee for soliciting a bribe."

Mack paused, as if expecting thanks. Bill merely grunted. So much for any hope of rescue. On the other hand, Ferguson would relish leaving Bill to Mack's devices, whatever they might be. Perhaps it was just as well that Mack had managed to intimidate him.

"Oh, yes. I just happened to lift the paperwork on your citation while I was wrestling with that man," Mack continued. Bill felt something being pressed against him on the seat. Hope flickered briefly. Mack would not be this accommodating if he were planning murder. On the other hand, he'd have to conceal any sinister designs until he reached his destination if he wanted Bill's cooperation. He glanced at the fuel gauge. It was low; another problem he'd have to face.

As they climbed into the foothills of the Theodore Mountains, Bill downshifted. He tensed when lights appeared in his side-view mirror until he realized it was just a tow truck laboring past with a wrecked Ford. A westbound trucker honked at him in greeting and he honked back, knowing there was no way of communicating his distress without alerting Mack.

A steady wind had risen, blowing away the remnants of the storm and revealing a sea of stars above second-growth pine. The tip of the old moon pierced a wayward cloud, but Bill was in no mood to appreciate its beauty. They finally crested, passing a McDonald's sign. The Golden Arches loomed behind a stand of trees. Mack was looking at his watch with increasing agitation as they started down.

"Drive faster, dammit!" Mack said, all gentlemanly airs abandoned. "If I don't reach Belleporte in time, neither will you!"

Bill's anger gave way to cold terror. There was no way he could possibly overpower Mack. "I can't, not downhill. If I lose control of this truck, we won't reach Belleporte at all."

They descended through more forest. Around a bend, the Atlantic Ocean gleamed in the first light of dawn, and a series of vapor lamps marked the Belleporte shoreline. As the highway started to level off, Bill noted the nearly empty gas gauge, and a plan began to form. He turned into a truck stop.

"Keep driving," said Mack.

"I've got to stop. We're low on fuel."

"Put in just enough to get us to Belleporte."

Bill thought it prudent to obey. He climbed down and phoned information from the diesel pump. After partially filling the tank, he went inside to pay then returned to the eighteen-wheeler. He noted that no other vehicles were in sight.

"Start the engine," Mack commanded.

Bill closed his eyes and turned toward Mack. "No. This is as far as we go for now."

Mack grabbed him by the shoulder, but Bill still refused to open his eyes. "I've just bought a capsule of garlic; you know, the souvenir item that's available in all stores on roads leading to Belleporte. I put it in my mouth back in the store, and if you don't let go of me now, I'll bite down." Mack jerked his hand away, and Bill thought he could sense the stranger's stunned expression, even through closed eyes.

"I'm glad I have your attention. Whatever you are, you can't stand garlic, and I could drive you out of this truck if I wanted to. You're also afraid that sunlight will kill you, and you can't operate this eighteen-wheeler, or you'd have taken it over a long time ago. I'm going to turn around, look straight ahead, and start my engine. If you try to control me again, I'll do what I said I would."

Bill pulled back onto the highway. A few miles down the road, Mack said "I'm surprised you didn't release the garlic anyway, no matter what I did."

"It's that inconvenient conscience I labor under. I can't risk killing a person who's just saved my job and kept me out of jail, even if he hasn't got a conscience at all."

Mack remained silent.

"Just how long have you been around?" Bill asked.

"Long enough to learn all I want to know about the great and famous. Captain Joseph Hill—remember him? He and his men massacred the Oweeran Indians in 1635, in violation of a friendship treaty, and became a Belleporte hero. I inhaled the stench from that slaughter the following evening. Oh, yes, and Percival Sloane, the great counterfeiter, who helped give Continental currency its bad reputation during the Revolutionary War—he even passed some of his fake money to me. His deeds didn't prevent Belleporte from gratefully accepting a portion of his land to build Belleporte College, never mind how that land had been acquired. I wish I'd feasted on him when I'd had the chance."

Bill opened his mouth to reply, but didn't know what to say. A portrait of Percival Sloane graced the Belleporte University commons, and history books glossed over his other accomplishments.

At the city limits, the eastern sky turned pale gold under a flaming cloud. "Where do you want me to take you?" Bill asked.

"To the Belleporte Cemetery—Colonial Section, and hurry!"

The sky was growing brighter as Bill turned onto Wolf County Boulevard. At length, he came to a halt, parking next to the burial grounds. The passenger door opened, and he heard Mack starting to climb down. Against his better judgment, he risked a final look. The closest graves were marked by thin rectangular stones and an occasional shrub. Mack had paused halfway down, and his features seemed to fluoresce in the dawn light. He regarded Bill with intense green eyes. His smile indicated that he could now resume full control any time he wished.

"I told you I'd make this run worth your while if you brought me to Belleporte," Mack said, "and I will. Whatever you may think of me, I keep my word." Mack placed a coin on the passenger seat, jumped down, and tipped his hat. "Till we meet again."

I keep my word! At that moment, Bill realized why he enjoyed the leap into the past that came with visits to Belleporte. In former times, ordinary people were dependent on their neighbors, and keeping one's word was a necessity in everyday life until it became ingrained in most people's behavior.

Bill examined the coin closely. It was a Pine Tree shilling in fine condition, bearing the date 1652 and worth at least a thousand dollars on the open market. It appeared to have dropped from the purse of an early American. When Bill looked up, Mack was nowhere to be seen, as if he had sunk into one of the Colonial graves.

At that moment, the sun burst over the horizon.

About the author:

Catherine A. Callaghan writes speculative fiction that emphasizes character and skirts the boundary between the real and the unreal. She has published a book of poems, *Other Worlds*, based on the prints of M.C. Escher, prints included. In her other life, she is a semi-retired professor specializing in Central California Indian languages.

The Waitress and the Serpent Priest

by Spencer Koelle

I kicked open the swinging doors and locked eyes with my favorite customer. Andrea looked like a plump princess, with her long red hair, tiny silver earrings and tight name-brand clothes. Her wide green eyes lingered on me before she even noticed the bowl of fried ice cream on my platter.

I strode between the tables, keeping my eyes on her. Customers waved their menus, shouting in English and Spanish. One drunken tourist even stood up and tried to block my way. I ducked past without even glancing in his direction. A good waitress controlled her gaze; I'd worked in Papa's restaurant for half my life.

Andrea turned to the window when I reached her table. The view out the window was pretty, especially to city girls from Iowa. Papa always set the chandeliers low and lit the tables with candles to keep interior lighting from overwhelming the view. I turned down the lights whenever he forgot or got into a mood.

The sunset streaked the desert foothills with bloody light and purple shadows. The haunted church loomed up at the edge of town, half-hiding its clutch of statues in deeper darkness.

"You better eat up before the center melts," I said, plopping her dessert in front of her. Andrea blinked and flashed a shy smile. She cracked the crispy shell and plunged a dripping spoonful into her mouth. She squealed. Then she blushed and covered her lips.

"Do you like it?" I said, holding back a sarcastic smile.

"It's amazing." She wiped her chin then took another bite.

I hovered over the table. Andrea tipped like royalty. "Is there anything else I can do for you?"

She opened her mouth, looked at me, then glanced away and

focused on her ice cream. If I didn't know better, I'd think she was bashful. What did she have to embarrass her? Skinny little me, in a baggy uniform that matched the checkered tablecloth?

"Maybe some hot chocolate?" I offered. I could always cajole her into an extra dish.

"I probably shouldn't," Andrea said, staring at her empty platters. The last crispy flakes floated in the melted remains of her dessert. She licked her full lips clean and wrinkled her pink pug nose.

"I think you *want* something to round off dessert," I teased. So many American girls pretended to hate food. Grown women skinnier than me tried to hide their appetites like a stains on a dress. "I could bore you with another splash of local history."

This clinched the sale. Andrea rubbed her hands together and sucked in an eager breath. She devoured every scrap of fact, legend, and time-seasoned village gossip I could remember. The last few nights I'd hit up Great Aunt Pilla for bedtime stories I hadn't heard in years. In return, Andrea shared some memories of modern art productions and fifteen-theater cinemas.

I looked out the window, and inspiration struck. "Tell you what, I'll get you a hot chocolate, and you can hear about the serpent priest while it cools down."

Andrea raised her eyebrows. "Serpent priest? Is that, like, something to do with Quetzalcoatl?"

"Do you want whipped cream on your chocolate?" My eyes focused on a point in the air inches above the back of her head. I'd held back this twisted tale for just such an occasion. I knew the mix of speculation, myth, and what Iowans thought of as "native customs", would more than satisfy her curiosity.

Andrea snorted. "Alright, a *small* hot chocolate, no whipped cream."

I power-walked back to the kitchen. Normally I didn't leave dirty dishes on the table. Putting off that chore would let me linger with the stylish city girl for a few more minutes. Then she might give me a bigger tip. I told myself that was the only reason I wanted to linger.

Old Man Enrique leered at me. "I need another drink over here. I'm not getting any younger, you know!" He waved a few bills. I stared at his ropy spit and shot past him. If I made eye contact, I had to serve the customer. Some other waitress could deal with Father's oldest drinking companion.

I swooped through the double-doors into spices and steam. Both cooks were busy, but I had learned to prep most popular dishes myself. I popped a cup under the wheezing nozzle and filled it up with chocolate-based drink product.

Father put a hand on my shoulder. I nearly spilled scalding chocolate all over him. He could move like a shadow when he was sober.

"Relax, little flower. What's the matter?" He smiled, wide and easy. His eyes were clear and focused, not bloodshot. I relaxed a little.

"Nothing's wrong," I said. His good mood might hold for the rest of the evening. "Is business going alright?"

"It could be worse." He chuckled and patted my back with his big smooth hands. They were gentle enough to brush away tears, but strong enough to leave dark bruises. "Does my favorite daughter need a break?"

"I can do my share, Papa. I'll just get back to my table." I gave him a one-armed hug and a quick peck on the cheek. Then I fled.

I navigated the maze of chairs and tables. The hot mug trembled in my hands. When I reached the circle of light around Andrea's table, the chills left my back. I realized how hot the cup was, and slammed it on the table.

"Are you okay?" Andrea said.

I shrugged and snickered. I fixed my gaze outside the window. The dusk lay too thick to tell, but the doors of the church may have swung open. The rushing clouds changed the play of shadows. Somehow, that old stone building could steal attention away from the strip malls and neon signs. I tried not to imagine the statues moving.

"Let me tell you about the serpent priest," I said.

Andrea pulled her hands back and sat up straight. The glow of sunset and candlelight turned her pale cheeks a deep scarlet.

"Sometimes he's called the fork-tongued man, or Father Two Tails. He built a church way before the bypass, before my Great Aunt's time, and before the fight for independence."

The ribbons of history pulled me back through the generations. A trance-like calm settled over me as I told the tale my Great Aunt had learned from her grandmother, who learned it from her elders before her. Everyone who belonged in our town knew the story by heart, but we told it anyway. Andrea leaned closer, hot drink forgotten. She brushed flame-orange bangs from her eyes.

I stared out at the church and took a deep breath. Andrea followed my gaze. I could almost hear her heart beat faster.

"Because he was a charming man, and because all the villagers were pious people—even the ones who followed the old ways—the church grew in power and wealth. You see that paved road, the clock tower over there, and the spring that's diverted to run through the fields on this side of the road?" I pointed to each land-mark. The shadowy blobs gained definition with my memory and words.

"All of those are the Father's 'holy works.' Of course, he set up the church with great gold crosses and wore robes of silk, too."

I brushed back my hair. Andrea blinked and took a sip of hot chocolate. She didn't lick or wipe away the mustache of foam.

I cleared my throat. "Old widows put their last pennies into the collection plate and prayed for ease and comfort. Lonely men turned in silver-crusted family heirlooms and prayed for beautiful wives and healthy sons. The lost and sick prayed for homes and healing. When their prayers were answered, the priest spoke of generosity and god's bounty. When misfortune and strife struck, he read sermons about divine retribution, pagan idolatry, and secret witchcraft."

Andrea nodded. Her legs swayed a little under the table, bare knees standing out in torn jeans. I couldn't believe that in the United States upscale stores sold factory-made torn jeans. Still, I liked seeing her knees.

I stared out the window at the tall, ancient house of stone. My shiver was only half-faked. My audience had grown restless.

"Everything changed when the priest noticed his unmarried sister was with child. At first, he denounced her and locked her in the cellar, but he couldn't stay angry at her for long. He decided it wasn't all her fault, and he called the entire village before him for a witch trial."

I spread out my arms and leaned back. Andrea leaned in closer, her green eyes wide. A desert wind whipped down and rattled the power lines.

"The preacher told them all that witchcraft had filled his daughter with lustful enchantment. He turned his wrath upon the most harmless widow in town, Marina the Ancient, in her ratty old rags and faded blue shawl."

"And she wasn't guilty, right?" Andrea burst in. She covered her mouth, like after a hiccup, and then gulped down chocolate, eyes downcast.

"He certainly said she was guilty when he put her to the stake, and all the married men and comfortable widows and healthy folk agreed with him. Whether his sister proclaimed the woman's innocence and threw herself on the fire, or whether she stood too close as she piled on kindling, I can't say." I hesitated, waiting for her comment before pressing on. "Your chocolate is growing cold."

Andrea chugged the hot drink and covered a burp. She even managed to burp in a cute way. "But, was the old lady a witch?"

I tapped my nose and shrugged. "Well, when the end came, something certainly happened. She proclaimed her innocence to the last. Some say she called out to the Virgin Mary, who appeared in the smoke to entreat the priest, but he turned away from her and was struck by the wrath of his God. Some say she really was a witch, and she laid a dying hex on him. Some say that the old lady was the last surviving priestess of Quetzalcoatl, who rose out of the smoke to punish the man for defiling his kingdom. You ask four people, and you'll get seven different answers."

Andrea nodded, but she looked a little lost. Her eyes drifted to the fading sunset, the flickering candle, and a small tear in the hem of my skirt.

"What I know for sure is that some power greater than his own took up the man and changed him forever."

Andrea perked up.

I leaned over the candle to put my face in shadow. "His tongue split in two, and his skin turned to scales, so that nobody would trust his lies ever again. He was bound to the church he misused until the town he built should fall into dust. His eyes filled with barren hatred, a spite so powerful..." I took a deep breath and glanced at the statue-filled church courtyard. I beckoned Andrea closer and whispered into her ear, "that anyone who met his gaze turned as stony as his heart."

Andrea jerked back with a gasp and shudder.

I nodded sagely and tried to hold back a smile.

She righted her chair and tugged down her shirt, hiding the pale bit of tummy that had poked out when she'd leaned forward.

"You mean, like Medusa?" she said.

I blinked. "Who?"

"You know, the Greek myth? She was some priestess cursed with snakes for hair and a visage so hideous that anyone who looked at her turned to stone. Perseus killed her by using his shield as a mirror, because the reflection wouldn't hurt him."

That didn't sound right to me. If it was the horrible appearance that turned you to stone, wouldn't a reflection be just as dangerous? I didn't want to push that point, though.

"Where did you learn about this? Did you live in Greece for a while?" I couldn't remember a time when I hadn't known about Father Two Tails. My friends and I had dared each other to go to the haunted church and touch a statue, and one boy claimed his big brother had stolen an altar cloth and closed his eyes just in time. That had been back when I was too small to help out the family business.

Nobody I knew had ever entered the church proper. Everyone

knew a friend of an aunt's cousin who'd stepped through those doors and never come out. The superstitious would leave a bottle of wine or some coins on the front steps of the church, to ward away sickness or ask for wealth, but always during full day, when cold-blooded creatures lay still to drink in warmth. The tourists might take pictures from a distance, but they didn't venture far from paved roads and soda machines.

"I learned it from books and stuff." Andrea shrugged. "I thought everyone knew about it. I mean, not that you should, of course, it's just an odd little story," she sputtered. Andrea turned to the window. "So, all of those statues used to be people?"

"That's what Aunt Pilla told me," I said.

"Why do they keep coming, then?" Andrea said.

"Well, because the fork-tongued man hoards up all the treasures he gathered during his mortal life, and everything he's stolen from victims or taken as offerings since. Aunt Pilla says half the treasure came from a blind widow who murdered her wealthy husband and fell in love with the serpent-priest." Andrea raised her eyebrows. Maybe she wasn't rich for an only child from Iowa, or maybe she had that relentless drive for money I'd seen in other teenagers from the United States.

"One of Mama's church friends, I mean, from the new church, not the haunted one, says . . ." I coughed and tried to regain composure. It was hard when Andrea stared at me. "she says that the people aren't dead, but imprisoned in stone as long as the serpent priest's heart keeps beating. The old corn farmer insists that all the statues will catch up with their human age and turn to dust the moment he dies. Some people even say that eating an eye of the holy snake demon grants you mystical powers."

Andrea stared hard at the church then she returned to me. She leaned over very close. "You're pulling my leg. I mean, you don't *really* believe that, do you?"

I cocked an eyebrow. "I told you about the time Father caught a green-skinned *chupacabras* attacking the chickens? It left four hens with tiny holes in their necks and less blood than a banana." I hadn't told her that we thought it would be a waste to throw out such neatly drained and butchered meat, so we'd served them in the quesadillas anyway.

"I told you about the red-eyed, headless, winged specter that flew over mom's house on her wedding night?" Andrea had called it a "mothman" and said they had a similar legend in the United States. My mother had called it a "godless angel."

"Okay, okay, I believe you," Andrea stammered. "I didn't mean to . . . like, I just wasn't sure."

I chuckled and patted her on the shoulder. "Another fried ice cream would do you good. You haven't tried the coffee-flavored one."

"Well, if you're positive," Andrea said. Her eyes drifted out to the long shadows of the haunted church. She smacked her lips, took a pocket mirror out of her purse, and dabbed away the chocolate foam with a napkin.

I straightened up and headed back for the kitchen. I looked over my shoulder, but Andrea didn't watch me leave this time. She kept her gaze on the haunted church, firelight glinting in her mirror.

Both cooks were busy, again. Father sat on a bench, sorting out receipts and muttering to a calculator. I skirted over to the industrial freezer and yanked it open. Somebody kept hiding the coffee ice cream at the very back, even though there was plenty of room.

"Pureza Mariposa Franchesco, could you come over here?" Father said, not looking up from his figures.

I shut the freezer and hurried to him. "Yes, Papa?"

"You know Mr. Enrique is still waiting." He kept his voice level and soft.

I nodded.

"Mr. Enrique has been my valued customer since before you were born."

"Yes, Papa," I murmured. I kept my head down.

"Don't you 'Papa' me, young woman. I will not have my long-standing customer listen to his stomach growl while you chat away with your little friend." He shook his head and sighed. He scratched out a line with his pen.

"Er, Father? I know Mr. Enrique is very important, but I just convinced this customer to order another dessert. Besides, mama said that people come here for the atmosphere as much as the food, and you told me that engaging the patrons on a personal level is important. So, I just thought, maybe it's good for the restaurant?"

Father smiled and shook his head. "Little flower, when you have worked for more than twenty years in this place, put the sweat of your back into the very foundations, and learned a little of the world, then you *might* understand how to run the Desert Rose."

I should have stopped talking, but some mad impulse pushed me on. Mother always said I didn't know when to keep my mouth shut. "But, Papa, I think it's for the best—"

Father locked eyes with me. I bit my tongue and stumbled back. His lips pulled tight. "Don't you try to walk away when I'm speaking to you."

I froze. He set down the pen and picked up the broom. The cooks and dishwashers took a renewed interest in their work. I braced for impact.

Father broke out into a peal of horse laughter. "You think? Little flower, when you bring home the eyes of the fork-tongue man, then maybe you can tell your father how to run his own restaurant."

I joined in the laughter, as did one of the cooks. I scurried out to take Enrique's order before Father's mood changed.

* * * * *

I bent under the table, scrubbing away something that I hoped was sour cream. The workers assigned to clean up this shift were late, again.

I could hear mother sobbing in the back and father begging for her forgiveness. Right now, I despised her more than absent workers or the sticky white mess under my damp rag. No matter what mother said now, no matter what father had done to her five minutes ago, I knew that eventually she would welcome him back into her heart.

Somebody rattled the door and shouted. I jerked my head at the "Closed" sign and returned to my chore.

Mother was weak. I hated her more because, in a while, I'd give in to the same weakness. I'd crawl back to her soothing words and bandages the next time Father lost his self-control. Mama said that she couldn't leave if she tried, because she had no livelihood. Father always told me that I must forgive him, because I needed him to take care of me. Sometimes, after a long night of drinking, he'd stumble into my room. He'd try to apologize, but he always ended with, "I did the best I could."

I cleared my eyes and scrubbed away the last curdled streak. Maybe Mama would learn not to bother Father this time. The man outside kept hammering on the door.

I looked up. He wore a tailored suit, but dust covered it. His red hair looked tangled and messy. Sweat ran down his face, and red rimmed his green eyes. A cold shadow passed over my soul.

I unlocked the door. "Sir?"

"Andrea! Where did you see her last? Is she in here? I know she's somewhere in town. I've looked everywhere else!"

I blinked. "Andrea? Are you her father?"

He stared at me. "You know her? You're the one she talks about? Did she come in for lunch?"

I shook my head. "I'm sorry sir." My voice wavered. I stuttered over my words. "She hasn't come around since closing time last night." I fell back on my default response to frantic strangers. "Do you want to see the manager?"

The man bit his lip and propped himself against the wall. He shook his head and mumbled. "Where's the police office? I was just there. You hear stories."

I wanted to reach out and take his hand, or to point him in the right direction, or say something. I couldn't move. The man stumbled away, oblivious to the blazing sun on his peeling red skin.

I didn't want to look. A bitter taste filled my mouth. My head jerked over to the foothills on the other side of the highway. The statues clustered around the haunted church. Light glinted off metal. I couldn't be sure at this distance, but maybe there was one statue more.

* * * * *

"I don't need to risk my flesh for some stupid tourist brat," I said, to the empty stretch of sand. A buzzard screamed at me, flapping its wings at such atrocious lying. I chucked a rock at it. The rock missed its mark, but the carrion bird flew further afield.

The wind whistled through the cracked stone. I gripped the bag at my side, filled with sharp knives, strong spices, and a silver cross.

I had only packed these items in case I ran into any wild animals taking shelter from the afternoon sun. I might find coyotes, or scorpions, or poisonous snakes.

Musical echoes rolled off the weather-worn church, filling the still air. A stink of incense and old leather rolled out from the gap in the doors. I tried to remember if the church doors had been open a crack when I'd arrived.

My skin crawled. I didn't want any treasure or riches. I didn't need to save stupid tourist girls. Andrea would turn up safe and sound the next day. I turned around and fled.

I stumbled when green and red screamed out of a clear sky. A quetzal bird perched on a stick-like shrub, right on the edge of the road. Great trucks roared past, close enough to make its perch tremble. The colorful bird didn't even blink.

The bird cocked its head my way. It focused its black eyes on the stone building behind me. The sun glinted in them. I felt puny, flushed, and awful in its presence. It stared me down like the coward I was, clicked its beak, and flew off.

I dusted myself off, wondering what a quetzal was doing so far from the forest. When I turned around, I saw only the profane house of worship. No hint of red and green glowed for miles around. I struck out for the church once more and recognized a terrible sight.

In the courtyard, one statue stood at the very edge, a plump statue with long hair. A pocket mirror glinted in its hand. I stepped closer.

I wanted to believe that some stonemason had spotted Andrea in town and chiseled a perfect likeness of her overnight, complete with a look of hurt shock. I knew that mirror trick wouldn't work. The reflected face of death was still the face of death.

My knees grew weak, but I pressed on. I prayed the story about the statues awakening when the serpent priest died was true.

Andrea wasn't the only slayer who had come prepared. All around me, big strong men stood with weapons in hand. Police aimed handguns they would never fire. Warriors with arms thicker than my legs brandished axes and spears.

None of them had struck. To take aim, they had to look at their target.

I shivered. Against the axes and rifles, my collection of kitchen tools seemed pathetic. I pulled out the cross and hung it around my neck. It occurred to me that a demon living in a house of god wouldn't flinch at one little cross. I left it on anyway.

"Hail Mary, full of grace," I whispered.

There was no question about it this time. The stone shook with a mocking, melodious voice. Out from the gap between doors, and out of every window and crack, an artful parody of "Ave Maria" rang forth.

I steeled my heart, and lifted another prayer to anyone who might listen. "To avenge, or to save, please, let me end this."

* * * * *

The courtyard had looked crowded, but it was almost empty compared to the inside of the church. Stone attendants filled every pew. Stone figures knelt before the altar, awaiting a communion that would never pass their hardened lips. Parishioners of quartz and marble lined the exits to leave a service that would never end.

I tried to sneak forward. The crunch echoed around the cathedral. I looked down.

The gems were the last thing I noticed. Emeralds, garnets, and moss agates carpeted the floor, spread among coins, Rolex watches, and even a few MP3 players. Here and there, a bottle lay, communion wine thick with dust or half-empty tequila. They hadn't gone crunch.

The second things I noticed were snake bones. Massive shed skins, glowing orange in the sunlight.

I wanted to turn tail and flee, but that would mean passing the statue of Andrea on my way out. Besides, where would I go then? To a restaurant where Aunt Pilla, Mama, and I did the real work so Father could drink the profits and treat us like sick dogs?

I heard a rustle. Movement flickered in the corner of my eye. I shut my eyes.

I couldn't even move. The serpent priest didn't move either. He sang to me, weaving together old chants and hymns about God's holy temple, living forever by the grace of Christ, and punishments for blasphemy.

I couldn't help thinking about the life of this lonely and bitter creature. The skeletons of fellow reptiles testified how he treated his closest kindred. I shuddered.

The song grew closer. If I didn't open my eyes, I wouldn't be in any danger.

Something lashed against my cheek and my head jerked back. I felt blood welling in the hot gash.

If I looked at his eyes, I was dead.

If I didn't open my eyes, I was dead.

I tried to back up, eyes shut, but I tripped over the rubble. The cold stone floor struck me, metal banging against my skull and cracked bones digging into my back. Violent pain slashed inside my dark spinning world.

Father Two-Tales hissed. His voice sounded too close, but I couldn't tell what direction it came from in the resonant chamber.

I couldn't look into those spiteful eyes. But then, maybe I didn't have to. I'd seen big strong men outside, warriors and police, but I hadn't seen any waitresses.

I curled upright, lowered my head, and raised my eyelids. The fork-tongued man loomed across the aisle from me, terrible and glorious. His tails lashed out, more than two meters long, but they weren't quite strong enough to support his weight. He used two holy staffs as crutches. He whistled at me and beckoned with the tip of his left tail.

As soon as my eyes ventured near his face, I locked on his smile. I didn't have to make eye contact if I could focus on his teeth. He had clean white human teeth, out of place in his lipless reptilian maw.

I knew that serpents didn't blink. I coughed dust and hunched over. He lurched closer. If this didn't work, my family would never find out what happened to me. Mother would weep for weeks. Sancho would never be able to catch up with his old school friend again. Great Aunt Pilla's heart would break, and the wild-eyed man from the States would never find out what had happened to his daughter. I reached into my bag and pulled out a vial of spices. Father, of course, would have to hire another waitress.

The serpent priest paused for breath. His tongue flickered in and out. Andrea had told me that snakes don't really "smell" the way humans do; they "taste" the air. As he leaned closer, sampling my aroma, I uncapped a bottle of hot sauce and the spice jar and flung them at his face.

The monster knocked them aside with his staffs, but the jar broke against one, and some hot sauce still splashed him. He unleashed a metallic scream when spices struck his eyes and tongue. He dropped the staffs to claw at his burning face.

I ran past him. If I could get behind him, I could manage a clean stab at the back without risking eye contact. I jumped over his tail, but the other one tripped me.

I tried to crawl away.

The serpent priest crawled faster than I could; he had more practice. His claws raked my back. His tails wrapped around me, crushing and binding.

I tried to reach my knife, but the tails pulled my arms back behind me. Every breath cost me more effort. I dug my nails in, trying to hurt him, but they couldn't break through his leathery scales.

The serpent priest hummed "Ave Maria" again. His bitter

tongue flickered across my face. I stared at the point an inch above his head, at his pale yellow neck, at everything except his eyes. He held my lids open and hissed in frustration, bringing his head closer to mine.

I opened my mouth wider, struggling for one last breath. Coils of muscle bound my chest tight. His tongue flickered out again, stroking my face from hair to chin.

I sucked in his bitter, spicy tongue. I bit down, hard.

The grip relaxed. The serpent priest rolled back, every limb thrashing, mad with agony. I rifled through my bag. The first knife clattered out of my sweat-slick hands. The second found my grip. I drew back, put all of my tender weight behind the blow, and drove it into his chest.

It broke skin then caught against the bone. I buried the next knife up to the hilt.

The body jerked, hissing, and tried once more to lock eyes with me. I waited until it lay still. I pulled out an empty case for chewing tobacco and a grapefruit spoon. I closed my eyes, groped around, and dug my spoon into the eye socket.

* * * * *

I opened my eyes after securing the tobacco tin. His empty sockets stared back at me from a peaceful scaly face. The trickle of cool blood at his chest ceased.

Stone cracked all around me. I stood up to see figures break free from their coating of dust and lichens. They all blinked, sighed, and aged away to withered husks. The church bell chimed thirteen. Decay claimed its back-rent before the last echoes died.

My throat closed up, and my vision wavered. Clotting blood and corpse dust decorated my work uniform. I didn't feel brave, or proud, or buoyed up by a triumph over evil. I wanted to take a long shower and weep where nobody could find me.

I stood like a statue myself. Wind whistled above the tower and old bones settled. A mouse crept out from the pews, half-climbing, half-swimming through the debris. Every whisker on its nose stood out in the glow of stained-glass, like a Fifth of May firework.

A sneeze brought me back to reality. More dust stirred up. I sneezed and coughed and shivered until thick mucus coated the inside of my mouth. I filled my pockets with as many valuables as my numb fingers could lift. Then I stumbled out of the empty church. A voice in my head warned that Father would throw a tantrum when he saw the state of my clothes.

Outside, the hot desert air scoured my face. A truck horn blared in the distance. The high sun blinded me with purple-edged whiteness.

I saw Andrea. I blinked and pinched myself. She dropped the mirror from her hand, worked her jaw, and rubbed her eyes as if waking from her mid-day nap.

"I was so stupid," she murmured. "I screwed up." Her voice rasped. Her legs trembled beneath her.

I caught Andrea by the arm. She steadied herself against me while I produced a water bottle. "Drink."

She almost sucked it dry, but she stopped herself. She offered it to me. I shook my head. She'd gone without water for a day.

"The last thing I remember is those bright, screaming eyes. They were the color you get when you stare at something too long, only, more light blue." She stopped and coughed out a hysterical giggle. "I'm babbling. Sorry."

I patted her on the shoulder. "It's okay. It must have been horrible."

She looked down at the blood on my dress. "Oh my God, are you hurt?"

I shook my head. "It's his, not mine. I mean, I killed the serpent priest." I felt absurd. My own knees started trembling. The insane day rushed over me.

Andrea stared at me. She shook her head, not in denial, but as if trying to dislodge water from her ear. "That's amazing. You're just incredible."

"Er," I stammered. I didn't know how to respond. "Thanks for going first. Really. I wouldn't have known that a reflection was just as deadly if you hadn't—" I mumbled. I didn't know how to deal with compliments.

"—been incredibly stupid." Andrea laughed. "I think you saved my life." She stared at her hands and blinked.

"Well," I stammered. What can you say to that?

Andrea didn't wait for me to respond. She jumped forward and crushed me in a big squishy hug, covering my face with sloppy kisses.

Andrea jumped back as if shocked by her own actions. She looked down and bit her lip. "Thanks," she said. "A lot."

My head spun. The dust and blood had smeared all over her perfect shirt, and some of it had even stuck to her cheeks. I knew I looked like a mess.

Still, that hadn't mattered to Andrea. I tried to catch my breath and felt a tingle run from my ears to my toes. Those hadn't been the kisses of an aunt, or the kiss used to greet an old friend.

Without actually moving, Andrea had started to shrink towards the shade. I reached out towards her and smacked my own wet kiss on her lips, dust and all.

This time, her freckles vanished in the heavy blush. I broke off to breathe. "Thank you, too. And, you're welcome."

Andrea rewarded me with her shy, unthinking smile. It lasted longer than a second. Her contentment broke.

"Dad! How long have I been here? He must be scared out of his mind." She bit her nails, then pulled them out and spat dust.

"I'll take you back to town," I said.

* * * * *

Three hours later, I stood on the broad green veranda of Father's house. Andrea's father had insisted on taking me to dinner somewhere I wouldn't have to help out. He didn't seem to believe most of the disjointed account Andrea and I relayed, but he didn't care either. His daughter had been returned to him, so he would express gratitude.

I looked over my shoulder at their black rental car on the cracked driveway. Andrea had offered to let me use the shower back at her hotel, but I had insisted on going home to change. This had all happened a bit too fast for it to feel real.

Inside the car, Andrea and her daddy laughed together, their eyes wet. I turned back to the battered screen door and opened it. My father always said he did his best with what he had, but then, I'd seen plenty of families in town with less money than us. Most of those families had children that didn't flinch when their parents grabbed a belt.

I knocked on the door. "Mama? Aunt Pilla?" With any luck, father wouldn't be home yet. How could I explain this to them? Aunt Pilla, at least, might understand.

Mama opened the door. She stifled a scream.

"Mama, I'm okay. I can explain," I said.

She grabbed me by the arm, kissed me, and began dragging me up around into the back room.

"Oh, baby, what happened to you? No, talk later. Your father is in a mood." Her eyes darted around. My strength left me.

Father strode out of the kitchen, cutting us off.

"Well?" he said, in a voice so soft I could barely hear it.

"I'm sure she just—" Mama said. Father cut her off with a glare.

"I'm sorry," I said, while I tried to think of which sin I had committed this time.

"You are sorry? Really, Pureza Mariposa Franchesco? Is that all you have to say for yourself?" He looked tired and sad.

Mother held my hand, but she started to lean away from me. Her eyes darted between us.

"It was terrible. I shouldn't have left work early," I stammered.

He raised his finger. "Be still."

I didn't move. He shook his head and took another step towards us.

"Don't try to play stupid with me. Do you think I'm an idiot?" He put a hand to his heart, and tears brimmed in his eyes. "I never thought that I had raised a little thief."

I'd told the cook about the spices and cutlery I needed to

borrow before I left, hadn't I? Had the cook passed the information on to my father? No point worrying now. I needed to make amends.

"Papa, it was just a mistake," I said with my eyes downcast. I didn't see the slap, but I had braced for it. I staggered back. Mama pulled me into her arms.

Father ignored her and kept speaking to me. "You're right about that, young lady. You have made a very big mistake."

He tapped my mother on the shoulder. "Go to the bedroom. This is between us."

She opened her mouth to speak. I looked at her, pleading with my eyes. He shook his head.

My mother gave me one apologetic glance then fled. While I looked after her, fuming at her cowardice, I felt the crack across the back of my knees.

I broke my fall. Splinters dug into my palms.

"You want to cry? I'll give you something to cry about," Father said. I struggled to my feet and backed away. One of the emeralds fell from my pocket. He picked it up. His face twisted with disgust.

"Where did you get this? Did you steal this too? You mean your own dear father isn't the only one you've been robbing blind?" Tears ran freely down his cheeks.

"No, Papa," I said through the lump in my throat.

I ducked the next blow he swung at me. He blinked, dumbfounded. Then his face went calm. I started backing towards the door as he reached into the closet. I turned and ran.

The broom stabbed into the back of my knee. My chin hit the floor.

"Don't you lie to me," Father said, striking after each word. He didn't stick to the places where it wouldn't show. "What else have you taken that doesn't belong to you?"

I reached into my pocket and pulled out the little tin. "Please, don't open it," I whimpered.

I closed my eyes and tried not to smile.

"You little—" His voice cut off with a sharp crack, like a chair breaking.

I felt my way upright and pried the case from the cold stone fingertips. I closed it up again. I opened my eyes, and stared at his terrified granite face. I ran upstairs to my room.

I tore off my uniform, tugged on my best dress, and wiped filth from my skin. I felt guilty for not feeling guilty. I dropped enough jewels to hire a new waitress on Mama's dresser. I left a note for Aunt Pilla. I packed the few things I owned and ran out the house. The door slammed behind me, just before Mama screamed. That sound touched my heart with a bit of grudging sorrow and a bit of sinful delight.

I ran up the driveway. Andrea got out and opened the door for me. I sighed and hopped in. The inside of the car smelled of disinfectant and pine.

Andrea squeezed in next to me and held my hand. "Are you okay?"

"I don't want to talk," I said. "Not yet."

She leaned closer and handed me a tissue. I clutched it tight. Maybe we could spend some time together, while she stayed in the town. Maybe I would strike out on my own. Wherever I went, I knew I didn't want to go back *home*.

"Can we go to the hotel? I'd like to use your shower."

About the author:

Spencer Koelle is a crotchety fantasy author trapped in a young assistant philanthropic consultant's body. He has written two novels, though neither is yet published. For more of Spencer's work, visit www.spencerkoelle.com.

A Leap of Logic

by Joseph Zieja

Kaslan looked down from the dais at the young man shuffling his feet. A nervous tension filled the chamber, the crackling of the torches the loudest sound in the room.

"Ten silver pieces, to be paid by the harvest." Kaslan clapped his hands, indicating that his judgment was complete.

Well, it didn't indicate anything, really, except that he felt the need to clap his hands. It was a sort of applause for himself, a pat on the back that he'd dispensed justice to another one of the cretins of Loamas.

The young man looked crestfallen. "Lord Magistrate," he began, an all-too-familiar whiny leer in his voice.

Kaslan silenced him with a wave of his hand. "I'll hear no more of this. You've already wasted enough of my time."

"But you haven't even heard me speak!"

Kaslan rose, staring down from his perch behind the long wooden table at the front of the dais. He leaned forward.

"Words," he said, "are the brush strokes of every con artist. And you, boy, are a con artist. You sold Finnel Brili sheep with no wool." He pointed to a dark-haired man standing to the side who failed to conceal a smug smile.

The young man gaped. "They're *sheep*," he protested. "It grows back!"

"Twelve silver pieces!" Kaslan roared, raising a finger. "And one more for every extra second you remain in this court!"

The man licked his lips, considering another smart-mouthed response no doubt, before turning on his heel and storming out of the room. The carpet that led to the exit was worn and frayed from many feet doing exactly that over the years.

Finnel approached the stand and gave a half-bow, his low voice bordering on snide mockery.

"I appreciate your objectiveness, Lord Magistrate."

Kaslan bristled at the flattery. "I warn you not to test my patience. You are just as much a fool as the fool who just left. Why you would buy a shorn sheep is beyond me."

"As I said, I have poor eyesight."

"Poor indeed," Kaslan said with a snort. "Now get out before I have the guards throw you out for malfeasance."

The dark-haired man looked up, shocked. "Malfeasance?"

"Wasting my time!"

"That's not what malfeasance-"

"Get out!"

The crowd shuffled, a murmur going up around the room. There seemed to be more and more onlookers every day, come to see him dole out righteousness. He wondered what they were smirking about.

"Next!"

A silver-haired woman with a face like a prune emerged from the dredges, hobbling her way across the floor. She tapped a gnarled walking staff on the ground as she walked, but it did nothing to accelerate her pace. Kaslan gave a sigh of exasperation as she crawled her way to the center of the room.

"Today, please," he said.

The old woman finally turned to face him, and for a moment Kaslan was taken aback by the color of her eyes. They matched her hair, a faded silver like worn steel wanting of polish, rimmed by the weak yellow of the many long years behind her. She gave him a placid smile, showing a set of crooked teeth.

To his surprise, two Loamasi guardsmen flanked her, expressions hard. They eyed her warily as though they expected her to strike out with her cane at any moment. A third man pushed his way through the crowd, a stout shopkeeper with a face as greasy as the insides of a hot meat pie. In not-so-short order, the four of them arrayed themselves before him.

"What's *your* problem?" he asked, locking eyes with the old woman.

"Actually, Lord Magistrate," the shopkeeper said, wiping off his apron with a pair of meaty hands, "I have the problem."

"I'll say you do," Kaslan said, switching his gaze to the man. "But I assume you came here to complain about something other than your obvious overindulgence in pastries."

The man swallowed whatever words came to his mouth. His face reddened.

"This woman," he said, pointing to the hobbling hag, "stole three crates of fruit from my stand."

Kaslan raised an eyebrow and turned his gaze to the woman. She changed her stance a bit, her back clearly unused to standing for long periods of time. Kaslan couldn't imagine her holding a single fruit, never mind three crates.

"Did she also steal your mule?" Kaslan asked.

The man frowned, confused. "No, Lord Magistrate. Why?"

"I'm just wondering how a woman who could be destroyed by a sneeze managed to carry off three crates of cargo."

The man cleared his throat. "They were small crates. And she took them fruit by fruit."

"Ah," Kaslan said. "And you, being hesitant to raise a hand without food in it, were powerless to stop her?"

"I didn't see it happen," the shopkeeper said, his voice trembling with barely-hidden anger.

"She stole it from somewhere below your knees, then? I imagine you have difficulty seeing anything in that region." Kaslan waved a hand below his own waist to accentuate his point.

The shopkeeper clenched his jaw. "I keep all my wares on the stand in front of me," he said. He slowly extended a flat hand above the ground, about the height of his collar bone. "Just about here." He waved his hand back and forth, drawing an imaginary line in the air.

Kaslan sat down, propping his elbows up on the table. A piece of parchment in just the wrong spot caused his arm to slip, and his hand slammed into the wood with a crack. The whole room jumped in unison at the sound.

That's right, Kaslan thought as he slowly peeled himself up from the table and glared at no one in particular. *I only did that because I'm angry.*

He cleared his throat. "Now, master . . .?"

"Shofann."

"Master Shofann. Am I to understand that a feeble old woman waltzed into your shop every day for the last month and stole a single piece of fruit, resulting in a total loss of three crates of merchandise?"

"Yes, Lord Magistrate."

Kaslan pulled out his favorite facial expression: a sardonic smile that, in the right light, could have been mistaken for genuine concern.

"You'll forgive me if I find that a bit hard to believe," he said.

"Oh," Master Shofann said, his face illuminating with the recollection of a forgotten piece of information, "she's also a witch." He turned to one of the guards. "I never remember to say that, do I?"

The guard shook his head.

Kaslan raised an eyebrow. "A witch?"

"You know," Shofann said, "a sly sorceress, a magical maid, a—"

"That's quite enough alliteration," Kaslan hissed. "I know what a witch is."

Or rather, what a witch was supposed to be. Kaslan had lived too many years in this boring world to believe such drivel. He turned to the "witch."

"And what do you have to say about all this?"

The old woman, her face still frozen in the pleasant smile of someone halfway in oblivion, shrugged.

"It's true."

"Which part?"

"Just the witch part."

For the first time that he could remember, Kaslan didn't know what to say. An uncomfortable silence settled on the room as he gaped at the woman, wondering from what astral plane she must have come to think that claiming she was a witch would earn mercy in the Loamasi court of justice.

"I'm sorry," Kaslan finally said. "What?"

"I'm a witch," she said simply. "But I never stole any fruit. It spikes my blood sugar." She tapped her foot with the tip of her cane. "Makes my feet swell."

In all his years as the Loamasi Magistrate, Kaslan had never heard anything so absurd as he was hearing at that moment. He'd dealt with liars, thieves, cheats, murderers, and encyclopedia salesmen, but never something as ridiculous as a witch stealing fruit.

But it didn't really matter. As with all other matters of the idiots of Loamas, Kaslan had no time for these games. Dinner was probably waiting for him.

"Alright, alright," Kaslan said, waving a hand. "I've heard enough. Normally I'd let you say your piece, but you're obviously insane. You are hereby guilty of theft, perjury, and diabetes. Pay double the amount of three crates of Master Shofann's fruit, and try not to curse anyone on your way out."

Kaslan looked down for a brief moment to collect his things, muttering to himself. The day was finally over, and he could go home to the only person in his life who wasn't a total moron: his wife.

A sudden silence made Kaslan stop what he was doing and look up. To his surprise, the population of the courtroom had vanished in an instant, leaving only the old woman. She stood as still as a statue, and the torches along the wall began to flicker in metronomic synchronization, casting pendulum shadows on the floor. The air felt thick.

"What are you still doing here?" Kaslan asked. "Too much fruit?"

"You ask all the wrong questions, Kaslan Virulle," the woman said, her voice echoing as though from the bowels of a dark, distant cavern. "I've been watching you for a long time."

"I only ask questions as a formality," Kaslan said, turning his attention back to collecting his papers. "I already know all the answers. Now go away before I call the guards."

"So be it!" the woman cried. He heard her shuffling around in her clothing, and the sound of a small bell ringing out. "Seek no answers, have no answers. Such will be the decisions you make. Let no utterance from your lips be drawn from the trails of the facts you so casually toss aside. *Malekh-sha na'ar soh remmini!*"

"Oh," Kaslan said, drawing the sound out. He still didn't look up. "A foreigner, too, eh? You're lucky I've already sentenced you. I detest foreigners."

Finally he'd finished cleaning up his things, and he found that the woman was no longer in the room at all. That was funny; he never heard the clicking of her cane. At least the torches had stopped behaving so strangely. Where had the woman gone?

The faint tinkle of a bell sounded from somewhere off in the distance at the very edge of his hearing just before he realized that the old woman had been a ghost.

He froze, the papers in his hand crinkling with the sudden tensing of his muscles. A ghost? He supposed that made sense, but why had he thought of it just then? And why was he so absolutely sure he was right? He wasn't even sure it was possible to be both a witch *and* a ghost. In fact, he hadn't believed in either until just a few seconds ago.

Kaslan blinked, then came back to life again. He walked out of the courtroom, muttering to himself and wondering how to solve this new ghost witch problem.

* * * * *

The streets of Loamas teemed with life, people scurrying about with harried expressions. The hum of conversation layered on top of the shuffling of feet and the crying of wares, creating a chaotic medley of human existence that grated on Kaslan's ears. All he ever wanted was peace and quiet, yet he never seemed to catch a moment of it.

As usual, Kaslan put his head down and pushed through the crowd like a gust of wind that would not be denied passage. Most of the citizens knew by now to step lightly around him, and they gave him a wide berth. Thoughts of the disappearing ghost-witch plagued his mind; it seemed such a silly notion, now that he thought about it, but he was absolutely certain that it was true.

Kaslan sighed. Tholas would be waiting for him at the tavern. Maybe an ale or two would help him clear his mind.

He became vaguely aware that someone was speaking to him.

"Please, sir."

Looking up, he saw a young woman, barely more than a girl, dressed in tattered rags looking at him with a pair of pleading yellowed eyes. Her face, marred with tear-streaked dirt, held desolation in gaunt shadows.

"Just a few coins," she continued.

Kaslan made a face, and was about to tell her to go away when he noticed a small boy, no higher than his knees, standing in front of her. The woman gripped him gently by the shoulders and pushed him forward. Kaslan could have sworn he heard the tinkling of that bell again.

"Please," she said, "for the child."

Kaslan's mouth dropped.

"Have you no shame?" he said, outraged. "I will not purchase your child!"

The woman looked perplexed. "I beg your pardon, my lord?"

Kaslan barely heard her. He spun around, searching the crowd.

"Guards!" he shouted. "Guards!"

A pair of them materialized from the mass of people moving around him, their faces wrinkled in concern as they moved toward him with hurried steps.

He pointed at the woman. "Arrest this woman!"

The guards exchanged glances. "Why, Lord Magistrate?"

Kaslan sneered at them. Were they so blind?

"She's attempting to sell me her boy!" he said.

"I never!" the woman cried. "Sell my child?"

"Oh please," Kaslan said, glaring at her. "Just a moment ago you offered him to me for a few coins. Why else would you be approaching someone of my stature? Don't you know that slavery is highly illegal in Loamas?"

Kaslan snorted and shook his head in disgust. "For a few coins! Isn't he worth more to you than that?"

One of the guards reached out to lay a hand on the woman, but the other guard stopped him with a wave of his hand. He turned to Kaslan and bowed his head.

"Lord Magistrate," he began. "This woman is clearly a beggar. She couldn't have been offering her child to you."

Kaslan narrowed his eyes, his voice becoming as cool as ice. "Do you presume to be more knowledgeable in the law than myself, guardsman?"

"No, Magistrate, but—"

"But nothing! I know what I saw. Is it not my job, my very purpose in life, to pronounce judgment?"

The woman, frozen in her spot, looked between the three men with an expression deepening from confusion to abject terror.

"I'm sorry," she stammered, trying to back away. "I must have offended you. I didn't know you were the Lord Magistrate. I'll be on my way."

"You will do no such thing!" Kaslan said, fixing her with a stare. "This boy is lucky you didn't know who I was. Someone with fewer scruples might be sending him off to work in the mines at this very moment. Shame on you, woman. Guards!"

The guards, their jerky motions betraying their hesitation, reached out and seized the woman by the arms. She tried to pull away from them, but she was as thin as string.

"Please!" she said.

"I already said no!" Kaslan said, incredulous. "Even in the face of the law you still offer your child to me for payment? You sicken me, woman. I am doing Loamas a great service by taking you off the streets."

Stunned, she said no more. Kaslan turned to the guard, who looked unfittingly nervous for someone on the right side of justice.

"There will be no need to bring her before me again," Kaslan said. "I've already done my job, and I won't do it twice. Straight to the dungeon with her. Take care of the boy."

The woman allowed herself to be led away by the two guards, the bewildered boy in tow. Kaslan watched them go, giving himself a satisfied nod.

Another job well done, he thought.

A crowd had formed around the commotion, creating a sort of island on which Kaslan now stood. He swept his gaze across the citizens.

"Do any more of you wish to barter your children?" he asked levelly.

That set them moving. Within seconds, the crowd had reintegrated with the rest of society, leaving the scene on the street exactly as it had been before he'd been approached by the disgraceful woman. He grunted and moved on. Now he really needed a drink.

The Jerry Rig sat in the middle of a small square in the center of the city, and Kaslan eyed its broad door with a sense of relief. Out on the streets, things were supposed to be orderly. At least inside the tavern he knew he could expect some degree of sanity.

The stout figure of Tholas waited for him at a table near the entrance, two mugs of ale already on the table in front of him. Kaslan sat down with a long sigh.

"Rough day?" His friend, the only sane person in the city aside from himself and his wife, pushed the spare mug toward him.

"I'll say," Kaslan said. He grabbed the mug and took a long draw. "I met someone claiming to be a witch, and someone just tried to sell their kid to me."

Tholas' round face lit up with surprise. "That *is* quite a day. I didn't think selling children was allowed anymore."

"It's not," Kaslan said. "That's what was so strange about it."

Kaslan paused. For the first time, he started to really think about what had just happened.

"The woman must have been from around here," he said. "She was too poor to be a traveler. She must have known that what she was doing was illegal. Yet she practically threw the boy into my arms and asked for a few coins."

Tholas raked a hand through what remained of his hair. "That is a little odd. Are you sure she wasn't just begging?"

"I'm sure," Kaslan said, but even as he said the words some of his confidence bled out of him. Was he really that sure? Now that he thought about it, he hadn't actually heard the woman say that she was selling her son. Yet he'd felt so certain. A bit of queasiness flirted with his stomach.

"You don't look very sure," Tholas said, reading his expression. "Are you feeling alright? You look a bit pale."

Kaslan shook his head. "Now *that* I'm not so sure about. I feel kind of funny up here." He tapped his temple with a long finger.

"Well, that's nothing new," Tholas said with a smirk.

Kaslan couldn't bring himself to grin at his friend's playful remark, and after another long moment of silence Tholas pried again.

"What's on your mind?"

Rubbing his chin, Kaslan sighed. "It's . . . I'm almost positive that the woman who said she was a witch was also a ghost."

"A ghost-witch?"

Kaslan's eyes snapped up to meet his friend's.

"You know of ghost-witches?" he asked, eager for some evidence that he wasn't losing his mind.

"No," Tholas said. "That's the craziest thing I think I've ever heard you say."

"But it's true!" Kaslan's voice was almost pleading. "I'm sure it's true."

Tholas fell silent for a moment, taking quiet sips of his ale while looking at Kaslan over the brim of the mug.

"Let's talk about something else," he said.

"Yes," Kaslan said. He squeezed his eyes shut for a moment,

though it did nothing for the fuzziness in his head. "Let's."

"I got a new job," Tholas said.

"Oh? Doing what, exactly?"

Tholas grinned. "Guess."

The man behind the bar grabbed a couple of glasses, and they clinked together with a sound much like a small bell. The sound shot through Kaslan's head as though it was the loudest thing in the room, and his head started to hurt.

"What did you say?" Kaslan asked, muddled.

"I said guess what my new job is."

Kaslan's face hardened. He slowly put his mug down and folded his hands in his lap as he glared at the man he thought was his friend.

"I can't believe you," he hissed.

Tholas' grin evaporated. "What?"

"I can't believe you!" Kaslan repeated. "I've known you my whole life. I've always thought you to be a man of honor, Tholas. But an assassin?"

"Kaslan," he said, cocking his head, "I didn't say anything about being an assassin."

Kaslan sneered. "You don't have to say anything." He pointed between Tholas' eyes. "You're an assassin. Who hired you? Who are you going to kill, Tholas?"

"You've lost your mind," Tholas said, his face turning red. "I can't even cut a pheasant properly. Why would I ever think of sticking a knife into a man?"

"Don't tell me I'm wrong," Kaslan said. He pushed his chair back, wanting to keep his distance. "You're a fool for taking this job, Tholas, and a dangerous fool at that."

"I'm going to be a dockworker!" Tholas proclaimed, his eyes widening. "A man who takes boxes on and off the ships! No killing whatsoever."

"Now you lie to me?" Kaslan said, furious. "I never—"

Kaslan stopped speaking as a realization struck him, and the blood drained from his face. He pointed a thumb at his own chest.

"It's me, isn't it?" he whispered, his eyes wide.

"*What's* you?"

"I'm your target. You've been hired to kill me, and you're here to rub it in my face!"

Kaslan's eyes darted to the mug of ale on the table. The half empty mug of ale.

"Poison!" he shouted, standing up so fast that his chair ricocheted off the floor and spun to the side. "You've already done it!"

"Calm down!" Tholas said, ducking his head down and scanning the tavern. The patrons of the Jerry Rig had already stopped their conversations and were staring at them with nervous expressions. "You're causing a scene."

"You're the one causing a scene, assassin!" Kaslan backed slowly toward the door, knocking into a tavern maid and causing a tray full of food and wine to rain down on the floor in a chaotic heap.

Kaslan didn't stop to apologize. Why would he, when the tavern maid was clearly in on the plot? He ran out the door, his heart pounding, hoping he could make it home in time for his wife to prepare an antidote.

* * * * *

Walking calmly down the street with the last remnants of sweat dripping down his face, Kaslan stared at the stones under his feet as they passed by. After running four or five steps out the door, he'd become so winded that he'd nearly collapsed.

He didn't feel poisoned. In fact, he felt pretty good, despite the sudden revelation that he was grossly out of shape. He could still see straight, and his ragged breath was more due to the physical exertion than any toxin. But he had been so sure that Tholas was an assassin, so sure that his ale had tasted just a bit strange, so sure that the tavern maid had tried to stab him on the way out.

Something was going on here. Every ounce of his intuition told him that, as usual, he'd been right about everything he'd concluded today, but hindsight was proving a bit of a pest. Ghost-witches and children for sale were one thing, but his friend, an assassin? He couldn't believe it. But he did!

After slapping the hand of a merchant who he was convinced had just tried to steal his beard, he knew for certain that something was wrong. He hoped Shirri could help him find some answers. The notion that he had perhaps been incorrect about these things haunted him more than the noose of a gallows. Death was nothing compared to the threat of not being right.

Shirri was fighting valiantly with a pile of vegetables when he entered their simple home on the edge of the city. She threw him a smile over her shoulder, which did wonders for his mood. That smile was all the antidote he'd ever needed.

"Hello, dear," she said, turning back to massacring the greenery. "Dinner will be a bit late."

"That's fine," Kaslan said. He walked over to his favorite armchair and sat down in a huff, his muscles all going slack. His eyes toured the room, looking at the places where his children used to play before they were all old enough to leave the house on their own endeavors. The house seemed very empty all of a sudden.

"Is everything alright?" Shirri called out to him. The rhythmic sound of the knife hitting the counter was steady and strong.

"I don't think so," he said.

The chopping slowed. "What's the matter?"

Kaslan sunk deeper into his chair, sighing. "Have you ever wondered if I might have been wrong?"

"About what, dear?"

"Anything."

She chuckled, and the knife resumed its steady pace. "What a strange question."

"Why is it so strange?" Kaslan asked. He moved his eyes to look at her slender form standing at the counter. He watched the rhythm of her shoulders and arms as they went about their work.

"Of all the things you've ever wondered," she said, "it was never whether or not you'd been right."

For some reason, Kaslan felt deeply wounded by that remark.

He fumbled for a defense.

"That's a bit ridiculous, isn't it?" he said. "I mean, it's my job to be right about things."

"I wouldn't say that, dear," she said. "It's your job to listen to other people's stories and make sense of them. One would hope you're right, but that's not the important part, is it?"

Kaslan swallowed. "Have I always been that way?"

The chopping stopped, but Shirri didn't answer immediately. Kaslan found himself leaning forward in his chair in the silence that followed.

"I have, haven't I?"

"It's not that, dear," she was quick to respond. "You're being too hard on yourself. Did something happen at work today?"

Kaslan didn't hear her question. The sound of a bell was ringing somewhere in the back of his mind.

"I see how it is," Kaslan said. He couldn't tell if he was angry or sad. "I'm too old for you."

Shirri finally turned around to face him, her face unreadable except for the slight cant of her eyes that told him she was concerned.

"Kaslan . . ." she began.

"No," Kaslan said, standing up. "You don't have to tell me anything. I know what you're thinking. I've always known. I fail to please you *one time*, and suddenly I'm the flaccid old geezer who has lost his spunk. Is that right?"

Shirri's expression darkened. "What's gotten into you?"

"Apparently not enough!" Kaslan shouted, his face hot. "You've probably already found some young stallion to replace me, haven't you?"

Shirri folded her arms and stared at him. "I will not tolerate this buffoonery from you, Kaslan. I know you better than this; something else is wrong. You come out and tell me what's on your mind right now, or you can find someplace else to lay your head at night."

"Oh, now the truth comes out," Kaslan said. "Now you don't

want me lying down next to you at all." He shook his head. "I devoted my whole life to you, Shirri. I gave you everything a man could give, and now you go running off with the first fop that comes flaunting his tight hindquarters at you." He whirled around and drew his robe taut against his legs, bending over. "Is this not enough for you anymore?" He wiggled.

"Kaslan!" Shirri said, appalled. "I will not disgrace myself by answering your absurd questions."

"You're in league with the ghost-witches and children peddlers!" he cried, pointing a finger at her as he stood back up and turned around.

Shirri's face set.

"I don't know what's come over you," she said with the tone she'd used with their children from time to time, "but you get out of this house this instant, and don't come back until you've regained your senses. If you won't bother to listen to me, if you won't bother to listen to the facts, then I have nothing more to say to you. Seek no answers, find no answers."

Kaslan harrumphed and left without another word, slamming the door behind him. He stormed through the streets with no particular destination in mind, fuming at the thought of his wife tossing him aside like an old rag. Seek no answers, she'd said. Ha! He didn't need to seek anything. He knew them all already.

He froze in his tracks. Was he really so arrogant? Even as he stood in the middle of the street gathering a collection of new and strange expressions from the passersby, the events of the day stacked on themselves in his head. Witches, assassins, his wife being unfaithful. Each conclusion more ridiculous than the last.

No, he decided finally. *It's all wrong. I've been all wrong.*

But how long had this been going on? He realized, with no small measure of panic, that he didn't know.

Something that Shirri had said echoed in his memory. "Seek no answers, find no answers," she'd said. He'd heard those words before, or something similar, anyway, just a few hours ago. The phrase rang in his head, like . . . .

Like a bell.

"Oh, damn it all," he said aloud. "She really *was* a witch."

* * * * *

Kaslan weaved through the crowds of Loamas, trying as hard as he could not to think about anything at all and staying alert for the sound of anything tinkling. His concentration faltered once when he ran in terror from a small puppy that he was certain was attempting to steal his soul, but mostly he maintained control. He had to find that witch.

But how was he supposed to find a ghost?

No, he thought. *Not a ghost. Not a child-seller. Not an assassin. Keep it together, Kaslan!*

Hours of walking brought the sun down past the walls of the city, bathing Loamas in turgid, multi-colored clouds. They also brought him a pair of swollen feet, which he recognized as somewhat ironic.

How was he supposed to find a lone old woman in a population of thousands? His eyes ached with the effort of squinting through the throngs of people, trying to pick out a head of scraggly silver hair and a thin walking cane. He even went so far as to pick up a forked stick and hold one end in each hand and wave it around. That was supposed to let you find magic, wasn't it? Or was that water? Either way, it didn't lead to anything except an increasingly wider separation from wary citizens.

Kaslan could finally walk no more, and moved to a small wooden bench in the city's main square. He sat with a groan, canting his head back to look up at the darkening sky. His muscles felt as weak as his brain, and his hope was quickly sinking to a similar state of exhaustion.

Would he snap at everyone he met for the rest of his life? What was next? Would he accuse an invalid of illegal acrobatics, or sentence a mute for lewd comments?

If only he could get rid of this curse, he promised himself, he'd never judge anyone again. He'd give up the position of Lord Magistrate and become a pensioner, or an apple farmer, or—he shuddered—an accountant.

With a sigh he rolled his shoulders forward to look back out at the street.

"Ah!" he screamed and nearly fell off the bench.

The witch sat next to him, that same unmovable half-smile on her face. She tapped her foot with her cane.

"Resting my feet," she said. "Too much fruit."

"What's happening to me?" Kaslan blurted. "What did you do?" He resisted the urge to shake her.

The old woman chuckled. "Nothing that you didn't already do for yourself long before I came around, Kaslan Virulle."

Kaslan sighed. "I know," he said. "I've been wrong."

He blinked. He'd just said he'd been wrong. Out loud. Had he heard a bell?

No, he realized. He hadn't, because unlike all the other leaps of logic he'd taken today, this conclusion was not an absurd one.

"That's comforting to hear," the witch said, nodding.

"Maybe for you," Kaslan muttered.

She reached out and patted him on the shoulder, her old, frail hand feeling more like a small breeze.

"You'll get used to it."

"I get it, I get it." Kaslan eyed her suspiciously. "Consider me a wiser man. You haven't said you're going to lift this curse yet."

He let the implied question hang in the air for a moment. The woman simply continued smiling at him.

"You…are going to remove the curse, aren't you?"

The witch laughed. "It's been gone from the moment you left your house."

Kaslan frowned. "But the puppy . . . ."

"A narrow escape—and good intuition—on your part. He really was after your soul."

Staring at her, Kaslan waited for her expression to crack, for her to tell him she was joking. She didn't even blink.

Kaslan cleared his throat. "Well, then. I suppose that's that."

They sat in silence for a moment, Kaslan trying to keep the

thoughts of demonic puppies locked away in some far-off corner of his mind.

"I have a question," he said finally.

"Asking questions already," the witch said. "That's progress."

Kaslan gave a wry smile. "I thought witches were supposed to be evil. Why are you helping me?"

"Sometimes we like a change of pace," the woman said. "But that doesn't mean I'm not a little evil."

"What do you mean?" Kaslan asked, a suspicious leer in his voice.

The witch grinned. "Nothing," she said. She reached behind her and produced a very small bell. "Nothing at all. Tell me, how do you feel about legalizing witchcraft?"

About the author:

Joseph Zieja was born in New Jersey and raised by a pack of loud Italians and Poles who forged the blade of his sarcasm in the fires of Christmas dinners. His fantasy, science fiction, and humor works are available in publications across the web and in print.

You can find out more about Joseph and follow his blog at http://josephzieja.wordpress.com.

An End to Half-Baked Schemes

by: Larry Lefkowitz

Albert Smith had a bent for half-baked schemes. So his wife exclaimed whenever one of the schemes, as she called his inventions, went awry. Her husband would not bother to deny it. On such occasions he took silent refuge in the knowledge that he persevered–that it was better to try to, "land the big one," as he put it, keen on fishing analogies, than to sit back and be carried along by the stream of life, without fighting. If he had failed to land the big one, it was only because they weren't biting that day.

He had come close. Even the missus had to admit that. There was the Even-Baker, for instance. Smith designed it to heat cakes consistently after his wife complained about her cakes coming out uneven. Even his wife had been interested, as well as her friends, in their weekly card-playing group. And though the trial run before the assembled ladies had proved a smoking disaster, he was convinced that if he were to use a porcelain liner the next time, the Even-Baker would bake perfectly. But his wife never gave him a second chance with anything.

Because his inventive road was littered with failed Even-bakers of one kind or another, Smith decided one day to leave his troubles behind. In anyone else this would have meant suicide, the throwing up of hands and saying, "Enough." But Smith's inventive bent refused to permit him to take this way out. If he were going to put an end to himself, it would at least be in an attempt to perfect a device that had long been on his mind, which the risk involved had caused him to long postponed. Now there was nothing to lose. To land the big one he had to wade into white water.

The idea had come to him one afternoon when his wife had dragged him along to the drug store to carry her purchases—those hair-curlers and other beautifiers with which she sought to preserve *her* youthful dreams. Being the belle of the ball was her secret equivalent to her husband's inventing something that would make him famous. On previous trips he had pleaded with her to let him experiment with an idea for a cooling device—he'd already named it the Face-Preserver. She could expose her face to it before going to bed, instead of her creams. It would keep her skin from wrinkling and stave off the effects of aging. Since she hadn't forgotten the Even-Baker, she refused each time he brought up the Face-Preserver.

While his wife was busy with her shopping, he picked a magazine off the rack. It contained stories about the future. Because he knew he had a spell to wait, he read the first story. It was about a man who was frozen for a thousand years and revived in the future. Smith was not a religious man, but he believed providence caused him to read that story. Because with some modifications of the Face-Preserver, which he had already built in his mind, he bet he could freeze someone like in the story, allowing that person to reach the future. Putting an end to himself while testing his invention, if it occurred, was not suicide. It was to die while going after the "big one" that he'd been waiting for all his life. If he succeeded with the Etern-a-Freeze, as he already referred to it, he would be the Thomas A. Edison of the future.

After telling his wife he was working on a better deep-freeze—she shook her head in resigned dismissal—he began work in earnest in his "lab", as he called his work shack in the yard. When the Etern-a-Freeze was finished, he would leave a note saying not to disturb him, but to leave it to the future to unfreeze him, together with a second note instructing the scientists in the future to thaw him out.

One day he brought a stiff, frozen trout into the house and dropped it onto the kitchen table. "Serve that for dinner," he said triumphantly. "It didn't come from the market." His wife knew it must have been from the deep-freeze contraption, but refused to give him the satisfaction of receiving any praise, yet there was no concealing the grudging look of respect on her face.

Weeks passed and the frozen fish, pheasants and deer that Smith put on the table confirmed the efficiency of his device. At breakfast, one morning, he puzzled his wife by saying, "If I don't appear for dinner, you'll find me in the lab."

Late for dinner again, while working on his contraption, she thought. She didn't know this was the day the Etern-a-freeze was ready for its ultimate test.

But her husband did. He dressed in his Sunday best, the string tie and black suit, lay down in the Etern-a-Freeze, and threw the switch which would send the proper amount of coolant into it to cover his body. As the numbing liquid poured over him, he had a sudden picture of his first success–the frozen trout on the kitchen table–which produced an urge to get up and go fishing.

* * * * *

Smith only gradually became aware of the warming current that invaded his body. He was surprised by it, remembered something about wanting to go fishing, and then he remembered the Etern-a-Freeze. The heat enveloping his body must mean that he had succeeded. The scientists of the future were thawing him out!

He opened his eyes and focused on the red source of heat above him that seemed to be coming from some infra-red device like a rotisserie but without any bulb. This caused him to recall an idea for a heating device he once had, but he couldn't put his finger on it. As his vision cleared, two figures hovering over him, dressed in white. Occasionally one prodded him gently with a device that looked like a stick, but which smith suspected was recording his temperature. The man with the probe said something to the other man in a language Smith couldn't understand.

"Howdy," Smith said to the closer of the two figures. "The name's Smith." He started to raise a hand to shake with his rescuers. It was then that he noticed his hands were held down at the wrists by clamps, as were his ankles. He had put no such devices in the Etern-a-Freeze. Raising his head, he saw the remnants of the Etern-a-Freeze in a corner of the enormous room. He had been transferred, frozen, to this thawer-outer. Other men in white were moving around the room, stirring vats of flavorful chemicals.

"Do you fellows speak English?" he asked amiably.

The man standing closest to him spoke: "Yes, we know all languages from the past. Our machines translate them automatically into our language—a language comprised of what you call mathematics. They also enable us to speak to you in your language."

"Then I succeeded in reaching the future?"

"Yes, your machine was primitive but effective."

"What year is it?"

"2668, according to the old calendar."

"Wow! Well, I'm all ready for the dinner," he said, noting that his Sunday best had survived the years in as fine fettle as himself.

"What dinner?"

"The chicken dinner. The awards. Say, you can turn off the thawer–I'm thawed out."

"There are no chicken dinners, since there are no chickens."

"No chickens?"

"No chickens, few animals. The last war eliminated them. There is very little food."

"No food? Say, do me a favor and turn off the thawer, will you? I'm getting cooked.

"Precisely."

"Huh?"

"There is very little food."

"You mean–" He thought fleetingly of the Even-Baker.

"Yes. I'm very sorry. You are–how did you phrase it?–'the chicken dinner.'"

About the author:

The stories, poetry, and humor of Larry Lefkowitz have appeared in many publications in the United States, Israel, and Britain. Among the publications: *A Cappella Zoo, The Literay Review, Thema, Third Wednesday Review, American Film,* anthologies and e-zines.

The Cave

by Terence Kuch

Waves shove against the shore. The dying cry out. Even so, it is quieter than the deafening noise before. Most of the invaders have moved on, pushing the enemy back, but Tom and his buddies are isolated in a shallow cave, cut off from their unit. Sounds from the distance tell them that not all the Germans were killed. Gunfire comes closer. A single shot, then another. Somewhere, a grenade explodes. In the cave the GIs sweat, tremble with rage and fright: Lopez, Jackson, LaGuardia, Cohen, Zaborowski. And Tom Sullivan.

Tom remembers that last Christmas with his family, especially with his son. It seems very long ago, or perhaps it wasn't the way he remembered it at all; or perhaps it never was. He wondered how Jimmy remembered that Christmas, and how Jimmy would remember him. And for how long.

* * * * *

Cracks made their random way across the parking lot. Some had been filled intermittently, but most were as nature, or the weight of passing cars, had made them. Today's cars had been confined to a corner of the lot, where they sat uneasily close to their fellows, ready to scrape against each other at the slightest driver miscue. This was a sure sign of December, when hawkers of Christmas trees and decorations, and assortments of holiday gewgaws occupied a good half of the lot.

Katie and Jimmy, the Sullivans' children, tumbled out of Tom and Helen Sullivan's Chevrolet and ran yelling into the ephemeral forest, accompanied by Mom's cries of, "Be careful!" and, "Don't get out of my sight." It was a perfect Norman Rockwell moment.

Jimmy Sullivan was just the age to pretend that he didn't have a sister. And so, seeing Katie zag left ahead of him, he zigged right and ran between stacks of trees, stray branches brushing against his face. He was happy, and being out of sight of Mom and Dad made him happier still.

Before he knew it, he was out of the asphalt forest and into a profusion of Christmas elves, lined up rank and file like so many soldiers. He stopped abruptly and stared around in wonder. Each elf looked pretty much like every other, all just slightly shorter than he. From their green pointy-caps and blue eyes and smiley faces to their little green jackets and curly-toed red shoes, they were the picture of Christmas delight. Immediately, Jimmy wanted one, that being his usual way of relating to things.

He considered if he should spend some of his hard-earned goodwill nagging Dad to buy him an elf. Yes, as he surveyed the green-and-red-clad warriors, he was very sure that he wanted one. No, make that two. And not to share with Katie, either. Two would be worth yelling and crying for, even getting spanked for and sent to bed. Jimmy weighed his options carefully, plotted his strategy like a general.

While Jimmy was in the midst of thought, a short, older man approached him. "Well hello there, young fellow!" He laughed. "How'd you like your dad to buy you a Christmas elf? They're great companions and fun, too. Wouldn't your friends envy you? Wouldn't you be really popular?"

Jimmy looked up. "Sure!" he said. He cast his eyes on the assembled elves, automatically looking for the perfect elf, "to die for," as Mom liked to say, or have a bawling fit for, which was Jimmy's version. He studied them carefully. They all seemed pretty much alike; how could he decide?

The man caught Jimmy's indecision. "Take your time, son. Each elf's different. Really. Some work harder than others. Some like t' smile and make friends. Some like t' grouch and shirk and go on sick call every day and use bad language!"

"They talk?" asked a surprised Jimmy. He had immediately picked up on "bad language," as any self-respecting grade-schooler would.

"Well, not really. I guess I exaggerated a little there. But they're pretty good about makin' their wishes known."

Jimmy frowned. He knew a few bad words, but he was sure there were some he didn't know. More important, he'd heard words that the older kids said were bad words but wouldn't tell him what they meant.

"How do I know which one to pick?" asked Jimmy. "Tell me everything each one does!" he added uncompromisingly.

At the intersection of the twelfth file and the eighth rank, one blue eye slowly moved.

"Well, that's a big order, little buddy," the elf-peddler said with a smile. "Why don't you just tell me what sorts of things you'd like your own personal elf to do, and I'll see if I've got a match somewhere here."

Jimmy surveyed the assembled elves. There seemed to be more of them now than when the elf-peddler had appeared.

"Ah," said Jimmy. "I can't decide. Can I just go look at them. Up close?" His eyes pleaded.

"Well, all right, but be careful!"

"Of what? Do they bite?"

The elf-peddler laughed like a bowlful of jelly. Before he could answer, Jimmy was out among the elves, peering, poking, touching. "Just take your time, sonny," the short man called out. "I'll be right over there helpin' another customer. Don't go away, now!"

Just as the elf-peddler said, from up close each elf seemed a little different. Jimmy wandered among them, trying to decide which to plead for. At first, he thought they were like the plaster statues his uncle Ralph liked to plant in his lawn, but he felt them calling to him. He remembered cats in the pound, how they reached their paws out to anyone passing by, as if they knew they would be killed the next day if they weren't admired, loved, taken home.

But the elves weren't pleading—they were demanding. He felt them struggling among themselves with, "It's my turn next!" and,

"That's not fair!" and, "Dibs!" and, "I saw him first!" and, "You just shut up!"

After a few minutes of wandering among the rows and columns, Jimmy found an elf he wanted, and then another. The first seemed smart and eager; shrewd; just right to play board-games with, or play war with little metal guns and tanks, squatting on the living room rug and yelling, "Bang bang!" The second elf was slow and dreamy, a good elf to have in one's bedroom at night, while the other one was maybe put away in a closet. Just for safe-keeping.

Jimmy threaded his way through the troop, back to where he'd entered it, and found the elf-peddler. He pointed out the two he wanted. "I want those two," he said.

Just then, Tom lurched out from among the trees, saw his son, ran to him and grabbed him by an arm. "Jimmy!" he said sternly, "your mother's been worried about you! Where have you been?"

"Now, now," said the elf-peddler, "your son's perfectly safe here. My name is Mr. Clausen, and this is my . . . Temporary . . . place of business. We've been discussin' the possibility of the lad's acquirin' one of these wonderful elves. Perhaps as a Christmas present?"

"Two elves!" said Jimmy.

Tom Sullivan calmed slightly and removed his hand from Jimmy's arm. "We were thinking of a sled," he said. "Or perhaps a set of Lincoln Logs."

"Want Elves!" said Jimmy. "Don't want any old sled or Lincoln Logs."

"Well . . ." said Tom, thinking that Helen might not approve this change of plan. He decided to find out more about the elves. She would be along shortly, and then blame for the decision, if needed, could be shared.

"Where did all these elves come from?" asked Tom.

"Well, sir," said Mr. Clausen, "these little buggers guard the trees. Out in the forest, I mean. That's kind of a tradition among 'em from the old pagan days. And when we start cuttin' those trees down, that magical transformation, you know, that turns those beautiful living things into Christmas trees for a week or so.... Well, as I was sayin', these elves live in caves out in the forest, and when there's any kind of disturbance they come on out. When we start to cut down the trees, we see 'em, skitterin' and hissin' and makin' gestures at us, and not very nice ones, either!"

The elf-peddler was silent for a moment.

"And then you capture them?" prompted Tom.

"Well, now, we do have to put most of 'em down, the ones that are fightin' the hardest, but some of 'em we catch, and train 'em to stand still in a row. If we didn't, it'd be like a barrel of monkeys around here!

"Now then," he continued at just the same time Jimmy was again yelling, 'I want an elf!' "sleds and play-logs are wonderful presents, but I think your son has his mind made up! So you'd better buy an elf or two."

Tom was at a momentary loss as to how to respond to this challenge to his fatherhood and perhaps his manhood as well. "I'm being called up!" was all he could think to say at the moment. "This may be my last Christmas with my son."

The elf-peddler didn't blink. "I really take my hat off to you, sir," he said, "and to all the other valiant fathers who leave their families and our shores to fight the Nazis. Or the Japs. Do you know which branch . . .?"

"No," said Tom. "I guess they'll assign me when I report. Infantry, probably," he added grimly.

"Well, sir," said the elf-peddler, "in the name of our glorious land of the free I'm prepared to offer your wonderful young son (Here he beamed his brightest beam in Jimmy's direction.) an elf to remember you by as you go off to defend our nation. Only nine dollars and ninety-nine cents!"

Tom looked surprised. "That's a lot of money!" he exclaimed. "That's almost what we spend on groceries for a week!"

"Well then, sir," said the elf-peddler, "as a patriotic citizen I'll tell you what I'm goin' to do: I'll give you two elves for that price, instead of just one; and I'll also give you, free and at no charge, two more as well, to honor your brave courage and sacrifice! That makes four elves, so that's only two and a half dollars each."

Jimmy jumped up and down, shouting, "Four elves! Four elves!"

Seeing Tom's hesitation, the elf-peddler added, "Besides; it's for a good cause. The widows and orphans, you know, from the war. Two percent of all my sales, after costs, go to help those in need."

Just then, Helen and Katie appeared. They stopped short at the sight of the elves. After a moment Katie burst forth with her news. "We've been picking out ornaments!" she said excitedly. "For the tree." She held up a paper bag. "Careful, now," said her mom. "Don't drop them."

Jimmy tried to explain to his mom and Katie what had just got! To happen now, or else! That is, acquire four elves, "For almost free, and they help widows!"

Tom Sullivan looked hopelessly at Helen, who turned her head. "What do you think?" he asked, and receiving no answer, shrugged and turned back to the elf-dealer. "OK," he said, "I'll take them."

"Sold!" said Mr. Clausen with overflowing jollity. He pointed to the two elves Jimmy had picked out, and two more. "Fall out!" he yelled. The four came forward and stood at attention. "Now," said Mr. Clausen to Tom, "let's see about that tree."

* * * * *

While the elf-peddler was packing up the four elves (who were struggling to avoid the gunny sack), the four Sullivans went back into the forest. Tom picked out a tree. Helen said nothing, but a look from her sent Tom down the row, desperately trying to read her mind for clues of tree-rightness and tree-wrongness. On the fourth try, he selected a tree that didn't bring forth a look.

"How about this one, Katie and Jimmy?" he said a little too loudly. "Isn't this a wonderful tree?"

Katie nodded.

Jimmy, caring only about his elves, said nothing, but was glad that the Dad and Mom Dumb Show had ended earlier than usual.

Tom paid for the tree, loaded it on the Chevrolet's roof, and tied it down with rope looped through the car windows. Seeing no other option, he placed the bag of elves in the trunk as gently as possible, an effort because there was kicking and shoving, mostly from the elves but also from Jimmy, who wanted them to ride in the back seat with him and Katie, although there was, as Tom pointed out, not enough room.

Smoothly, the car pulled away from the parking lot and purred, ascending to the three-lane state road and then on to 504 Buttercup Lane. A friendly shine of red and green lights greeted the returning Sullivans. They were not four, anymore, but eight.

* * * * *

Sounds approach. The six GIs hear shouting in what must be German, and then whispering. There are drones of warplanes overhead, and a distant thud of bombs. The GIs are as quiet as possible. They aim their M-1s toward the cave entrance and wait. Tom Sullivan aims his weapon, and waits.

* * * * *

Tom lifted the sack of elves out of the trunk. It was heavy, and the elves' constant jostling and jumping made the job harder. Finally, he got them through the garage and into the toolshed. Jimmy would want to play with them right away, but Christmas wasn't for five days yet. He'd have to wait, wailing or not.

And indeed there was wailing and gnashing of teeth and perturbations and recriminations and sobs and sadness. Helen and Katie tried to ignore the unpleasantness.

To an audience of the two children and their mom, Tom set up the tree in its red and green metal stand. He turned its screw into the trunk. He strung lights around the tree and plugged them in. No light. Laboriously, he tested each bulb in turn until he found the dead one and replaced it.

Helen, after watching this fatherly process, said that Tom had strung the tree-lights all wrong. No one would see them in back of the tree, there against the wall, she informed him. And she didn't want those hot bulbs touching her good wallpaper. Tom made acceptable changes.

Then Helen and Katie decorated the tree until it shone through the un-silent night. From the background, Christmas carols could be heard, like some ghostly underscore.

During these events, Jimmy continued to raise loud objections to any delay in the satisfaction of his desires. Finally, and after much raucous debate, a resolution was reached: Jimmy could have his elves the next morning, four days before Christmas. At least, Tom reflected, not that very same day. Jimmy would be learning patience and responsibility.

Jimmy wiped his eyes and settled down with his map collection. Every day, it was his habit to commandeer the previous day's newspaper and cut out the war maps, paste them into albums. Jimmy only dimly understood what the little cartoon figures were doing (white for us, black for them; soldiers, planes, tanks), or why their lines zigzagged across Europe and the Pacific, or why they changed positions, perhaps only slightly, every day. He knew he was supposed to root for the white figures, but some days he couldn't help appreciating the black ones, especially when they were advancing.

After dinner, Tom retreated to the backyard, which he intended as a more permanent home for the elves than the trunk of his car. He studied the fence he'd built years earlier for a long-departed dog. Good; it should keep the elves in. He didn't think they could climb. He regretted not having asked Mr. Clausen about that. Satisfied, he went back inside. It occurred to him that he didn't know if the elves ate or drank or even generated waste products from these activities. He hadn't thought to ask Mr. Clausen about that, either. There were other things he might have asked Mr. Clausen about, too.

As it was Sunday, all worries about how to occupy the family's after-dinner time had been temporarily banished: it was comedy night on network radio. The two shows that the family, even Jimmy and Katie, most enjoyed were Red Skelton and Jack

Benny, back-to-back on the Red Network.

The family gathered around the big floor-model radio. Jimmy's job was to keep the station tuned in until he got bored and stopped. Then Tom would do it. And that's how it went until bedtime. Tom read Jimmy to sleep from a *Popular Science Monthly* magazine article about the wonders of the postwar world to come: television for everyone; vacations on the moon; unbreakable phonograph records; dinner in a capsule, including dessert; turnpikes everywhere; miracle cures from large doses of ionizing radiation.

Tom kissed his wife and told her he was afraid of battle, afraid of being killed. She sympathized with him; what else could she do?

They slept. Suddenly, sounds of warfare ripped through the night. Tom and Helen both jerked awake. "Jimmy's room!" both said, as they ran to it and flung the door open. There was Jimmy in his pajamas, marching around the room, trailed by four Christmas elves. They were waving and twirling and aiming the toy rifles and pistols that were Jimmy's presents from the Christmas before, and his birthday, and Christmases and birthdays before that.

"Bang bang you're dead!" chanted Jimmy.

"Bang bang you're dead!" responded the elves, one after the other, aiming their weapons at Jimmy and then, after the door had opened, at Tom. "The enemy is here!" they chanted. "The invaders are here!"

Meanwhile, Katie had begun to cry, and Helen ran off to comfort her. Tom stood there looking at Jimmy and at the elves, all now standing startled and still in the middle of Jimmy's bedroom, no longer shouting.

"Get to bed!" He looked at Jimmy and grabbing the elves by the nearest available limb. He dragged them away, all four of them. As he proceeded down the hall, Tom heard the elves chanting, "Bang bang. Bang bang. You're dead."

Tom tossed the elves into the backyard. Jimmy, meanwhile, was screaming and throwing his toys all over his room, breaking his bedside lamp and a framed Uncle Sam poster in the process, all the while continuing to yell, "Bang bang you're dead!"

The elves immediately marched to the center of the yard, formed themselves into two rows and two columns, and glared at Tom as he shut the backyard door behind him. "Bang bang," they said again.

* * * * *

Four days later, the family gathered around the table for Christmas dinner: Tom; Helen; Jimmy; Katie; Helen's dad and mom; Tom's mom, Tom's dad having died some years before in a place called Ypres. For once, the elves were banished from the dinner table. The food was enough, and plain. There had been rationing, after all, for the past year. The little stamps with pictures of tanks, and the little stamps with fighter planes, and the little stamps with aircraft carriers, were precious, not to be splurged even for Christmas, not even if the Sullivans had any stamps to spare, which they didn't.

Tom's mom thanked God for everything but the current state of the world, which she was reluctant to blame on Him, then they ate. During dessert, Tom played a few of his favorite Bing Crosby songs on the family phonograph: White Christmas, Silent Night, I'll Be Home for Christmas, then The Vict'ry Polka (with The Andrews Sisters):

There's going to be a great Hallelujah Day
When the boys come home to stay
And a million bands begin to play.
We'll be dancing "The Vict'ry Polka."
And we'll all give a mi-mi-mighty cheer
When the ration book's a souvenir.
And we'll heave a mi-mi-mighty sigh.
When each gal kisses the boy she kissed good-bye.

Tom seemed a little sad after, "The Vict'ry Polka," but he perked up for one of his favorites, "The Bombardier Song."

He saw the target and locked the target
And suddenly bombs away.

The Air Corps, he reflected, might be a safer place than the infantry. Or maybe not. Less dirt and mud, anyway. But it wouldn't be his choice.

Tom helped clear the table, and their guests went home. Jimmy was, finally, exhausted and asleep on the living room floor, surrounded by maps and pieces of newspaper. Katie had long since fallen asleep at the table, after playing with her presents all day. Tom picked up Jimmy, and Helen picked up Katie. They put the kids to bed and went to bed themselves.

Tom had a dream. Not the dreams he'd been having for weeks, not the war-dream or the POW-camp-dream or the shot-to-death-dream. Tonight, it was about the elves.

The elves had figured out how to get out of the backyard. This involved standing on each other's heads, three deep, and then hauling the fourth up and over the fence, and then the third, and so on. It took a long time, and there was much complaining, but at last they were over, running and yelling and dodging, as they pointed elvish fingers at each other, alternating, "Bangs," and, "Pows."

With a shock, Tom saw that the last one over the wall was Jimmy, following the elves, becoming an elf himself. It was disturbing enough to Tom that he woke. He scrambled out of bed and peered into the backyard. The elves were still there, shuffling their feet and glaring at him. He checked Jimmy's room. Jimmy was asleep. Tom went back to bed. As he did every night, he counted the days before he'd have to report for duty. "Six," he whispered.

* * * * *

The Germans have discovered the cave. A figure appears, and Jackson blows his face off with a well-aimed round. Then more firing. Tom is hit. Above the elbow, his right arm is shattered. Tom turns to the other five GIs, but they are dead. Time seems to slow, stop. He has always been here this day, jumping from the landing craft, rushing up on shore, firing, being pinned down, finding a place to hide, taking refuge. There is a moment of silence. Tom Sullivan remembers Christmas. A grenade rolls gently into his cave.

About the author:

Terence Kuch is a consultant, avid hiker, and world traveler. His speculative fiction stories and the occasional poem have appeared in paying markets including *Dark Fiction Spotlight, Arct, Ballista* (U.K.), *Fusion Fragment, Niteblade* (Canada), *Noctober, Polluto* (U.K.), *Roar & Thunder* (Australia), and *Sybil's Garage*. His work has been featured in anthologies from *Pill Hill, House of Horror* (U.K.), *Static Movement*, etc.

His work in literary and other genres has appeared in the U.S., U.K., and India, including *Commonweal, Diagram, Dissent, Foundling Review, Journal of Irreproducible Results, New York magazine, Penguin Review, Stray Branch, Thema, Unlikely 2.0, 5923 Quarterly, North American Review, Slow Trains, Worm-Runners' Digest, Yellow Mana, Washington Post Book World, Washington Post Magazine*, and others.

The Time Guard

by Richard Zwicker

Jon Bailey was a man of deeply held but superficially examined beliefs. He believed in God but didn't understand him. He believed in his marriage vows, though he and his wife bored each other. He believed in doing the best job he could, even though he'd had a lot of jobs: short order cook, orderly at a crematorium, and presently, security guard at Time Research. So when fellow guard Trevor Mellman told him Time Research was taking advantage of them, Bailey became defensive.

"C'mon, Mellman," said Bailey, as the two shared a pitcher of beer, sitting across from each other in a dimly lit booth at Crowley's Restaurant. "We get pretty good pay for, let's face it, mostly sitting around eight hours a day. We have good benefits. Four weeks' vacation a year."

"I'm not talking about that," Mellman said. He was in his mid-30's and still possessed a hint of youth, as opposed to Bailey, who was on the far end of 50 and supported a bushy gray mustache. "Something's going on and they're not telling us what it is."

"So why don't you ask Delahanty about it?"

"Yeah, right. They're up to something and the president of the company is going to tell me? It's for people like us they coined the phrase 'need to know basis.'"

Bailey took a big gulp of his draught, getting foam on his mustache. It tasted better than this conversation. "I don't want to talk about conspiracy theories today, okay? You'll get all worked up for nothing."

Mellman's eyes narrowed. "Is that so? You remember the power outage we had three months ago?"

"How could I forget? We got three days off."

"Right. And we were told it was because the time machine prototype caused an overload. But that's not what Frank Salmon told me." Frank served as Time Res' chief electrician. "After he rewired the lab, he checked the time machine. It's still no more effective than a washer/dryer as a means of time travel, but electronically, there was nothing wrong with it."

"So what caused the power to get knocked out?"

"He saw this eight-foot square box sitting in the far corner of the lab, that wasn't there before. It was locked but he could see three chairs and a control panel inside. He didn't know what it was, but I do. It was a real time machine, from the future."

"Yeah, right. Maybe the 31st century is trying to warn us that it's going to rain tomorrow."

"Let me ask you this. When's the last time you saw Luke Kennedy?" Kennedy was one of the more tightlipped scientists at Time Res. His automatic response to "Good morning" was a barely audible "Mmm."

Bailey thought. "Now that you mention it. Is he on vacation?"

Mellman waved his hand dismissively. "He's out of here. He took his whole family into the time machine and vanished. They're not coming back."

"How do you know that?"

"I tried to call Kennedy yesterday." Mellman frowned. "Disconnected. No new number. "

"He probably just got a better job somewhere. Anyway, why would anyone want to leave everything you know to go to another time?"

Mellman pushed his drained mug to the side and looked Bailey in the eye. "Because he knows something about the future we don't. Keep an eye on Time Res's admin. If we start to experience major turnover, I'd start worrying."

Bailey left the bar feeling unsettled. He knew Mellman dealt with stress by complaining, but Frank Salmon wouldn't have said anything without some factual basis. The thing to do would have been to talk to Salmon, but the chief had spoken to Mellman in confidence. Bailey wanted to confide in his wife, but she'd probably overreact. He shrugged. Time eventually revealed its secrets, and the revelations invariably proved less extreme than Mellman's suspicions.

In the next two weeks, four high-ranking scientists abruptly left Time Research. This made Mellman unbearable.

* * * * *

"What can I do for you, Bailey?" Strom Delahanty asked as the security guard, head slightly bowed, stood in front of his desk. Framed degrees and pictures of Delehanty shaking hands with important people covered his office walls. His bushy head of hair and tucked skin made him look ageless.

"Mr. Delahanty, something's been bothering me lately."

"My door is always open . . . Bailey." Delahanty' read the guard's name tag. His forced smile barely masked his impatience.

"Well, as you know, there has been quite a bit of turnover lately."

"That's correct. It's always difficult when people leave. We do everything at Time Research to hold onto our workers."

"Right. What I'm wondering is, well, people are talking . . . ."

"What are they saying?"

"That we've had some kind of breakthrough with the time machine and discovered something bad is going to happen, something unavoidable, and that the people who have left haven't just left for other jobs. They've left for another time."

Delahanty leaned back in his swivel chair, searching for a comfortable position. "Bailey, I'm going to level with you. As president of Time Research, it's my responsibility to make sure each worker has the conditions necessary to do the best job he or she can do. Do you understand?"

"Sure."

"OK. Now you're right. We have, to a limited degree, been able to make the time machine work."

"That's great."

"It is great. Great for humanity, for Time Research, for you and me. I can't give you specifics because we're not sure ourselves, but by going into the future we have learned some things. Now we need to figure out how best to use this information."

"I understand."

"As with any healthy organization, not everyone agrees on what to do. After making their views known, some people have decided to go elsewhere. We want to reward people in our organization, even if they decide to leave. I assure you, if for some reason you wanted to move on, you could depend on a glowing recommendation from me."

"Thank you, sir. I'm happy here."

"Good." Delahanty leaned forward and looked squarely at Bailey. "Your job is important. If just one person got by you and went to the past, it could change . . . everything." Delahanty stretched out the last word for emphasis. "I know it sounds melodramatic, but the future of the world depends on the vigilance of people like you. All I can say is, keep up the good work." He shook Bailey's hand.

Bailey left Delahanty's office feeling a lot better about everything, until he punched out for the day and ran into Mellman. They didn't even make it to Crowley's before they had an argument.

"So he didn't tell you anything," Mellman said disgustedly.

"He told me what he could. I got the impression that he wanted to tell me more, but couldn't."

Mellman grimaced. "That's the impression he wanted to give you. If our job is the most important, why don't they pay us more money? Why don't they trust us? Why are you so dumb?"

"Which question would you like me to answer first?"

Mellman sighed. They stood on the far edge of the sidewalk, exposed to a light rain. Roiling clouds darkened the sky. "Forget the questions. This is what we should do."

* * * * *

Both Mellman and Bailey worked the day shift but managed to trade with two other guards for the 1:00 to 9:00 AM shift two nights later. The building was dark and quiet as Bailey fingered his holstered pistol.

"I'm glad I don't normally work this shift. Every time I look at my watch it seems like it's gone backwards."

"Things are going to pick up. Salmon told me Dr. Oblomov was going to use the machine tonight for a one-way trip." Maia Oblomov was co-founder and vice president of Time Research.

"She's not going to just leave."

Mellman looked ahead with steely eyes. "Time will tell."

As it turned out, 2 AM had little to say, as did 3, but at exactly 3:19, the main entrance door to the third floor opened with a clank. In walked Dr. Oblomov, Dr. Delahanty, another scientist by the name of Kenneth Greene, and three people they'd never seen before: a forty-year-old woman and two sleepy pre-teen girls. Greene wheeled in two stuffed suitcases, while Mrs. Greene pulled one. Each of the two girls struggled under the weight of an overloaded fanny pack.

"Working late?" Mellman asked as the group of people walked up to the entrance he and Bailey guarded.

Delahanty nodded gravely. "Yes, we are going to be doing important work tonight. We don't want to be disturbed. Is that clear?"

Mellman nodded. "Couldn't be clearer." He put his thumb on the scanner and the door opened. After the six people entered the room, he closed the door and glanced at Bailey. "I guess I was wrong about Dr. Oblomov, but you've just met the family of Dr. Greene. Don't expect to see any of them before quitting time. Or ever again."

"I wish we could hear what they were saying."

"The only sound we can hear through these walls will be the time machine when they activate it. At that moment, they'll never hear us opening the door. Vision is another thing though. If they're looking in our direction, we're going to have to come up with a story about an unexpected emergency, which may or may not keep us from getting fired. I'm willing to take the risk. Are you in or out?"

Bailey didn't like it, but he'd come this far. "I'm right behind you."

They waited, the time inching by. Both heard the grating sound during experiments and knew there would be only about sixty seconds for them to open the door and find a place to hide in the room.

The noise of the transporter hit them like an unexpected drill. Mellman jumped to his feet and stuck his thumb onto the entrance scanner. The door swung open, revealing a machine-laden room of about twenty square feet. Powerful overhead lights threw every lever, cable, and wheel into sharp relief. Mellman pointed toward the tilted capsule of Time Res's failed time machine. Bailey ducked behind it while Mellman pressed the scanner, closing the heavy door. He then joined his partner in hiding.

Peering from behind the capsule, they saw five people standing intently in front of the other time machine, which looked like a detached elevator. Dr. Greene was missing. Bailey noticed a burning, unsettling odor that made him nauseous. It apparently affected Dr. Oblomov as well, as she had grown pale. With her shoulder-length hair piled on top of her head, she looked older than her 35 years. When the sound stopped, her legs nearly buckled, and she grabbed onto Dr. Delahanty for support.

"It's done," Delahanty said. He manually opened the time machine door to reveal it was empty, then turned to the forty-year-old woman. She looked drained. "Are you ready, Mrs. Greene?"

"He said he would write a message to me once he got there. That he would put it inside that clock," she said softly, pointing to the grandfather clock that stood like a sentinel against the wall.

"Oh yes, he did mention that to me." The clock is the one thing we know had been in the building since its construction seventy years earlier. Delehanty walked over to it, unlocked its lower cabinet, and extracted a yellowed piece of paper. He handed it to Mrs. Greene. She read it and teared up.

"He made it." She folded the paper, placed it in her pocket, and turned to her two children. "We're ready."

Bailey and Mellman watched as the Greenes stepped inside the time machine. They looked like hitchhikers unsure of what to do with their hands. Delahanty reminded Mrs. Greene to press a button marked "engage" on the inside panel, then patted her on the shoulders and secured the door. The machine began to hum, the sound slowly ascending in scale. After the hum stabilized, a grinding sound predominated. Bailey's teeth hurt, while Oblomov put her hands over her ears. In sixty seconds it was over. Delahanty opened the door of the empty reeking machine.

Delehanty glanced at Oblomov. "How's your headache?"

She shook her head. "We had no right to fake that note."

"The important thing is they're together and safe."

"We don't know that!"

"We both used the machine. You don't believe your own eyes?"

"I'd like to know why Greene didn't send us a message back."

"Maybe in seventy years someone took his message out. Maybe travel to the past doesn't work that way. Maybe he's gone to another strand of time that doesn't affect ours. As scientists, we have to accept some uncertainty."

"And try to figure it out. Not save our own asses."

"You know we've been able to get the machine to work only in five-year intervals. There's only so much we can discover. Maybe just by sending so many people back, we will disrupt the continuum enough so the destruction of Earth in five years won't happen."

"We should be asking who sent this time machine."

"We are asking that. But until we get an answer, we can interpret it as a warning from the future."

"What future?"

"Maybe some people survive on another planet and sent this when they developed the technology."

Oblomov looked at him as if he were crazy. "We are not going to have the technology to go to another planet in five years."

"All I know is, we shouldn't look gift horses in the mouth."

"That's exactly what we should be doing." She glared at him. "So why haven't you left yet? Is it because you want to save more lives, or you're not sure about it yourself?"

Delehanty's face hardened. "At some point, I will join them. If you don't believe in it, why are you even here tonight?"

Oblomov struggled to answer. "I may be asking myself that for a long time. I'm going home," and she turned to leave.

"Do what you have to do," Delehanty said quietly, following her. As Oblomov opened the entrance door, Delahanty noticed Mellman and Bailey absent from their posts. "Where the hell are the two guards?"

Oblomov walked to the elevator, while Delahanty stalked angrily down the hall, calling the guards' names. Once he turned the corner, Mellman and Bailey dashed out of the lab. "Go to the bathroom and stay there until I call you." He rushed after Delahanty, armed with a story about how he and Bailey, prior to reporting to work that evening, had shared a large order of colon-purging fried seafood. To their astonishment, Delahanty didn't fire them on the spot.

After Mellman's confrontation with Delahanty, the two security guards had nearly five hours on duty to digest what they had seen and heard. Mellman was energized.

"That's where company loyalty gets you: a third class ticket on the Titanic. The world's going to end in five years and what does Delehanty tell us? Guard the escape hatch. That bastard."

"So why hasn't he escaped yet?"

"He's probably selling tickets to anyone with lots of money, for crissake. The question is, who is going to be left behind."

* * * * *

Because they had traded shifts with the night crew, neither Bailey nor Mellman had to report back to work for 24 hours. Bailey spent the first five of those hours fitfully sleeping, his body too tired to argue against the changed schedule. When his wife came home at six from her job as a sales clerk, she asked if something was bothering him, but for the time being, he kept his concerns to himself.

The next morning at work one of the guards from the night crew told him Oblomov had resigned. Bailey took his place on the chair to the left of the lab entrance and watched forlornly as Mellman strode up the hall.

"Did you hear the news?" Mellman asked, standing in front of Bailey.

"Yeah."

"That's why we didn't get fired. What do they care? Oblomov's probably buying up southern real estate after the Civil War."

"I can't believe she left."

Mellman snorted. "You thought she had more honor than that? What's honorable about waiting for the Earth to explode if you can escape?"

"She didn't do it two nights ago."

"Nothing like a day closer to the apocalypse to strengthen your resolve." Mellman put his hand on Bailey's shoulder. "Jon, listen to me. I don't know exactly how or when, but I'm going." He motioned toward the empty corridor. "When the news gets out, mobs will storm this place. They'll kill you and they'll break the machine."

That week while Bailey guarded the entrance, a trickle of important looking people filed into the laboratory. None came out. Delahanty told him it was his duty to keep unauthorized people from using the time machine. But if all it took to be authorized was money and position, what was the point? After he punched out on Friday, he felt so enervated he almost didn't notice Dr. Oblomov in her office as he walked by.

He did an abrupt u-turn. "Dr. Oblomov, I thought you were gone." She looked up from her desk, her eyes veined and tired. With the walls bare and her desktop clear, the diminutive woman physically dominated the room. Only a coffee machine standing at attention on a small, low stained table remained.

"I am gone. I'm just picking up some things I left in my…this office."

He hesitated. "I thought you'd transported to the past."

She took her hand out of a drawer and stared at him. "You are one of the guards who left his post last week?"

Bailey nodded. "We saw you transport the Greenes. I was impressed that you didn't go."

She stiffened. "You impress too easily."

Her weakness emboldened him. "What did you see in the future?"

She brushed some dust off her desk, then met his eyes. "As you already know about the transports, I will tell you. Then you'll have to decide what to do with the information. Twice, I went into the future. The first time was utter chaos. Earthquakes ripping the land apart, tidal waves, gale force winds, all at once. I saw hundreds of people fall into a bottomless chasm. That's five years from now. I spent one hour there, but what I saw is seared into my brain. It also gave me the worst headache in my life."

"What causes it though? An alien invasion, an asteroid?"

"We don't know. We couldn't learn anything from five years in the future, so of course we went ten years ahead. We could only get it to do five-year intervals." She shook her head. "There was nothing. The time machine just floated in empty space."

Bailey frowned. "How could you keep this information to yourself?"

Her body slumped. "If the Earth is going to be destroyed in five years, the only chance for our species to survive is the time machine. That chance will vanish the moment this hits the news. There will be riots, death, and a destroyed time machine." She turned to him helplessly. "What would you do?"

Bailey felt the discomfort of being put on the spot. "I'm just a security guard," he stuttered.

* * * * *

Mellman transported to 1950 over the weekend. He'd sent a lighthearted text message to Bailey before leaving: "Couldn't wait any longer. I'll be able to experience the birth of rock n' roll and, with luck, I might be able to save Marilyn Monroe from self-destruction. Whoever designed this machine made it user-friendly. You just get in, set a time, and press the engage button. I would have talked this over with you, but I knew you'd want more information. Dig a one-meter hole exactly two meters to the left of your sundeck. There you will find a small metal box in which, if there's any justice in the world, you will see confirmation of my safe arrival. Then GET OUT OF HERE!"

Bailey wanted to see that box before he told his wife everything he knew, but she gave him such a hard time about digging a hole in their backyard that he relented. It didn't come out very well.

"Are you crazy?" she asked, her formidable body shaking, her long brown hair hanging in her pinched face. "You've known about this for weeks and we're still here?"

He dropped the shovel. "Darcie, you think transporting to another time is going to be like getting on a plane to Florida? We won't belong there. We won't have any of our possessions or money."

"It won't be as bad as falling into a bottomless pit. Dear God, Jon. You never take advantage of anything. This isn't a hot tip. It's life or death."

He sighed. "Let me see if Mellman's message got through. Then…we can figure out what to do."

That didn't placate her. Instead, she grabbed another shovel and both dug. It reminded him of his childhood, digging a hole to China, fueled by a video version of Jules Verne's *Journey to the Center of the Earth*. That enthusiasm had lasted a day or two, halted by an unmovable rock. A pathetic four-foot deep hole remained in his parent's backyard for the duration of his childhood, a reminder of the limits of youthful enthusiasm.

They found no metal box.

"This machine was tested, right? By Time Research?" Darcie asked.

"Yeah. I talked to Dr. Oblomov on Friday. She went to the future twice."

"Did she go to the past?"

"I don't know. Other scientists did, but the only confirmation we've been able to get is from people who went to the past temporarily. As far as I know, there's been nothing from the hundreds of people who went to stay. Something is not right here."

"Yeah, us."

"Maybe, but we're not using that machine until I have proof it's safe. I'm a security guard. I'm supposed to protect people. I am going to call the newspapers and tell them what I know about the time machine."

Darcie stared at him in disbelief. "You are a fool. I may have to stay in this time, but I don't have to stay with you." She threw some clothes into an overnight bag and left. He guessed she'd stay with her mother, though she refused to confirm this.

After she left, Bailey called the three local TV sites. They sent reporters to his house and for several hours, he told them what he knew. Afterwards, exhausted, he realized he hadn't eaten and did something he hadn't done in many years: cooked himself a hamburger. It wasn't until the smoke alarm went off that he realized he'd burnt it. He ate it anyway, too lonely to cook another. It didn't go down very well.

He could still taste the burnt burger when he woke up the next morning. In seconds the memory of divulging the time machine story to the TV stations jolted him. The media was probably screaming about the end of the world.

Then he realized what the hamburger reminded him of.

* * * * *

Bailey found a crowd of two hundred people milling around the entrance of the Time Research building. Four armed cops stood in front of the door, their fearful eyes trained on the mob. As Bailey pushed to the front, two police pointed their pistols at his head.

"Don't shoot! "Bailey said, waving his identification card. "I'm a security guard with Time Research."

One of the two cops lowered her gun. "Go home."

"What's going on inside?"

"We're securing the building."

Bailey helplessly peered at the third floor windows. Gunshots, crashes, and screams rang out like a haunted house soundtrack.

"Look out!" someone screamed, and Bailey whirled around, covering his head with his arms. Someone pushed him to the ground. A foot stepped on his head as he rolled back to his knees, then scampered to his feet. A truck roared past him, amid bullets, crunching metal and snapping bones. A rush of bodies carried Bailey into the building, toward the stairs.

"The time machine is on the third floor!" someone yelled.

"They got the door to the lab open!"

Bailey yelped as his body got jammed against the railing between the second and third floors. He saw no cops. With a jerk he pulled himself out of the stairwell and into the third floor corridor. He looked in horror at the metal door to the lab, dangling like a partially removed incisor, the bottom hinge still attached. Over the chaos he recognized the voice of Delehanty screaming for everyone to get back or he'd shoot. He said it twice, then a gunshot rang out, followed by silence.

Delehanty waved his gun like an admonishing loaded finger. A fat, balding man lay sprawled and leaking on the ground. "No one is going to transport in the time machine today," he said, to boos and hisses. "I know you've heard . . ." and he paused for emphasis . . . "the theory about the world ending in five years."

"It's no theory!" someone yelled, but Delehanty ignored him.

"People have been predicting the end of the world forever, and they've always been wrong. You have a greater chance of getting killed by this mob than by going home and living your lives for the next five years. We have no proof a cataclysmic event will happen in our lifetimes." Bailey couldn't believe his ears.

"The only proof is if it happens," someone said.

"You want proof?" Delehanty asked angrily. He pointed at the body of the man he had shot. "That's what's going to happen if we don't remain calm."

"You're a murderer!" someone shouted.

"Shut up!" Delehanty yelled. "If I hadn't done that, more of us would be dead right now. So listen. This machine is going to be under a 24-7 police guard. It's impossible to get to, and even if you could, you wouldn't know how to use it."

"How do we know you won't use it to escape?" The words came from Bailey.

Delehanty's eyes lit up in recognition.

"Come here every day at 9 AM. You'll see me walk into this building. I'm not going anywhere, and neither is anyone else. Now I need a brave person to be the first to turn around and go home. Then I need the rest of you to follow him."

Bailey stood helpless as the crowd muttered for a few minutes, then teetered on compliance. Heads turned for corroboration, then glanced back at the lab. The standoff broke when Delehanty dashed into the time machine and slammed the door. The machine came to life, emitting an otherworldly hum, followed by the dissonant roar of the transport process, which energized the mob like electricity. But just as quickly, the explosive reports of a gun once again stilled them. Eyes fell on Bailey, who had emptied his bullets into the time machine. The roar, sounding like a garbage disposal, became lower pitched, slower, hollow, then silent. Surprised but relieved that his pistol had such an effect on the machine, Bailey tossed the gun onto the floor. A burly policeman grabbed him.

"What the hell are you doing?" the cop asked, shaking him.

"Check the machine," Bailey said.

Someone wrenched open the door of the time machine. Inside was a pile of ash.

"You killed him," someone said.

"The machine did," Bailey said. "I used to work in a crematorium. That smell of burnt flesh was present after every so-called transport. This wasn't a time machine. It was a death trap."

The crowd looked helplessly at the broken machine for several tense minutes, then someone swore and turned to go. A few people followed suit, building to a desultory flow to the street.

Later in the day police questioned Bailey but did not arrest him. When news of the event reached Dr. Oblomov, she released a statement. She believed some kind of drug or advanced wireless technology caused identical images of the Earth's destruction to play in the scientists' brains. In her view the machine came either from the future or an alien civilization. Either way, its source was foreign to present-day Earth. As for its purpose, since it could dispatch only a handful of people at a time and it proved to be easily destroyed by a handgun, she did not believe it to be part of a hostile attempt to conquer the planet. Instead, she theorized that it was part of an experiment that Earth might never fully understand. None of this could be proven as an hour after its destruction, the remains of the machine disappeared without a trace.

After releasing her statement, Oblomov treated Bailey to dinner at a restaurant fancier than those the former security guard normally frequented.

"How does it feel to be a hero?" Oblomov said as she cut into her baked haddock.

Bailey struggled with his lobster, trying to extricate some meat from the shell. "I'm separated from my wife. My best friend is dead. I'm out of work. If this is what happens to heroes, I can see why there aren't more of them."

"I'm sure there's a market for someone who does his job to the best of his ability. If not, you can work for me."

"I don't know if I'll be able to blindly guard something ever again. Mellman was right about one thing. I was used."

"If this machine was an experiment, then we've all been used."

"What kind of creature would set up such an experiment?"

She frowned. "One that saw us like laboratory rats, the scientist's best friends."

About the author:

Richard Zwicker is a high school English teacher living in Vermont with his wife and beagle. In addition to reading and writing, he likes to play the piano, jog, and fight the good fight against middle age. His short stories have recently appeared in *Stupefying Stories*, *Mindflights*, and *Flagship*.

Gravity and Grace

by Stevie Schafer

Usually, it started as she walked the tarmac. This time it started when she climbed into the rickety plane for the hundredth time and settled in for the ride. The prospect of jumping from a plane into open sky excited Bonnie so much sometimes it hurt. Twisting her fingers around her wrist until the skin turned red, she fixated on the thought of falling. Her back crawled with goose bumps, and all she could do was imagine it. She dreamed of the moment of contact; the touch, the pressure of connection.

She watched the pilot. He expertly eased the craft across the runway. She tried to count the jumps she'd done since her leave started three weeks earlier. It was over twenty-something.

Takeoff brought another rush of adrenaline. The anticipation started in her gut. It moved into her throat, restricting her airway, and then her vision. The world blurred. She secured her goggles. By the time she swung her legs off the edge of the hatch, she'd gone into the bliss of it. The anticipation killed, wound her jaw tight, and lit up all her nerve endings. If she weren't dying to jump, she would have fucked anyone in that moment.

Going to space used to give her all these feelings.

But instead of her jaw rattling from exit velocity, she had to settle for it rattling from the battering wind. Falling towards the earth, she prayed to be saved.

Afterward, she got into her car and drove fast.

* * * * *

From where Bonnie stood at the center of the spherical observatory, vast empty space surrounded her. Except for the small hatch that led back to the station, high pressure viewing windows paneled the entire room. She took a detour on the way back to her quarters every day to spend some time with the distant gas giants. In the center of the platform was a sweet spot: a place where she could feel completely alone with the universe.

When Bonnie noticed herself floating, she turned. Paul Grace stood next to the hatch, watching her, his fingers locked around the gravity dial.

"Hey, Grace," she said.

"What are you doing in here?" he asked. Latching the door shut, he pushed off the wall.

"I was thinking about you," she said. The honesty felt uncomfortable.

Grace extended his arms, drifting through the sphere towards her. She caught him, his momentum sending them into a slow spin.

"You were thinking about Comet Galaxy or Andromeda, not me." He brushed a hair out of her face and behind her ear. "You belong in the stars, don't you?" he asked. His dimples accentuated the small age lines around his lips, even when he barely smiled.

Everything felt surreal. Bonnie tried to remember the last time he spoke in such an intimate tone. She couldn't remember if he had ever smiled with those bedroom eyes. He maintained his gaze for longer than usual, and it made her uncomfortable. Her gut told her to withdraw, to look away, but it was just the two of them and the stars. If she looked away she would simply be alone again. Solitude wasn't what she really wanted—she wanted to connect.

He looked down. His hand followed his eyes, his fingers trailing across her forearm. "I don't mean to make you uncomfortable." He glanced up at her. She sensed a question in his eyes.

His heart-stopping eyes.

"I care about you," she whispered.

Gently, they collided with the viewing windows, their bodies pressed together. He was so close. She didn't dare move. He might change his mind, he might leave.

"We've shared something, Lindstrom," he whispered. "We've been to a place no humans have experienced that way, together, alone, in space. Your design is genius. Without your beautiful mind, the suits wouldn't—"

She panicked. "Don't talk about the suits."

The moment broke. Like all the dreams, she woke up trembling. Her bed was empty but for her own shivering body and her sweaty sheets.

* * * * *

Driving back to her hotel she fought off the assailing memories of things she'd seen. She couldn't get the images of bloated bruised skin, black-red shriveled eyeballs, and the violent convulsions of death out of her mind.

Her cellphone rang.

It was the Department of Outer Space headquarters. She jabbed her stereo, switching it off, and snatched the phone.

"This is Payload Specialist Lindstrom," she said.

"Bonnie, it's George. Listen, I'm calling with an update."

"Hey, George. What's the status?"

"I've got good news. Transdrive Corp got back to us. They decided that your tech is still viable. They're moving forward as planned on the suits' production schedule."

Bonnie veered around a slow driver. The sound of his blaring horn followed her as she sped forward. "What does that mean for me?" she asked.

"I'm not sure. But your name will be famous for a very long time," he said.

"What about re-entering orbit? Continuing my work on the space station?"

"You've got an appointment at headquarters on Friday morning, right?"

"Yeah."

"Then go to that. You should find out there. Take care, Lindstrom."

She sighed and looked at the DOS I.D. photo on her phone before dropping it in the passenger seat. At the hotel, several functional second-gen prototype suits waited for her. But without authorization to study his suit, she could only speculate about how it failed. It didn't matter now. Transdrive Corp still planned to manufacture them and staring at the suits wouldn't help her figure it out.

She didn't want to sit with them, watch them, and wait for an answer.

Parking her car at the hotel, she stuffed the key into her pocket and headed down the street on foot. It only took about fifteen minutes to get to the bar. The Small Step Pub was where all the local space rats gathered when they were stuck planet-side. It was quiet that night. The abundance of empty stools at the bar offered solace. She relaxed into one.

She nodded to the bartender. He opened a bottle of her usual Guinness.

"Bonnie fucking Lindstrom, Department of Outer Space failure," a loud voice called. "Finally grounded for manslaughter. You should be locked up or shot, if you ask me."

"Bonnie Lindstrom? The astronaut? No way!" another guy added.

Two men slid into the seats on either side of her. So much for solace.

"I don't want trouble," she said, eyes glued to the alcohol rack.

"They were talking about you on the news—did you know that? Did you ever think you'd be so famous?" the loud man asked. "Let me ask you something. How exactly is it that someone could die in one of those suits with the inventor right there with them? Those suits must be pretty damn broke. Transdrive cancelling production of those things?"

She glanced at him. The set of his shoulders was youthful, but his skin had been sun-aged, dried and cracked. Something about his face bothered her.

"It didn't go down that way, so I'd appreciate you leaving me alone," she said.

"Why don't you tell us why the good U.S. government hasn't locked you up?" the smaller one asked.

"I bet she's got some sort of diplomatic immunity, you know, for being a brainiac or a national asset or something." The tanned one leaned in, crowding her space.

"Just fuck off." Bonnie's voice cracked. She swallowed half her beer in a few gulps.

They eyed each other. The smaller guy was about to get up, to back off, when his friend put his hand on her back.

"I'm not going anywhere, Lindstrom. You know I knew him?"

All warmth drained from her face. She turned to the man. She examined him more closely this time. The sun had weathered his face, but the underlying features could have been sympathetic once. How many hard losses in a life made a man look like that? She wondered if she was on her way to looking like him. Underneath the layers of time, she felt a familiar twinge.

"Who are you?" she asked.

"I shouldn't be surprised. You never did see me after Grace fucked up my nose," he said, touching the swollen bridge that looked to be poorly healed. "Then again, I didn't get much sun when I lived on the station, either."

She recognized him in an unpleasant wash of emotion. James Patton, biologist, rabble-rouser, and former astronaut who'd been grounded for at least five years. She had barely been zero-g for a week when the fight between him and Grace happened. Of the two hundred and fifty astronauts and scientists who lived aboard the space station, every single person had to pass a series of psych exams before their commissions were approved. Patton's psychotic break spawned that particular rule.

Grace told her the story, once. He said that Patton had come to his quarters in the middle of a rest cycle and begged then threatened him. Said his life was in space. Said he'd die planet-side, that gravity would slowly poison him. Grace said Patton had attacked him with an old hull fragment, almost slit his throat, but his old hand-to-hand training saved him. Grace cracked him once in the nose, broke it well and good, and saved himself enough time to hit the comm and broadcast to the entire station.

The story was, Grace and Patton had been friends before that.

"What do you want from me?" she asked. "You want me to tell you what it was like being there? You want me to describe it step by step?"

He grabbed her wrist, stopping her in mid drink. "You're a fucking heartless bitch."

"Let go of my hand, you ape."

"Hey, uh . . ." the small guy mumbled.

Bonnie lifted her free hand, balled a fist, thought about Grace, and clocked Patton right in the nose. He stumbled back.

"Break it up!" someone shouted. The burly bartender wrangled Bonnie to the back door. He tossed her out on her ass.

Sucking in a deep breath, she took a moment to let the red clear from her vision. Her stomach turned and she wished she'd had the opportunity to wreck Patton. She gritted her teeth and tried to push Grace out of her mind. The smell of smoke punctured her rage.

She noticed a lanky, greasy blond-haired man perched on the curb with a cigarette dangling from his lips. He smiled at her. Looking again, she recognized him.

"I love a lady who gets thrown out of a bar." His voice was higher than she expected.

The last time she'd seen the punk he was jumping out of the Cessna C-182. She'd noticed him once or twice before that. He seemed to also frequent the Harrington Dive Center.

"Do I know you?" she asked. "From diving?"

"Yeah. You're Lambda, right? I think you took my record for most dives in a week." He laughed. "I'm Mitch."

* * * * *

It was a beautiful day—great for a jump. Bonnie drove to the airport with her windows down and her music up. The weather was freeing in its warmth. She felt giddy, buzzing with excitement.

Mitch leaned on his car, waiting for her. A limp cigarette hung from his lips. He grinned as she drove up. They had time to talk before the jump. He kept asking the strangest questions, things like,

"Does taking off make you really horny?" and "When you're entering low orbit, do you ever pee yourself?"

For once she didn't fixate on the idea of falling, not until they were well into the air. Halfway through a shouted conversation she realized they'd be jumping soon. She turned to him. He smiled. His warm expression gave her solace. He distracted her from all her frustrations.

"This is my favorite part," she shouted.

"Yeah, me too."

"Really? Why?"

"Because right when you start falling, for a split second, you have no idea if you are going to live or die."

Bonnie blinked at him. "When you make that decision you give up control and everything that happens is a matter of timing and luck."

Mitch's smile widened, dominating his face. His eyes squinted with the force of it.

* * * * *

"We've shared something, Bonnie." The heat in Grace's breath touched Bonnie's lips.

"We've been to a place no humans have experienced that way, together, alone, in space." He continued, "Your design is genius. Without your beautiful mind . . . ."

She leaned in. His breath hitched. She swallowed the taste of his air.

She pushed his crew jacket off his shoulders and pulled the standard issue tank up over his stomach. She knew each garment intimately. Each piece matched her own. He smoothed one hand across the dimpled 'v' at her lower back. She noticed all the places they touched: knees, thighs, hips. He pulled her shirt over her head. His hand reached up and spread to cover her shoulder-blade. She leaned into him, their chests pressing together. The beat of her heart matched his. She sucked in the taste of his breath once more, hesitating.

He may have kissed her first, she wasn't sure. The pressure of his lips aroused her. It awoke something inside her that she'd long forgotten.

They drifted in tandem towards the center of the observatory. She tugged the zipper of his trousers down, fingers grazing more intimate parts in the process. He watched her with an amalgamation of hunger and adoration. She slid out of her own trousers.

Normally, being alone with the black vacuum and its vast field of stars outside, Bonnie felt infinitely insignificant. Now, naked with Grace, every star was a point of burning passion; they fed her. So bright, even from hundreds of thousands of light years away. She thought only of sating her roused passion. The desire to touch him everywhere, to hold him tighter, overwhelmed her.

She reached for him.

He stopped her, circling her wrists with his fingers. He ran his warm tongue gingerly down her jaw. She caught the lilac and musk scent of his thick brown hair. Her lips parted and she rolled her head back.

"Let me show you how space makes me feel," he whispered, cupping her shoulder and turning her around. They neared the metal platform. Bonnie gave a small push off the surface with her feet, sending them back towards the viewing glass.

Grasping her hips, he tugged her into his lap. He kissed her throat and nipped the yielding flesh there. At the tenderness of his teeth on her skin, she arched her back and reached out to clutch him. Their legs entangled, their bodies pressed urgently against one another's. Floating weightlessly, the sturdiness of his body was her only anchor. His fingertips skated across the tender skin of her belly, brushing across her navel and down her hips. She turned to press her lips against his cheek, feeling rough stubble across her cheek and mouth. The touch of his hands drew a euphoric moan from her.

As he rubbed and encouraged her, a feverish pressure built in the cradle of her pelvis. He played the warm cascade of his breath and the velvet caress of his lips across her earlobe and throat. His free hand rested over her heart, holding her body near and protecting her quickening desire. A bead of sweat dripped down her back. The thrill rose—an internal volume that became louder with every tantalizing sensation. She struggled for breath in the frenzied throes.

Her body undulated and she lost herself to bliss.

The sweat of their connected bodies gave way to the emptiness of her bedroom sheets. She opened her eyes from the dream. Numb and dry-eyed, she stared at the ceiling.

* * * * *

"You know, I've been in bar fights before," Bonnie said, popping the top off her bottle.

"Oh yeah?"

"Yeah, I'm a regular badass."

"Did you wail on ten guys?" Mitch asked, eyes fixed on her face.

"No, but I saw these two beating the shit out of each other. The one guy who was down was really torn up. There was blood everywhere," she said, leaning back in her seat.

"Sounds pretty normal for a bar brawl."

"Well, I yelled at the guy. This was right before I went zero-g for the first time, so I really couldn't risk getting injured. I knew I'd fucked up when he turned at me and got this, like, wicked raging look in his eyes. I did almost piss myself that time."

Mitch laughed. "I knew you had a dark past."

"Well, he came at me, and you know what I did?"

"What?"

"I hugged him."

"What? Seriously?"

"Yeah, I just wrapped my arms around his neck and my legs around his waist and held on for dear life."

Mitch snorted. "Sounds like me when I was a kid."

"Eventually, he stopped trying to hit me. When I let go I ran for it, though. Didn't want to risk getting pummeled and losing my ticket to space."

* * * * *

Bonnie got up at five thirty on Friday morning. She tossed the still-packed suits and her suitcase into the trunk of the Honda, gulped a hotel-sized coffee, and hit the road. The drive to DOS headquarters only took an hour, but she wanted to arrive promptly. The stress of constant tension from her skydiving habit left her emotions raw. She hoped that by getting back to work she might ease the pain. At the same time, she hated the idea of going back to the station. Outer space reminded her that she'd watched the vacuum consume a life in ninety seconds flat.

The night before she'd spent a good four hours staring at the ceiling. She'd only managed about two hours of solid sleep. Her nerves pulsated, raw from coffee and constant adrenaline baths.

The bright platinum lettering on the sign at the gate declared: "Department of Outer Space." She dropped the unopened suits at the front desk with a receptionist and headed up to the top floor.

George and the other DOS executives sat around a long conference table when she entered. The Secretary of Outer Space sat at the head of the table, shuffling through a large stack of paperwork with a glinting metallic pen in her hand.

"Welcome, Payload Specialist Lindstrom," George said. "Have a seat."

She could tell from the looks on their faces that something was wrong.

"Miss Lindstrom, you have, no doubt, made one of the greatest contributions to modern space travel in the last fifty years," the Secretary said.

Bonnie held her breath. She felt the 'but' hang in the air.

"We reworked the contract agreement with Transdrive Corp to increase your commission payout to ten percent."

"Excuse me?" Bonnie cut in. "Ten percent is outrageous. How did Transdrive ever agree to something like that? They might as well put me on payroll as a senior executive."

"It is my belief, Miss Lindstrom, that they would like to do something along those lines," the Secretary said, shuffling through her folder. "I'm sorry, but we have decided to end your contract with DOS and let you go so that you can pursue this other opportunity."

"Unfortunately," George said, "what this means for you is that your space station access will be revoked."

Bonnie almost wretched on her way out. She had to stop in the restroom and hang her head between her knees until the dizziness passed.

* * * * *

The heat was stifling as she parked in front of Mitch's house. What possessed her to show up at his door, she didn't know. The heavy blue wood swung inward. He stood there in a pair of torn-up jeans, his long scraggly blond hair pulled out of his face. A tattoo she'd never seen covered his chest.

"Holy fuck, what happened to you?" he asked.

She shook her head.

"Come in." He stepped out of the way.

She crossed the threshold, and soon they ended up in his bed. She felt empty until he started talking. She stared at the long wiry muscles in his arms as laid there, a cigarette burning between his lips, staring at the ceiling. He reminded her of herself, lost and empty with no reason not to die.

"I know what happened to you," he said. "At least, I have a good idea."

She watched him, taking in the details of his profile.

"Everyone knows you were in that space accident. But I think there's more to the story. I think you're damaged because you lost someone."

She'd never thought of herself that way: damaged. The word fit.

"I lost someone too. About ten years ago." He shook his head. "When we were skydiving."

"Who was it?"

"My brother."

His gaze fixed defiantly on the ceiling, moisture catching the light in his eyes. "We both went out at the same time. I lost sight of him when we were going down, but I wasn't looking that hard. I should have been looking harder. When I landed, one of our dive instructors was there in his Jeep. He ran over to me and, God, I had no idea what was wrong. I remember thinking he had a funny run. And then he told me."

He closed his eyes. "Between you and me?"

"Yeah?"

"I've been fucked up ever since." He took a long drag from his cigarette.

* * * * *

Space surrounded them. Blackness stretched on forever, except for the peacefully onlooking Mother Earth. Bonnie relaxed her eyes and leaned her head back. The emptiness was visceral for her. As a child, she captured the desperate feeling by staring at the stars. Now she moved freely through space, protected by an inconsequential layer only as thick as a Kevlar vest. She was free, unbridled by a safety lead.

This was the beauty of her design.

Paul Grace's voice clicked through the comm. "Hey, Lindstrom. I think something is caught on my movement generator. Can you take a look?"

Grace pushed his hands back, spreading his fingers out and activating the internal movement sensors. His thin suit propelled him towards her. It seemed to be slower than normal. He smiled at her through the clear glass of his visor. She grabbed onto his shoulder and turned him around, examining the lightweight pack that housed the movement computer, generator, and wiring.

A small globule of blue liquid seeped out from the bottom corner of the pack.

"You've got a fluid leak, Grace. Hold on. I can patch this. Then we need to head back."

She opened a small toolkit on her belt, pulling out a tube of fast-drying gel to patch the damage. She lifted the pack away from his suit. A burst of gas vented out.

"Fuck!"

She'd accidentally exposed or possibly extenuated a massive

defect in his suit. The first layer of protection had fractured; it was only a matter of seconds before the second would follow. It was too much to fix with a bit of fast-drying gel.

"We have to go, now!" she commanded. "You've got no time."

"No time?" He turned to look at her. "Bonnie, my propulsion is shorting out."

"Grab onto me, I can get us back. Come on." She held her arms out to him. He took her hands instead.

"It's a five minute trip back. How long do I have?"

"Shut up and come on!"

"Listen!" he shouted. "Bonnie, I care about you. I just wanted to tell you that before . . . ."

She saw it happen. All the oxygen in his helmet expelled from the back of his suit. He'd had the training; she saw the retching motion as he exhaled everything in his lungs. Exposure to the vacuum was possible for almost ninety seconds, but that exhalation was key. She distantly felt the tears wetting her cheeks. She couldn't travel the distance to the station in ninety seconds by herself, let alone pulling him. All she could do was hold his hands and watch him die.

She watched him panic. The moisture in his mouth and eyeballs quickly evaporated, followed by the moisture in his muscles and soft tissue. The swelling started next, all parts of him expanding. A blossom of bruises discolored his skin as his capillaries broke. She knew what she couldn't see—the nitrogen that was dissolved in his blood bubbled with the agony of the Bends.

It still wasn't too late, he could still survive. But she was frozen.

She held his hands. He began convulsing violently. By the time his body calmed, his skin was cyanotic.

The next two minutes felt like an eternity. And then, she was alone with his body. Staring through the fogged glass of his visor at his discolored face, she cried uncontrollably.

She would use up all of her oxygen sobbing.

Somehow, she made herself move. She held his hand firmly, never letting go, and dragged his corpse through the vast black space back to the station.

At the station, they couldn't get her to let go of his hand.

After that, they sent her planet-side on mental leave.

* * * * *

Bonnie thought about Mitch as she approached the airport. He skydived almost as fanatically as she did. Like her, he needed the thrill of the possibility of death. She could see he felt nothing inside. He hated the world. The only life he could find was in the violent contact of drunken bar-fights and diving through the sky, like she did. She loved him in a strange way, like she had always thought she should love herself. She wondered if she even came close to filling the hole left by his brother.

He leaned against the hood of his car, like every time she'd met him at the small county airport. This time, when she approached him, he pushed off the car and planted a small kiss on her lips.

"Hi, killer," he said.

The jump was all Bonnie could think about. She wanted it more than anything. Twisting her fingers around her wrist, she fixated on the thought of falling. Her back crawled with goose bumps and all she could do was imagine it. She'd dreamed of the moment of contact, the touch, the pressure of connection. Standing beside her, she knew Mitch understood. She silently thanked the universe for bringing him into her life.

She didn't notice the pilot as they went airborne. She stared at Mitch. He watched the ground recede.

"Thank you," she shouted in the windy cabin. They approached the jump spot.

"Thank you. You've been so good to me," he yelled, looking at her.

She nodded.

Together, they fell. Blissful, unending waves of atmosphere

pushed into their faces. Bonnie wished silently that she had an angel to save her. She prayed for one to bring her a violent end. And then she committed to her only good deed. She straightened her arms and barreled towards Mitch. Extending her arm to him, he took her hand. They looked at each other through the barrage of oxygen.

It felt so real.

Bonnie pulled him closer.

They made eye contact through their goggles. He mouthed something, but she couldn't read his lips. She wrapped her arms and legs around his body, tightly.

They fell for too long like that.

Finally, Mitch touched her hips. He stared at her, eyes wild, he knew what was coming. Fear burned in her throat. She clutched him with every ounce of strength. The ground rose towards them. The wind battered her face. Somehow, this dive reminded her of floating with Grace in her dreams. Mitch kissed her as they plummeted towards the earth.

About the author:

Stevie Schafer has been writing since she moved to Colorado in 1998. She studied creative writing and art at the University of Colorado. She's devoted to creating strong female characters, mostly due to her massive Xena obsession. One day, she hopes to defend the universe in an epic space battle.

Sweet Little Princess Irene

by Talia Haven

Dried leaves crunch under my bare feet as I leave the dirt path and enter the clearing of the three ancient oak trees. Overhead, their leafless branches resemble the arthritic fingers of an old weaver woman. Clinking and rubbing against one another in the moonless dark, they dance to the silent tune of a warm spring breeze that pushes them about.

A lone field mouse, spooked by my footsteps, darts over the dead plants covering the forest floor. Flapping, heavy wings announce the presence of an owl as it leaves a limb. Swooping down, it finishes the brief life of the tiny rodent.

Hesitating in the center of the clearing, I wait for the voices. Every time I get angry at Lenora, I end up here. The voices from the trees talk to me about my problems and make me feel better.

"Why are you so upset Irene?" whispers voice number one.

"Her older sister," says the other.

"Yes," declares the third.

"Mother says I can't go to Lowender AnNorvys Flogh." My hazel eyes dart from one tree to the other. I absentmindedly pull on a single dark-blond braid that runs down one shoulder. "Lenora gets to."

"The Festival of Earth's Children?" questions the second voice.

"Charms and wishes made tonight are some of the strongest," says the first.

"Tonight is a very dangerous night," agrees the third.

"Perhaps if you can't go," the first voice suggests, "you could make a wish?"

"She has no charm," says the third.

"She doesn't need a charm here," says the first, "just a wish,"

"What is it that you want the most?" asks the second.

Encouraged by the unseen voices, I stand in a place that I think is just a dream and speak aloud my heart's desire.

"I already know what I want," I tell them. "What will make me happy? I wish I was the oldest."

* * * * *

The next morning Lenora doesn't wake up.

Father and Mother tell me Lenora died in her sleep. They say the physician examined her, and it was the only explanation he had.

Hot and smelling of lavender, water soaks one side of my dress as I push open the door to Lenora's room. Dim sunlight beaming through narrow-slotted windows is not enough to justify extinguishing the touches that hang on the stone walls.

Women servants surround the bed. Their shadows dance in the smoky flickering light while they work on a body tipped to one-side. Shoulders shaking with hic-cup sobs, Mother's back is toward me as she washes a flesh-colored and bare back.

"Irene!" She can hardly get out the sentence. "Bring that bucket of water over here, then go over and wash your sister's face."

Wet cloth in hand, I stand at the head of the bed and stare down at Lenora's hair-covered features. Mother finishes drying her back, and the servants roll her off to her side. Tenderly, mother leans over and brushes away blond strands of hair that are so close to her own in color. Lenora's lips are light red, her skins not blue as I expect it to be but full of warmth and life. The hot cloth, now just lukewarm, smells of lavender. I take a tiny step forward, just close enough to do what Mother expects of me. Timidly I reach out and start to clean Lenora's cheek, accidentally touching her with my hand. Instead of cool, she feels warm. Droplets of water run like tiny rivulets down one side toward her ear. Not wanting to get the bedding wet, I lean my face in closer to hers. I pat at the drops. That's when Lenora, who everyone says has died, looks at me.

Desperate hazel eyes follow me as I drop my cloth and back

away.

"Mother." My voice shakes. Mother's hand calmly continues to stroke her hair. Lenora watches every move I make. I back towards the wall. "She's alive."

Mother thinks I have gone mad. She says Lenora's eyes are not open, even though I stand here and point it out to her. She closed them herself, she insists. Then she orders one of the servants, whispering among themselves at the foot of the bed, to escort me out of the room. I am not to come back in, she tells me. I won't be needed until the service.

* * * * *

My gown itches at the neck as I sit in the pew beside Father and Mother. Family and friends fill the remaining sections behind us. Our household servants quietly gossip as they crowd the area behind them. Face up, Lenora rests on a wooden bier and stares at the simple smoke-stained stone ceiling. Her uncovered head is directly across from me. I try hard not to look her way, but I glance up anyway and spot her staring at me out of the corner of her eye.

Alarmed, I touch mother's arm to point it out to her, but she gives me a warning glare to be silent. So I keep my head down and play with the rings on my fingers while I sit and listen to the service. It is a long ceremony, filled with crying, prayer, and frantic eyes. Everything smells like lavender, even though I had taken off my other dress and scrubbed myself with rose-scented water.

Father and Mother get up to leave, and I'm forced to follow them as they walk up to view Lenora. I tag along close behind Mother with my head still down. We pass by. I sneak a peek at my sister. Anguished eyes look back. A thin tear runs out of one corner and disappears into the hair covering one ear. I know Mother will not listen, so I decide Father might as I follow them outside to wait.

"Lenora's crying," I tell him in a low voice. Mother grabs my elbow, a warning for me to be quiet and not make a scene. "She's not dead," I continue, ignoring the increasing pressure of Mother's hand. "It's a mistake."

"The dead sometimes cry," my Father mumbles as people

begin to file out to take their positions. Turning his face toward the open-doorway, he accepts condolences from a growing line of mourners on behalf of Mother and me. "Sometimes they even moan."

Father and Mother walk behind the bier, and I walk behind them, barely able to make out Lenora. Dressed in her favorite green gown, she is hoisted on the wooden funeral bier. The bearers, six of them in all, march in step. A basil-filled turbine swings on one of the briers wooden legs. A curl of light-colored smoke drifts out to purify the air around them. I know it's not lavender, but it smells like it. The scent of it makes me sick to my stomach.

Lenora should be beside me, during this agonizingly slow walk toward the necropolis. Her ringed fingers should be flashing in the sun as they clutch the skirt of her green dress to keep the hem out of the mud. Instead she looks like she is in prayer. Hands bound by strips of braided white velvet, she's carried from home to grave.

The solemn procession continues through the village. It grows long as mourners and the curious follow a respectful distance behind. I wonder how many know that I think she is still alive.

A simple wooden box for a princess who never married lay on the ground next to an open grave. The musty smell of freshly shoveled earth becomes stronger the closer I get to the gaping dark hole. At the foot, a simple unfinished headstone with the word LENORA chiseled on it lays on the ground. Surrounded by grey flecks of newly chipped stone, it will be finished and set in place after the entombment. The stone worker is nowhere nearby, but two gravediggers stand off to one side. One holds a hammer and iron nails while the other leans on the handle of a spade as he waits to finish the job.

Mother and Father put me between them as we take our positions at the head of the coffin.

Hands folded, we wait. The bier bearers lower Lenora to the ground. Mourners gather silently. Two of the carriers pick her up and place her into the casket.

Rolled up so far back in their sockets, the whites of her eyes are almost all I can see. Silently pleading now, Lenora looks like she is on the verge of hysteria as I stand looking down at her.

Help me! They beg. Don't let them do this to me! I'm your sister, save me! Finally, I will not be hushed anymore. Weeping, I step forward. Dropping to my knees, my hands grab the rough wood, and I start to leap over the edge, into the casket with my sister. My mother grabs hold of me and pulls me clear before I can.

"I'm sorry Lenora." My words are all broken up by panic-stricken sobs. I stare into the eyes of my older sister for the last time. "I tried to tell them, but they won't listen."

Lenora no longer looks hysterical. Her accusing eyes remind me of what I have done. You did this to me.

One female servant lifts me up by my elbow. Another puts an arm across my shoulders. Most of the crowd look at their feet or off at something in the distance. They step aside to make a path.

Eyes red and puffy, I tell anyone who meets my glance, "Listen to me. It's a mistake." I continue as I am lead past, "Can't you see her looking at you?"

"It's your grief playing tricks on you," one of the servants says. Quickening her pace, she tries calming me. The other gives my shoulders a tight sympathetic squeeze. "Her eyes are shut," she says as I am lead away.

We barely get past the edge of the crowd before I hear the sharp ringing sound of metal against metal. The grave keeper, performing one of his final duties, is starting to drive the nails deep into the wood, sealing in Lenora.

* * * * *

I don't go to the feast afterwards. Mother thinks I should just retire for the night. So she has sent one of the servants instead with a supper of cold meat, cheese, and bread. The meal she has brought remains untouched where she sat it beside a pitcher of water on the table. The maid nervously busies herself in my room for a little while then asks if there's anything else I need.

I tell her, "No," and she leaves in a hurry, shutting the door behind.

Lenora's eyes watch from the shadows of my room. I pretend to sleep, but I can feel them staring, accusing me while I toss and turn into the early morning hours.

Outside it is pitch black, and one of the guards has called the hour. I know her eyes are still there, staring even though my own are tightly closed. Sleep does not come easy when you're constantly watched, and all you can think about is a simple wish made in a place that you thought was a dream.

Dried leaves crunch under my bare feet; I walk once again through these familiar woods. Tonight the wind is calm and a full moon casts long shadows as I wander up the path. But no matter how hard I look or what paths I go down, I cannot find the clearing with the three old oak trees.

Dawn is just beginning to break off in the east. Its dim light starts to show through the branches. I do not have a lot of time so I shout my questions to the still forest again. "I want to take back the wish," I yell. "Where are you? Why won't you answer me?"

Just before I wake up to the gentle-tapping knock on my door and sound of people moving out in the hallway, I feel Lenora in the shadows, waiting while three voices taunt me from the distance.

"A wish was made," mocks the first.

"A wish was granted," sneers the second.

"Sweet Little Princess Irene," the third sarcastically says, "she's the oldest one now."

About the author:

Talia Haven was born in Michigan, raised in Michigan and still lives in Michigan. Her most recent works have appeared in *The Scareald* and *Stories for Children Magazines*. *Sweet Little Princess Irene* is her first short story for Loconeal publishing.

The Curse of Nao

by Dan Hart

A foreign presence invaded Tatsuya's mind when he was eleven, the night after a stray Frisbee collided with his forehead and caused a half-inch bruise on his temple. The wound hadn't hurt much at the time, but now Tatsuya's head felt swollen and fragmented memories he'd never known rushed into his mind. He screamed out for his parents, but only his dad stomped up the stairs to his room, wearing a stained brown suit with a loose black tie—he must have been working late, again. He scowled at Tatsuya with practiced wrinkles.

"You should stay quiet," the presence said to Tatsuya, using the boy's brain to think as if it were its own.

Tatsuya reached out for his dad, kneeling on the covers of his bed. "Dad! Something's in my head!"

His father's frown relented. "You mean a headache?"

"Don't tell him about me," the presence said in a singsong voice.

Tatsuya tightened his face and panted. "No. Like, something's talking to me."

His father's scowl returned. "You're too old for imaginary friends. Go to sleep."

"But Dad, I—" The sight of his father's lowering eyebrows interrupted him, and Tatsuya reconsidered the presence's advice. "Okay," he said, barely audible.

His dad grunted approval, and shut the door. But Tatsuya wasn't alone.

"Don't worry, I won't stay very long," the presence said. "My name is Nao. Thanks for letting me into your brain."

"I didn't say you can stay," Tatsuya said, aloud.

"Well, you should." Nao sighed, which made Tatsuya sigh involuntarily. "It's so hard to find someone new."

Tatsuya clenched his teeth, closed his eyes, and imagined a bulldozer plowing through his mind and destroying the presence. In his imagination, Nao appeared as a middle-aged, round-cheeked man wearing geta sandals and a bamboo hat, much like the traditional figures his mother drew on greeting cards.

Nao deftly evaded the bulldozer despite his plumpness. "Just a short while, honest," he said. "And in the meantime, I'll tell you secrets."

Tatsuya was not a quiet boy, and his blabbing had cost him the confidence of many friends. Nobody ever told him secrets, anymore, even though he loved them more than ravioli. "What secrets?" he asked.

"Let's see. Do you know how to light a candle with smoke?" Tatsuya shook his head. "You put the candle out, then just light the dark smoke that comes off. The flame will burst back to life."

Tatsuya frowned. "Neat, but not really a secret."

Nao made them both grin. "Did you know the president ate glue as a kid?"

"Really?" But only dumb kids did that, Tatsuya had thought.

"I'm serious. I shared his brain for a few years, many decades ago."

"A few *years*?" Tatsuya pulled his eyebrows together, and fought the panic that grew in the stem of his brain and between his lungs. "You can't stay a few years!"

Nao chuckled, bouncing his gut, which made Tatusya's belly tingle. "Oh, but I must," Nao said, and in Tatsuya's imagination he patted the boy's head. "Only eleven years old, and already you can read between the lines." Nao chuckled again.

Tatsuya mimicked his father's most menacing scowl. A surge of anger pressed against the back of his eyes. "Go away. Get out!"

Nao's grin became a smirk. "Don't worry about it for now. Go to sleep."

Against his wishes, Tatsuya fell backward onto his bed, and

started to snore before he could protest.

* * * * *

Over the next week, Tatsuya barely said anything to either Nao or his parents, and he had no desire to leave his room. Nao could hear Tatsuya's thoughts as easily as his voice, so Tatsuya tried to think as little as possible, too. He shambled more than he walked, and when he spoke, he muttered.

His mom patted his head as she poured his orange juice. "Feeling better today, honey?"

Tatsuya shrugged, and his mom sighed.

"Just ignore him if he's still moping," his father said, not looking up from his newspaper. "If he wants to ruin his summer vacation, then that's his choice."

"He's not supposed to be depressed at eleven," she said. "Don't you think—"

"No, I don't." Tatsuya's father sipped his coffee. "Leave it be."

Tatsuya peeked beyond his downward stare to look at his mom. She stood unsteadily, shifting her balance between her feet, and Tatsuya felt certain she wanted to say something. Then she sat down, placed her left palm atop her right knuckles, and smiled.

Tatsuya's shoulders slumped deeper, and his gaze returned to the grain in the wooden table. Golden sunlight beamed through translucent curtains. Birds chirped, singing above the growl of morning lawnmowers. Tatsuya imagined he could smell the freshly cut grass, and wished Nao wasn't in his brain so he could escape back into his fantasy summer world and be happy again.

"But I can help you," Nao said—the first thing he'd said that day.

Tatsuya hoped that if he ignored him, Nao would go away. He closed his eyes and tried to focus on happy green fields with running dogs, towering redwoods, and flying Frisbees.

"I won't go away; not yet. But I can help."

"Just shut up," Tatsuya thought.

"I can help."

Tatsuya clenched his teeth. In his imagination, Nao tapped his foot and crossed his arms, smiling and calm. Tatsuya tried to ignore him but the effort was too much. He opened his eyes and relaxed some of his tension. "Fine. How?"

"Why does your father seem so strict?" Nao asked.

"I dunno. Maybe he hates me, or maybe he's just mean."

Nao laughed from his belly. "He loves you and you know it." A parade of memories asserted in Tatsuya's head at Nao's urging. Birthdays, vacations, the night his dad stayed up until three in the morning to work on the Stegosaurus costume he'd procrastinated for over a month. "So why's he so strict?" Nao asked.

"I don't know."

"Don't you? He works late and sometimes doesn't come home until after your bedtime. He says you're too old for imaginary friends, and he prevents even your own mother from coddling you. Those are facts, yes?"

"I guess."

"So why do you suppose he does that?"

"He's just strict."

Nao laughed again. "Do you really think so? Doesn't he usually seem more laid back?"

"With other people," Tatsuya said, pouting a bit. "He's only mean to me."

"So it seems," Nao said. "But why?"

Tatsuya shrugged.

"How does he feel about his own parents?"

"He hates them," Tatsuya thought, and exhaled a loud sigh. His grandparents were so loving and nice, always toting handbags of gifts. But Dad would glare at them like they were horrible people.

"Do you know why?" Nao asked.

"He just does."

"But why?"

Tatsuya grew frustrated at the question and his mind wandered. He slurped a straw-full of orange juice.

"Ask him if he felt overprotected as a child," Nao said.

Tatsuya snorted, but decided the question was interesting enough to ask. "Dad, were you overprotected as a kid?"

Both his parents stopped eating, and his father lowered his newspaper, seeming to stammer silently before finding his voice. "Your grandparents?" he asked. "Why do you want to know?"

"See?" Nao said. "Ask him if that's why he's so hard on you."

Tatsuya didn't completely follow Nao's logic, but decided this was the right question to ask. "Is that why you're so mean to me?"

"Tatsuya . . ." His dad stared blankly.

"Go on," Tatsuya's mom said, smiling and tapping his dad's shoulder. "Didn't you say it would be good to talk about it?"

His father's cheeks reddened, and Tatsuya wondered if it was a blush, not anger. "With you," he said, sounding embarrassed.

"Talk about what?" Tatsuya asked, not following the shift in his parents' mood. "About why you're mean to me?"

His father sighed. "I'm not *mean* to you. I just want you to have the opportunities I never did." Tatsuya's mom smiled as his dad spoke. "Your grandparents—I know you like them, but yes, they were very overprotective. Paranoid, really. People called them hippies but they weren't. They just used the label as an excuse to hide up in Humboldt, away from the world—and to hide me from it. From any pain or disappointment. Nothing was ever my fault— they thought they were protecting me . . . ."

His father trailed off, but Tatsuya was too curious not to press. "So, what?"

"Tatsuya, remember what you did when the Cub Scout pack leader wouldn't let your car race in the regional Pinewood Derby? Because he said your car was too ugly?"

Tatsuya did, and he frowned at the memory. It was the first time he'd said the "F" word to an adult. "Yeah. I'm sorry." Tatsuya found it odd that his dad smiled.

"No, that was the healthy way to react. That's why I'm hard on you—I want you to be independent and capable of surviving on your own. My parents protected me from everything, so I never learned how to respond to things like that. I never tried out for anything, and your grandparents isolated me from any potential rejection or pain. I missed so many opportunities because of it."

Tatsuya's mom clapped her hands together, her face radiant. "You're a smart kid, Tatsuya," she said. "You know that?"

His father nodded, raised his newspaper, and hummed.

* * * * *

Nao's insights helped Tatsuya resolve the conflicts with his schoolmates by convincing them he'd learned the value of secrecy. Nao taught him card tricks, clever jokes, and ancient undiscovered riddles. All he asked in return was that Tatsuya spend an hour or three each day reading, watching documentaries, or otherwise furthering Nao's centuries of knowledge. Within a year, Nao had become Tatsuya's best friend.

"No—don't say anything," Nao said, instructing Tatsuya as he courted Jennifer Landing. Tatsuya had just turned thirteen, and she was his first girlfriend. "Just listen to her," Nao said.

"—and I never had a horse, but my grandparents have a ranch, and I know it's cliché, but—"

"I really don't care about this," Tatsuya thought *"Do I have to?"*

Nao shrugged, and laughed. "Do you want to be her boyfriend?"

So Tatsuya listened to Jennifer detail her summer vacations, favorite books, and anecdote after anecdote about her love-hate relationship with her little brother. But most of his thoughts were focused inward, on random chit-chat with Nao.

After a month, Jennifer gently took his hand in hers, hugged him, and said, "I can't be your girlfriend, anymore."

"Why not?"

She laughed and shook her head. "I thought you'd understand after listening to me for so long."

"I'm sorry?" Tatsuya cursed himself for not paying attention. "What do you mean?"

"You're way shorter than me." She shrugged as if that

explained everything.

"So?"

Jennifer laughed again, and Tatsuya felt very small. "You weren't listening at all, were you? I'm sorry, Tatsuya. You're too short. People are saying things."

Tatsuya felt only a moment of hurt before his veins pulsed hot anger. How dare she dump him over something so trivial and stupid?

"Don't say anything," Nao said, quietly but firmly. Tatsuya felt Nao hug him in his imagination. "If you explode, she'll tell her friends, and they will tell their friends. Accept her rejection gracefully."

Tatsuya closed his eyes and managed to contain his anger. He nodded and excused himself. That afternoon, he biked to the Santa Cruz mountains to hike and lose himself in the redwood canopy with Nao.

* * * * *

After almost five years, when Tatsuya was fifteen, Nao felt like an inseparable part of him.

He enjoyed the solitude of California's coastal redwoods most of all. Here the air was crisp and the world beneath the trees spread out like a lush emerald fantasy. He shared his deepest conversations with Nao on these trails far beneath the canopy, and experienced his most life-changing awakenings. It was here Nao helped him get over Jennifer, and it was here he fully comprehended the simple beauty of evolution, discovering his passionate interest in biology.

And it was here Nao told him that he would soon leave.

The panic Tatsuya felt dwarfed any fear he'd ever experienced before. He was walking when Nao said it, and a jolt of cold shot up his ankles, turning his legs to rubber; he stumbled. "You can't," he said, groaning as his palms scraped against the rocky dirt trail.

They sighed as one. "I told you I wouldn't stay long," Nao said.

"That was different. Now I want you to stay."

Nao smiled, but Tatsuya maintained his frown. "I can't," Nao said. "Don't you want the rest of your brain back?"

Tatsuya did, but not at the cost of losing Nao. His head throbbed, stabbing his left eye from behind and signaling the start of a migraine. "No," he said. "I want you to stay."

"You're a smart kid. Just think of what you could do if I wasn't stealing some of your brain."

"But I'm smart because you tell me the answers. If you leave . . ." Nao said nothing, and Tatsuya knelt quietly for over a minute imagining how awful it would be to exist in such silence for the rest of his life. "I don't want to be alone," he said.

Nao nodded. "You won't be alone. You'll find someone to be with. Someone like Jennifer or Stacey. Someone even better."

"Yeah, but you should stay, too."

"I would," Nao said. "But I've already stayed too long. Your headaches are getting worse."

"So?" Tatsuya's head throbbed so hard he wondered if his veins pulsed visibly. "They're worse because you keep poking me with crap like, 'Oh, now I have to leave.'"

"It's my fault, yes." In Tatsuya's imagination, Nao's typical jolly fat cheeks turned sad and sullen. "You are growing up fast. Your head hurts because I'm in too much of your brain. Your adult mind needs the territory I possess."

"It doesn't hurt so bad," Tatsuya said, even though each word struck his throbbing head like a hammer to an anvil. "It's okay."

"No it's not. You say that now, but later—"

"I'll say the same thing. I'll never care. So stay." Tatsuya felt an odd gratitude for his headache, and embraced the feeling as if it were righteous. "I'll give everything to you, Nao. Just stay. Please?"

Nao shook his head, and a long silence ensued. A strong wind swooshed through the tops of the trees, but at their trunks the air stood still. At length, Nao spoke again. "I don't want to stay, Tatsuya."

Tatsuya felt eleven, again. Suddenly, the world didn't make sense. He sniffled and clutched his backpack like a teddy bear. His brain felt cold. "You, you don't want to?"

"I'm sorry, Tatsuya. But you're almost sixteen now, and your mind is becoming rigid. You are maturing into a wonderful young man, with your own dreams and your own thoughts. That is too constricting for me."

Tatsuya stood upright and balled his fists. "Don't be so selfish! I put up with you, gave you a place to stay. And now you're bored with me? Just because I grew up?" He punched a tree beside the trail, and was angry he hadn't punched hard enough to break the skin on his knuckles, so he punched it three more times. Then he punched it with both hands, until his fingers were swollen and numb, and speckled with red holes.

Nao said nothing until Tatsuya's tantrum was complete. "Feel better?" he asked.

"No." Tatsuya dropped his head. "You have to stay."

"Not for long," Nao said, then went mute for the rest of the day.

* * * * *

Three days passed before Nao spoke again. Tatsuya's parents worried about their son's sudden depression and the wounds on his knuckles, but Tatsuya made up a story about a new girl who had broken his heart. His mental solitude and lack of energy forced him to introspection, and although his heart hurt just as badly as before, he began to accept the inevitability of Nao's departure.

"Thirty days," Nao said while Tatsuya stared at his ceiling from his bed. "That much longer."

"Thirty days," Tatsuya echoed. It was more time than he had expected, and part of him felt joy at this. The rest felt only despair. "Who are you leaving me for?"

Nao giggled, and lifted his bamboo hat to scratch his ear. "I love the way you phrase things. But I haven't chosen. That is your responsibility."

"Mine?" Tatsuya blinked twice, then said: "I choose me."

"You can't choose yourself. It needs to be a kid under thirteen. Preferably at least ten. A pliable brain that's not too stupid."

"How about a cat? Or a sloth? I think a sloth would fit you. Or how about a horse with a broken leg? Ever been inside someone who died before?" Like bile, spite festered in Tatsuya's tongue. "I'll send you into a quadriplegic. Or into someone who can't feel pain." He was surprised at the plethora of ideas he thought of to punish Nao. "Or a brain-dead vegetable. What do you think about that?"

"I think you're acting like a selfish child," Nao said. "And are missing the point. I am the greatest gift you can give. Who will you give me to?"

"No one," Tatsuya said. "You've hurt me too bad." He wanted Nao to hurt, too.

"That's mean," Nao said. "This is hard on me, too, you know. It's always so hard to find someone new."

Nao had said something similar when they'd first met, and the memory caused a brief grin to mar Tatsuya's frown and disrupt his emotional turmoil. He felt as if his sorrow crystallized in his veins.

Twenty-seven days, and he had already wasted three.

"Nao, I . . ." Tatsuya had never told Nao he loved him as much as he loved himself, but since Nao shared his brain he hadn't thought he needed to. Now the words stuck, both vocally and as thoughts.

"So let's celebrate these final days," Nao said, leaning forward and grinning as if he had some ultra-clandestine secret to share. "It won't be as bad as you fear; honest."

Tatsuya forced a smile even though his heart palpitated and cold, tingling wires twisted around his nerves. He stood, waited until the weakness in his ankles relented, and said, sheepishly, "Okay. Let's go hiking, Nao."

* * * * *

Tatsuya told his parents he was working on an ecological summer project for school and wouldn't be home much the next few weeks; only for meals and to sleep. They were eager to see him active again, and didn't ask many follow-up questions.

Nao hid in the corners of Tatsuya's mind most of the day.

When he emerged to engage in conversation, Tatsuya's head pounded in pain.

Tatsuya didn't much care about this. "We only have twenty-two days left," he said. "You still have too much to tell me to stay quiet."

"I don't want to hurt you," Nao said.

"It's a bit too late for that." Tatsuya's head pounded and he stumbled on the trail, tripping over a small exposed root, and only regained his balance after wildly flailing his arms.

"Are you okay?" Nao asked.

"Yeah," Tatsuya said. "Just tripped." He breathed several deep breaths before resuming his forward shamble down the trail. He forced another smile, trying hard to enjoy his time with Nao.

But Nao continued to hide in the recesses of his brain, only coming out when prodded.

"How many times have you done this?" Tatsuya asked.

"Two hundred eighty-three leaps so far."

"This must be so different for you," Tatsuya said, interrupting a sniffle with a laugh. "I'm just another random face."

"Never. I only pick the best and brightest. I remember everyone."

Tatsuya snickered. "I thought I got to pick. Or were you lying?"

"You will go on to do great things. I promise."

Tatsuya shook his head and snorted. "So do I get to pick?" he asked.

"Yes," Nao said. "If you are able to come to terms with my departure."

"It's inevitable. I understand that, now. But you have to help me. I need to know something, first."

"Of course. I'll do anything to help."

"Then tell me who chose me."

Tatsuya didn't expect Nao to answer, but he did. "Alex Peterson," Nao said.

* * * * *

Alex was a tall, skinny college student with wireframe glasses who lived down the street from Tatsuya. They had rarely interacted before, and Tatsuya's sharpest memory of Alex was the awkward visit he had made to "interview" Tatsuya before he'd entered the eighth grade. Tatsuya had found it strange that Alex only asked questions about his dreams, goals, and how he felt about imaginary friends—but Nao had warned him to keep quiet.

Tatsuya knocked on Alex's door, and the twenty-year-old greeted him with a warm, expectant smile. "Tatsuya," Alex said, nodding his head with respect. "I'm glad to see you."

"Thanks," Tatsuya said. He shifted his weight between feet. "I wanted to ask you some questions."

"Of course," Alex said. "Is Nao still with you? Or has he already left?"

Tatsuya had come to see Alex to discuss Nao, of course, but Alex's awareness of the entity still caused Tatsuya to flinch. "He's here," he said.

"Hi, Nao."

Inside Tatsuya's head, Nao said nothing.

"He is leaving soon," Tatsuya said. "I need to pick someone."

"Do you hate him for it?" Alex asked, smirking. "Did you tell him to die in a fire?"

Tatsuya shook his head. He was beyond anger—whenever he felt mad at Nao, the anxiety of imminent emptiness squelched these feelings as petty and irrelevant.

"Do you hate *me* for it?" Alex asked, quieter.

"No," Tatsuya said. "But why did you choose me?"

Alex shrugged. "You lived nearby. I had to choose someone, and you were at the park with your dad. He was ignoring you, and you were playing an imaginary game with pinecones and twigs."

"Helicopters," Tatsuya said. "Maple seeds." The day came back to him in vivid detail—sunny, fluffy clouds, several annoying dogs, and a stinging Frisbee to the head. It was that night, nearly five years ago, that Nao had leaped into his mind. Tatsuya had almost forgotten about his day at the park.

"You were all alone, but smiling and entertaining yourself. Other kids were there playing games, but you ignored them, living inside your own imagination." Alex shrugged again. "You seemed right."

"I thought you said you only picked the best and brightest," Tatsuya thought to Nao.

"Everyone has that potential," Nao said. "It doesn't matter if you choose or I choose. What matters is what the recipient does with me. What their brain becomes."

"Who should I pick?" Tatsuya asked out loud, to both Alex and Nao.

"Only you can know that," Alex said, and smiled—but Tatsuya thought it was the kind of smile one gives to cover deep, unbearable pain. Alex must have loved Nao, too.

"I don't want him to leave," Tatsuya said.

"Of course you don't. Neither did I. But why not?"

"Because he's the greatest thing in my life. Because he's always there, always listens—because he has all the answers and knowledge and fun and . . ." Tatsuya snickered, then chuckled, feeling incredibly selfish. He wanted something no one else had, and because he had it now, felt entitled to keep it.

"He changed your life, right?"

Tatsuya nodded. He knew where Alex was leading. Nao stood in the background, his face in shadow beneath the brim of his hat. "I should let someone else share him, too," Tatsuya said meekly. His vision blurred, and he sniffed hot pre-tears away, maintaining his composure.

"It's not an easy thing to do," Alex said.

"No," Tatsuya said. He didn't want to give Nao up. Besides, wouldn't it be wrong to inflict Nao's inevitable pain of departure on someone new?

"Is five years better than none?" Nao asked.

Tatsuya needed time to unravel the knot of emotions arguing inside him, and he turned away from the doorstep to leave.

"Tatsuya," Alex said. Tatsuya stopped moving, but didn't look back. "I'm here to talk, whenever you like. When Nao leaves, I mean."

Tatsuya tried to thank him, but the words wouldn't pass through his constricted throat. He nodded and walked away.

* * * * *

Maplewood Park had barely changed since Tatsuya was little. He sat cross-legged in the grove of maples where he used to play, or on a nearby bench when his feet fell asleep, and watched distant children climb jungle gyms and squeal on slides and swing sets.

"Any ideas, yet?" Nao asked.

"Nope. They're all extroverted and happy. They'd all hate you."

"You hated me at first, too."

"That was different. Besides, I don't want to curse another innocent kid with you." He paused. "Can't you just stay with me, Nao? Maybe I can survive. I'm more scared of you leaving than of dying."

"I'm a gift," Nao said. "Not a curse."

The golden hour before sunset approached, casting long shadows across the open grassy fields of the park. Tatsuya stood, stretched, sighed, and plodded home.

* * * * *

He came back to the park every day. Only four days remained of Nao's deadline, and every conversation now hurt like icepicks were ramming through his skull.

"You need to choose someone," Nao said. "The migraines will be fatal, soon."

Tatsuya nodded, and tried to feel enthusiastic about a goal he did not want. "Tell me about the first ones you leaped into."

"That was a long time ago," Nao said. "I didn't have many to choose from. Most people were peasants or slaves and lived lives I loathed to be a part of. So I chose noble children, at first. I lived in the palaces, which comforted me."

Listening hurt very much, but Tatsuya gave Nao his full attention. "How did it start?"

"It actually was a curse, at first. For having what my mistress called 'unnatural desires.' No mortal should thirst for knowledge as much as I did, or wield as much arcane power. So she bound me inside her daughter's mind, and exiled us into the dungeon."

"Her own daughter?" Tatsuya asked.

"It was a different culture," Nao said. "But our time in the dungeon was tolerable, and I taught her how to control the magical ether. We escaped into the forest, but her headaches didn't cease. She died not long after, in the arms of a nomadic healer."

"Will you teach me magic?"

"No," Nao said. "There are too many people alive now, and the ether is spread too thin already. When I tap it—" Nao interrupted himself with a shake of his head. "Well, never mind that." He slunk toward a dark corner of Tatsuya's mind.

"What happened next?" Tatsuya asked.

"I leaped into the healer's son. From there I leaped into a nobleman's son—I was happy to be back in the palace—and didn't leave for nearly a century."

"Why did you, then?"

"Boredom. Each life I leaped into was a new experience, and my consciousness grew exponentially. After a time, the homogeneity of royal life became mundane. I wanted new lives to experience. So I journeyed."

Tatsuya's head thumped with a pounding, burning pain, and he didn't noticed the tears that formed in the outer corners of his eyes until a small girl asked, "Are you okay?"

The girl couldn't have been more than ten, and she stood hand-in-hand with her empty-eyed mother whose blouse had been buttoned incorrectly. The woman stared blankly at the trees, craned her neck back to look up, and chuckled at the breeze.

"I'm fine," Tatsuya said.

"You don't look fine," the girl said.

"But I am."

"Okay." The girl turned away. "Over here, mom." She pulled on the woman's hand and tugged her down the path.

"Is she okay?" Tatsuya asked the girl, nodding at her mother. He wanted to return the annoying question.

"She's fine, now," the girl said. "But she was in a car wreck. It took her mind."

"I see," Tatsuya said. The girl acted more like an adult than a child. He thought he could see resentment in her eyes and cheeks, and decided she was cursed already. "What's your name?" he asked.

"Sarah," she said, hesitantly. Then, to her mother: "Come on."

"What about her?" Tatsuya asked Nao in his thoughts. She reminded Tatsuya of himself at her age, only sadder and more lonely. She would love Nao, without question. But could she give him up, at the end? Was it right for Tatsuya to inflict Nao upon her?

"She is a good choice," Nao said. "Strike her in the head to cause a bruise and mark her. I'll leap over tonight."

"Tonight?" Tatsuya pounded the bench he sat on. "But I have four days left!"

"What if you don't see her again? You don't even know where she lives."

"I'll find out." Tatsuya closed his eyes and tried to push back against the pulsing torment inside his skull. "Not yet. Not now. You're *my* curse, Nao. Not hers."

"Tatsuya." Nao said nothing more than his name, but his scolding tone made Tatsuya relent.

"I'm being selfish," Tatsuya said.

"Yes. But it's okay." Nao smiled at him. "As long as you do the right thing."

"Fine. I'll give her the opportunity to love then hate you." Before he could reconsider, Tatsuya scooped up a golf-ball sized rock from the ground. He stalked within twenty yards of Sarah and threw it at her, beaning her in the back of her head.

Sarah shrieked, spinning around to locate the source of the projectile, wearing a scowl Tatsuya had never seen on a little girl's face before. Then she sighed, took her mother's hand once more, and pulled her back toward the trees.

"He's your curse, now," Tatsuya whispered to Sarah's back.

"You did the right thing," Nao said.

Tatsuya nodded. His head still throbbed, but somehow it didn't hurt quite as bad, anymore. He wondered what kind of adventures Sarah would share with Nao, and almost smiled. "What now?" he asked.

"We have about seven hours left," Nao said. "We can do whatever you want."

* * * * *

It was after six before Tatsuya reached his favorite redwood trail, and he only managed to hike a mile into the forest before the sun threatened to set.

"How will I ever be able to come here again without thinking of you?" Tatsuya asked.

"Why would you want to?" Nao's chubby frown showed wrinkles Tatsuya had never noticed before.

"I don't want to remember you, Nao. I want to forget."

"You say that, but you'll change your mind."

Tatsuya sighed, and sat on a rock beside a ravine filled with fallen, moss-covered logs. Nao had always been right before. "Okay. I guess I'll believe you."

In his imagination, Nao ruffled his hair. Nao draped his arm around Tatsuya's shoulders and squeezed. "You're very special, Tatsuya. You're unique. You've had experiences that billions of others will never have. Be grateful for that. I love you, Tatsuya."

The salty drops that streamed from Tatsuya's eyes didn't feel like tears or sobs. They just were. Like the tension in his joints or the soreness in his muscles. Like his blurry vision and stinging nose; the taste of blood deep in his sinuses.

This was what the end felt like.

"I love you too, Nao," Tatsuya whispered.

And then there was a silence and emptiness Tatsuya hadn't known since he was eleven, and though he struggled not to, he wept.

* * * * *

Tatsuya was twenty when Sarah knocked on his apartment door. He wasn't surprised she had tracked him down, or that she'd traveled across the country to visit him. She wore blue jeans, a yellow shirt, and a bamboo hat that approximated Nao's. "Hi, Sarah," he said.

"Hi." She tapped the toe of her left foot in a circle on the ground, probably searching for courage. Tatsuya waited for her patiently. "Nao says he has to leave," she said at last.

"Do you hate him?" Tatsuya asked.

She shook her head. "No, I understand."

"You're a better person than I was, then." Tatsuya smiled, and chuckled to fend off the nostalgic sadness that tried to grip his heart as if it were new.

"What is it like?" she asked. "What was it like when he left?"

"Emptiness, at first. Then . . . . It's hard to explain, but imagine you were trapped in a box. You loved the box, and never noticed how confining it was. Then it bursts, and you find you have an entire new field to play in."

"But it's empty," Sarah said.

Tatsuya nodded, and sighed. "Yes it is. It's empty and cold and indifferent." Sarah's lower lip quivered, so Tatsuya hastily added, "But it's not all bad. He leaves residual neural pathways. Some of him is left—some of his knowledge, anyway."

Sarah blushed, and Tatsuya realized she must have had an entirely different relationship with Nao than he had had. "I don't care about that," she whispered.

"Life goes on," Tatsuya said. "That's the end of it. It's up to you to decide how to live the rest of your life."

"How can I without him?" she barked, her voice strained and hoarse. "He's all I have! I never had a father; my mum's been dead for three years. I have no family. No friends. Only Nao."

"I'm sorry. Do you wish I hadn't chosen you? You can blame me, if you like."

She didn't look at him, but smiled. "Why would I blame you for the happiest years I've had?" She shook her head. "I just wish my life hadn't peaked so soon. What will the rest be but nostalgia?"

Tatsuya shrugged, and found he couldn't disagree with her. He still couldn't spend a day without thinking of Nao. "It will be okay," he said, wishing he could make it sound more convincing. "Nao was the greatest thing in my life, too. I'm here to talk, if you need. After Nao leaves, I mean."

She nodded, and turned away. "Nao asks if you have anything to say to him," she said.

Tatsuya had thought about this often since Nao had left. Just as he had sought out Alex, he had expected Sarah to seek him out, as well. And just as he had never returned to visit Alex again—such a meeting would cause too much pain, Tatsuya was certain—he suspected Sarah would never return, either.

He strove to focus on only the good Nao had brought into his life, but these glorious memories still hung under the pain of Nao's departure.

He wanted to thank Nao and reminisce about their happiest times together. He wanted to feel Nao's comforting, imaginary embrace again. He wanted to share all he had come to understand since Nao had left, and again dream of a majestic future together.

But his time with Nao was over; had ended five years ago. It was Sarah's turn now, and part of Nao's gift was learning to deal with the torture of his departure. To learn how to withstand harsh independence and make the most of her opportunities, no matter the pain.

"Nothing," Tatsuya said after a hard swallow. Sarah nodded and her eyes frowned, but behind them, Tatsuya knew Nao was smiling.

About the author:

Dan is a systems engineer working, reading, and hiking in Silicon Valley with his boyfriend.

He maintains a blog at http://www.danhartfiction.com.

The Three Sheriffs of Churningfoss

by Robert Lee Frazier & David A. Hill

Have you ever thrilled to the great tales of yore, where men of valor pitted their strength and courage against immense evil? Have the tales of St. George, Roland, or El Cid stirred your blood? Have you sat enraptured as you were told a legend of mythic power?

Did you also know that most of them were nothing more than a wagonload of dragon tripe not worth the paper they were scrawled upon? Now don't look so surprised. Noblemen and their hired scribes have been reworking history since the beginning, particularly to make themselves look good.

How do I know? Well, I was in one of those stories. You know the one. It's practically the most famous tale to come out of our little kingdom: The Three Sheriffs of Churningfoss!

The one and the same.

It all started in the tiny shire of Ritecross, where I was the second son of the local blacksmith. Nib was my name then. Not a very heroic sound to the ear, but mine just the same. All of us had different names at the start, but the storytellers have changed them over the years to those more stirring to the blood of the audience. Nothing matters more than the audience—except for the tossed coins. There would be no tales without the appreciative masses, after all.

I wasn't a Sheriff then—only a squire. Squire to Sheriff Asper. At the time Asper was a lean and weathered middle-aged man who carried his responsibilities high on his shoulders. I had been in his service for about a year when a royal messenger appeared in our village. This messenger spoke with Asper and demanded we come at once to Castle Churningfoss, and so we did.

* * * * *

It took us three days to make the trip to Castle Churningfoss. Yes, three days. This is a story after all, and three days is the usual span for just about any journey. Upon arriving, we were taken to our quarters in a long, low building behind the castle proper, but inside the walls of the bailey. Here we were introduced to the two other Sheriffs with whom we were to be working. The first was Otto, a wily-eyed and heavily bearded fellow who was posted to the northern city of Klaptrappe, and he was glad for the reassignment. The second was the proud and handsome Sheriff Cluny. Cluny was not only Sheriff of Churningfoss city, but acted as its jailer and warden. After we had freshened up and gotten a meal into us, we were all shuffled off for an audience with the King.

We were escorted to the throne room where great painted murals adorned the walls. I'm not sure what I thought I was expecting, but this was definitely not it.

We all stood trying not to make eye contact when from one of the side doors a valet stepped in and bellowed, "His Majesty, King Nigel of Anju, Master of Castle Churningfoss, and Defender of the Faithful!"

"And a right stuffy shit," added a voice at my shoulder that nearly made me jump out of my britches. I turned to stare into the grinning face of the Court Jester. He winked at me and then, leaning in confidentially, said, "They always forget that part."

The King stepped forward, cleared his throat, and opened his mouth to let out the strangest little voice I've ever heard. It wasn't quite bird-like, more of a squeaking sound. He gave us the most outlandish mission I'd ever heard of, as well. He said the following, "I, your lord and King, have decreed that the head of the noble house of Argo is a Necromancer and a lapsed pagan from our country's beloved faith of Nigelism. I am sending you men to arrest this heretic."

The Jester was at my shoulder again. He asked, "So the fact that one of your number is diddling the princess makes no never mind?"

He pointed at the door from which the King had entered, and

standing there doe-eyed, dressed in a blue gown with a plunging neckline and a small tiara on her head was Princess Virgina. She had her shimmering eyes locked on Sheriff Cluny, who was staring off into the distance in mock contemplation.

"I'm empowering you," the King continued, "to capture, if possible, kill if necessary, this enemy of the people."

"Of course, if that cheeky bloke Cluny happens to get killed during the mission… well, let's just say we won't be crying our royal eyes out," whispered the Jester while rolling his eyes.

Two days later, each of us received a fresh horse plus Sheriff Asper's mule, aptly named Bull. Bull was laden with a huge load of provisions. Directions were given, and we sallied forth with fanfare. Four horns blew our departure from the battlements. It was all pretty exciting, and a bit frightening, I must admit.

* * * * *

We rode all day, each man telling bits of stories about himself and his previous assignments and experiences.

Spread out amongst the trees were a great many black ravens. They seemed to be watching us. When not in conversation, Asper would practice mimicking their strange calls and vocalizations, for lack of anything better to do. Evening came, and we found ourselves in a forested stretch of country. We dismounted and walked up to a small hill with a great oak on top. Asper tied Bull, the mule, to the tree, and we started to set up camp.

Otto slapped Cluny on the back, asked, "Are you going to pitch a tent on a night like this?" then scanned the darkening sky.

"I'd been wondering about my choices," Cluny answered as he eyed his pack and the camping gear Asper had handed him.

Otto smiled and said, "What say we sleep out under the stars?"

Meanwhile, Asper and I started a fire and pitched our tent as Otto and Cluny lazed around. At one point I whispered to Asper, "Shouldn't we sleep out too, Master?"

Asper, in his usual slow easy way considered my question along with the sky then said, "No boy. I don't fancy getting wet."

About an hour later, while Cluny was gathering firewood, he

stopped under a small elm tree. There, perched on a branch just above his head, was a large grey squirrel.

Cluny said, "Hello?"

The squirrel, which was busy chewing, turned around and faced him. Then, the gods as my witness, he looked Cluny in the eye and said, "Give me a piece of silver, and I'll tell you a truth."

Cluny stood mouth agape. Having never even heard of the mischievous squirrels of Bantam Wood, he was shocked to find himself spoken to by a small furry woodland creature. Just then, Otto wandered over and in his gruff voice asked, "What's distracting you, mister rich britches?"

The squirrel put his hands on his hips and said to Otto, "Bugger off hair-face, we're in the middle of a financial exchange."

Both man stared from the squirrel, to each other and back again. Cluny shrugged his shoulders and handed the squirrel a silver piece. The squirrel grabbed up the money, bit it experimentally, nodded his approval, and leaned in conspiratorially. Both men also leaned in, and the squirrel said, "What kind of idiots wander around in the woods handing silver to squirrels and talking to strange animals? You two!"

Cluny and Otto looked at each other in bewilderment. Cluny whispered, "I don't get it."

It was at that exact moment in time that three things happened all in a rush. First, it began to rain. I don't mean a few drops. I'm talking a deluge. Secondly, a band of ravenous squirrels (The one Cluny and Otto had been distracted by was obviously the lookout.) sprang up out of nowhere and invaded our camp, grabbing up bits of gear and foodstuff and running away in all directions. Lastly, realizing that Otto had become aware that he had been duped by the squirrel's little stunt, the talkative grey squirrel leaped at the Sheriff. The squirrel grabbed onto his arm and proceeded to bite hard into his hand, as Otto reached for the axe in his belt.

Comic mayhem ensued. The crackling campfire was quickly extinguished. As our camping equipment was being stolen, Asper and I ran around in a futile effort to retrieve it. Otto shook off his attacker and grabbed up his weapon. He bellowed out a great oath of vengeance and began swinging his axe at everything cute and fuzzy.

Seeing the axe-wielding madman, Cluny screamed out like a little girl and tried to jump up on a stump. However, because everything was now soaked, he lost his footing, stumbled, and landed on his ass in a large mud puddle.

To make matters worse, Otto was shouting and swinging his axe so vigorously that he spooked the horses. They broke free from their tethers and ran off into the woods. We all stopped and stared at the fleeing horses.

Asper spoke up, "This can't be good."

Off we ran in desperate pursuit of our mounts.

Four hours later we stopped. We were hungry and soaked to the bone. Being great heroes, the Sheriffs naturally fell into blaming each other and hurling ugly accusations.

When looking around I spotted a light. It wasn't much, but after I pointed it out the men feel silent.

Asper said, "Let's go and see if they will put us up for the night."

No one argued, and we all followed. We were in luck. It was the hovel of a family of poor beggars, and for a fee and the promise to hire their son as a guide, we were allowed to spend the rest of the night in front of their fire.

So there we were the next morning. We had lost our horses, most of our gear was spread across the hill, due to the ravenous squirrel troupe, and Sheriff Otto was nursing a nasty bite wound. Only our pack mule, Bull, remained. True to his name, he stubbornly endured the rain by standing still under the oak. The only one of us with any sense, really.

Our new guide, Turk, the son of the poor family who gave us shelter from the storm, told the following narrative to me.

'I smelled the four of them before ever laying eyes on the lot. The man that was to become my master reeked of sweet oils and aromatic pomander. I should have paid more attention to that singular point, but my family was starving and beggars, as they say. We cannot be too particular about the company we keep. The one to whom I wished most to become squire smelled simply of new leathers and fresh soap. Clean as a shiny new pennywhistle, inside and out. The third constable wore the earthy, musky aromas of artless Nature—and he wore them with considerable pride. The man smelled like an animal and certainly preferred their company to that of civilized folk. Therefore, after they gathered their kit and found their mule, we were off. My Ma cried and my Da patted me on the shoulder and wished me luck. I looked over that miserable pack of King's Men and shook my head. Luck was exactly what that lot needed, that and a hot bath.'

Turk was small and nimble with a good sense of direction and even a bit of cunning for one who was never educated.

* * * * *

We walked for hours the next morning. Honestly, my mind had wandered, and I wasn't paying attention when a large man dressed in the remnant of a military uniform stepped out from behind a tree. He was a brigand. The woods were rumored to be full of them.

This brigand walked out onto the road and while waving his sword around yelled, "Your money or your life!"

Our troupe came to a stop and stared. One armed man threatening five just smacked of complete desperation. We each exchanged glances and sly smiles, feeling we had the upper hand.

Sheriff Cluny stepped forward, took a sweeping bow and announced in a deep theatrical voice, "I am Sir Virago Amelio Cluny, Sheriff Warden of Castle Churningfloss and Servant of the King."

The robber stared open mouthed at Cluny, who continued, "Now, before we start swinging weapons at one another, I'd like to point out that this is a brand new doublet I am wearing, and it is of the very highest quality."

The highwayman paused in his threatening advance and took a moment to look the dandy up and down.

"So?" retorted the ruffian.

"So," replied the dandy with a hint of pique, "I'd rather not get any blood on it, if you please."

"Yours or mine?" The other considered his rusty blade.

"None at all," said the dandy, "but mine especially."

Lowering his weapon and shaking his head slowly, the ruffian answered, "You've never been robbed before, have you?"

Turk spoke up then, "Oh he's been robbed before, sir. Why just last night he was robbed and assaulted by a band of evil-talking squirrels!"

We tried hard to suppress our laughter. Now the ruffian was leaning on his blade like a walking stick and scratching his head, his brains clearly over taxed.

Otto spoke up, "Well you great stinking pile. Are you going to fight or what?"

This seemed enough to revive the brigand who picked up his sword, lifted it above his head, screamed out a terrible battle cry, and ran straight for us. A group of ravens, who had been watching from the treetops, screamed out and took flight.

No one moved. It really shouldn't surprise you, gentle reader, to learn we were not the magnificent fighting force that the story claimed.

It turned out to not really matter. Over a small hill a wagon pulled by two horses appeared, bearing down upon us as if on a mission. Just as the brigand reached the middle of the lane, three or four steps from Sheriff Cluny, the horses ran him down then came to a complete stop just a few feet farther.

We looked from the now-trampled brigand's corpse to the wagon and back again. A slim hand with many bracelets waved to us. We all stepped over the corpse and around the wagon to view the driver. Even under a cloak and wide-brimmed hat, you couldn't help but notice her beauty.

Asper cleared his throat and asked, "Greetings, strange lady. You've run over a brigand. What's your name?"

The woman scrunched up her face and said, "Brigands?

Detestable. I have many names; you may call me Abbey."

"Abbey," Sheriff Asper repeated. "The side of your cart reads, The Great Majorca."

"It is no matter. Majorca is the name I go by for my day job."

Cluny bowed and in a mock-heroic voice announced, "Dear Lady, I am Sir Virago Amelio—"

Before he could finish Abbey interrupted, "Yes, yes I know. Your master's herald announced you to me two days ago."

A collective moan of surprise went up from us all.

She sat, bridle in hand, the afternoon sun playing across her face, looking lovely. A slight smile, and she continued, "In fact I came searching for you. It was said you are going to face the necromancer in Chateau Argo." She reached her hand through a curtain behind her and rummaged around a bit. Then she pulled out a small oaken box. She looked up at us and asked, "I'm a fortune teller. Would anyone care to hear their futures?"

"A gypsy." Otto spat. "Pagan witch."

Abbey turned up an eyebrow and in a loud voice asked, "Well then, would any of you care for an amulet that will ward off the undead?" She opened the box and there inside, laid out on a bit of silk, was a collection of golden talismans.

We offered her a trifling for the set, one for each man, and she accepted. I for one, felt much better with it around my neck. With another smile, she pulled down her hat and coaxed her horse team forward. As they pulled off, she raised her voice and announced, "Farewell, Sheriffs of Churningfoss. Until we meet again."

* * * * *

I couldn't help but wish for another meeting with that lady—without the company of the Sheriffs. Those hands, so nimble and pale.... Fingers like alabaster and with nails to match. Translucent nails that neither gleamed in the light like... well, that is here nor interesting, as they say. Right. She was a toothsome wench who happened to come along in a dire moment to offer her able assistance.

"Onward, my friends," exclaimed the redoubtable Sheriff

Cluny, "to glory—and to lunch!"

He was right, that watery-bowelled poseur. By the position of the sun above our weary heads, it was just about noon, and the perfumed dandy was striding, with rare confidence, down the lane.

In the shade of a tree, I spied a sign. It had a crow sitting atop it. The sign swayed a little in the feeble breeze from the end of two short chains.

-THE GOOSE & GANDER-

I had never heard of the place and soon found out why.

"Can't have been here much longer than a season," mused Otto.

We stood atop a last rise, gazing out at the inn. The moment would have made a nice painting for the cover of some popular adventure chapbook. Cluny was halfway there already, and we were all content to let him, 'scout out the situation and not report back.'

My Lord Asper regarded Sheriff Otto with a speculative glance. The grizzled ranger met the other man's gaze with a level stare.

Otto shrugged.

Asper nodded.

Down we went.

The place looked brand-new. Bright-blue paint fairly shone from the outer planking. Three stories of shelter and refreshment for the bone-weary traveler and a wide and welcoming stable for our noble . . . uh—mule.

A bevy of scantily clad young beauties leaned, with provocative intent, over the second-floor balcony.

I did a double take. Cluny was already climbing a rose trellis to reach the girls. Otto had spit into his hands and was slicking his hair back. My own Master checked his breath surreptitiously against the inside of one cupped hand while I could but sigh quietly over my own lack of entertainment expenses.

Leaving Cluny to his fate, the rest of us went inside while our faithful beggar guide led stolid old Bull to the stables.

Fresh and clean.

These two words described the insides of this place as accurately as the outside. And so many women! A very solid-looking matronly type welcomed guests from behind the innkeeper's counter. Her name was Mug . . . or Meg, Mog—I really didn't catch it. To my shame, I was distracted from my duties by Lily, Wisteria, Holly, Daisy, Maisy, Mimsy . . . oh . . . it really made no matter.

There was the usual laughter and merry sounds of the late afternoon roister from downstairs. I could hear it all from my Master's room where I was eating a small meal, alone. The lamps lit, the gear had been unpacked, the bed checked for vermin and suspicious stains, the windows latched securely, the laundry sent out to wash, the complimentary wine and cheese sampled and approved, and the bathwater set to heat. As the day faded, the night seemed to be full of promise, particularly as my now-inebriated traveling companions gathered some cash for me to . . . entertain.

We woke the next morning, renewed and empowered! Well, at least I was. The Sheriffs had drunk themselves into stupors, and our guide Turk looked bedraggled because of sleeping in the manger to guard our equipment. Truth be known, I think Sheriff Cluny just wanted him out of his hair for the evening. If anyone other than us had gotten near Bull, he would have lived up to his name and kicked the stuffing out of them.

* * * * *

It was the third day of our journey and I honestly had no real idea where we were. We still followed the King's Highway, so I felt some relief knowing all I had to do was turn around.

For the better part of the morning, the road cut through thin forest. We came upon a stretch of raised land. Grasslands stretched out for as far as we could see. The old broken fence that marked the edge of the roadway now turned into a small stone wall. It reached no higher than my hip and was broken in places and in need of repair.

My Sheriff Asper noticed the horse first. Off to our right, it grazed as if it hadn't a care in the world.

"Well now," said Otto, "the gods are smiling on us today. We have found a mount."

He crossed the wall and started walking towards the horse, all the while making little whistles and nickering sounds.

While we stood watching, Otto crossed into a patch of taller grass and stopped suddenly. Turning back to us he yelled, "You'd better get over here and have a look."

"Why, what is it?" called Sheriff Cluny.

Otto didn't answer; he just kept looking down at something on the ground before him.

We strolled over to him, greeted first by the smell of death.

Sheriff Cluny covered his nose with a silken tissue and announced, "I think we can safely say the Herald will not be announcing us anymore today."

We moved about a mile farther, more to get away from the stench of the dead man than to make up any real distance, seeing how we were now in the lands of the necromancer, Lord Argo.

We lit a small fire then found what shelter and comfort we could. It didn't rain that night, however I know I wasn't the only man missing a bed.

* * * * *

We traveled almost all of the next day until we came to a slight rise in the ground.

We halted.

Turk raised his arm and pointed to the top of the hill. There stood the remains of a once-great house, a ruined chateau complete with crumbling tower and ramparts.

"What a dump!" Otto sneered and spat.

"Could be something—with a little work," mused Cluny with a definite air of covetousness. "Just look at the stonework in those groins."

"I'll not be lookin' at nobody's groins, ya daft effete lecher!" Otto's hand strayed to rest upon the hilt of his axe.

Asper simply stood and shook his head, trying to keep his snorts of laughter to himself. He started towards the ruins.

Sheriff Cluny spoke up, "Asper wait!" his voice rising.

Asper stopped and turned towards Cluny. "Yeah?"

Cluny didn't take his eyes off the broken entrance when he said, "Maybe we should have someone stay behind? Guard the door? Watch over Bull, that sort of thing?" Asper and Otto exchanged looks, as if to say, I told you so.

Asper looked over to me and for one fleeting moment I thought he was going to tell me to stay, and honestly, I would have, gratefully. I was so full of fear. However, slowly he turned back to Cluny and said, "Good point. Turk, stay here. If you see or hear anything, you start screaming your head off." Turning back to us, Asper said, "Now, let's go. I want to get this over with."

We all followed him into the ruins.

* * * * *

We formed into a line. Asper took the lead, followed by Otto, Cluny, and then me. We passed through the splintered and broken-down remains of the doors of the outer wall, in silence.

Upon entering the courtyard, I noticed a wagon off to our right. The Great Majorca was painted in bold letters on the side. You would think this would have been enough to raise suspicion, but all it did was provoke each man to consider the possibility that he might meet Abbey again.

Trooping forward, we mounted the stone steps up to the great house.

The Chateau was big. There were three levels, and on the left hand side a roofed tower had been attached to the building. The grey stone of the house appeared in good order, but paint was peeling and the wood trim rotted.

We paused under the raised portcullis. The large oaken front door was unlocked so Asper pushed it open. We stood staring into the house. Nothing moved. I could feel my knees knocking together, and I had to swallow hard several times to keep from shouting out.

"Asper whispered, "Onward Sheriffs. Let us be about our duty.""

All four of us tiptoed into the house. It was a wreck. It looked as if no one had been on this level in a long time. The ground floor was originally designed as a set of triple open rooms. To our left rose a tower room that at one time must have been a bedroom for a door attendant. A quick search found nothing. All the time we could hear the rise of some strange chanting off in the distance. It was enough to make your hair stand up.

We gathered at a set of stairs. One set led up to the next floor, and an identical set led down to a cellar and a closed door. We had a whispered discussion at the steps and decided to go down instead of up to the second floor. Otto was of the opinion that the basement was the most logical location for a necromancer.

We began descending the stairs. A few steps down we came to a halt as the chanting grew louder. As if it weren't scary enough, a female voice shrieked out with what sounded like an evil incantation. We heard the following:

Slain by the hand of man
Arisen by the dark of the moon
Nevermore to fall again.

Without warning, Sheriff Cluny let out a scream of fear and spun around, pushed me aside as he ran away. Asper and Otto exchanged nervous glances as we listened to Cluny's heavy boots moving across the floor above. The door opened then slammed shut.

"So much for surprise," Otto said in a conversational tone. We continued down the steps. The chanting was now more rhythmic and insistent. Asper reached for the cellar door.

Because I survived our encounter, I think this will be a good time to break off from the main narrative and tell the events that transpired outside. As told to me by our guide, Turk.

'I knew something had gone wrong. Old Cluny came running

out of that house as if he'd just robbed the place. I tried to question him, saying, "Oye, pretty boy, where's the others?"

He ignored me and tried to rush by. Old Bull, bless him, never thought much of that smelly old windbag, Cluny. He stepped into Cluny's path, forcing him to halt.

I suspected treachery, so when he didn't answer me the second time, I reared back and delivered a kick to the seat of his pants. Bull, sensing I was taking action, moved out of the way. My foot connected. Cluny flew forward and slipped in the mud. He ended up, face first, in a manure pile. He jumped up and ran off. Never to be seen again.'

Asper opened the cellar door, and we stepped in. Torches on the walls lighted the room. In the far corner, indistinct shapes were tending a fire. A caldron bubbled and hissed. As we moved forward and arranged ourselves, a female voice called out, "Right on time. Slaves, seize them."

Three cadaverous shapes moved toward us. Shambling would be a more accurate description of their pained movements. I've seen grandmothers move with more agility.

I wish I could report that each of us struck down one of the fiends, but that isn't true, regardless of what the story says. Here's what really happened. We were evenly matched, one man for one undead servant, as they lumbered towards us. The one I should have faced stumbled over something on the floor. There was a loud popping sound, and the creature's hip slipped out of joint. It wobbled then fell forward. Face down onto the stone floor, it stayed, writhing in an ineffective attempt to regain footing. It was pitiful to watch, as it tried to pull itself up onto that shattered pelvis, only to fall to the floor again.

Asper's adversary proved to have far more endurance and moved to close the distance. A simple feint and lunge from Asper's drawn sword was all that was needed. However, when he pulled his blade from the chest of his enemy it emitted a horrid stench of rot and decay.

Asper stepped away and waved his hand under his nose.

"That's enough to peel the paint off the walls. Smells like that girl Nib slept with the other night."

"Hey!" I shouted, trying to force my voice into a deep baritone.

"We wasted our money," Otto spat. "These amulets are crap!" He swung his ax with great fury, wedging the weapon into the iron collar the undead thing he faced wore around its neck. The force of the blow disconnected the rotting head and sent it sailing across the room.

A large form that had been tending the caldron now stepped forward, wearing the tattered remnants of the livery of Argo. We recognized the now-undead master himself. The ugly monster growled and slowly raised a loaded crossbow.

"Get behind me," Asper yelped, as he wrenched a large shield from the wall.

The living corpse hesitated then turned to the final form standing behind the caldron.

"Do I have to do everything myself?" Abbeys voice rang out as she stepped forward around the great caldron and into view.

"Abbey?" a collective question, tossed out from behind the shield. "You?"

She took another step and placed her hands on her hips. In the lilting voice, used days before on the road, she answered, "The one and the same."

"So you're the power behind the throne," Asper questioned in an attempt to win us some time.

"Behind!" She answered with scorn. "I'm the only power here boys."

"So, you planned all of this?"

Just like every storybook villainess, Abbey couldn't resist the chance to gloat:

"Planned right down to this very event." She waved her hand at the undead thing in front of us. "Here is the original male necromancer, now an undead thing that is teaching his foul arts to his surviving wife."

"How?" Asper asked, obviously trying to keep her talking.

"I killed him. He was trying the same curse, but a woman instead of a man slew him so the curse reanimated him as a mindless zombie instead of a powerful undead lord."

There must have been some small bit of humanity still alive because when born-again bad Lord Argo heard that, his face crinkled up in a teeth-baring sneer. He pulled the trigger on the crossbow, and the bolt shot out. It pierced the shield inches from Asper's arm.

Abbey and her undead hubby took a step forward.

Otto whispered, "Let's give them a push."

We all nodded and moved with the shield still in front of us while shrieking.

We ran right into Lord Argo, impaling him with the feathered end of the crossbow bolt and knocking Abbey to the ground. We all pulled together, and the bolt slid out of the undead lord's chest with a disgusting sucking sound.

Otto winked at me and said, "Reminds me of how that lady you slept with sounded when she kissed you, Nib."

"You too?" I asked in agitation.

Asper, looking down at the now-dead lord. He said, "Sorry about your husband. Why did you help us out on the road?"

A beautiful angelic smile beamed up at us from Abbey. "Oh, don't be sorry. You saved me the trouble. Why? So you would reach my lair. I want you—need one of you—to kill me so I can finish the necromantic curse and rise up into my power."

"No-one's that foolish," Otto shouted.

Abbey stood, and picked up a loaded crossbow from a small wooden table and took aim. "No? I think you may be wrong."

With that, she took a shot. It was high and to our right. It grazed my right shoulder and bunching up inside my fighting leathers, pulled me back, and nailed me to the wall.

Abbey, with a smug expression said, "Now, let's just see about this. If I kill two of you, the last will surely want to kill me." She dropped the spent crossbow to the ground and picked up another loaded one from the table. She laughed and said, "I can do this all day."

Before she could take up her weapon and let fly a second bolt, the house sounded as if it had come under attack. From above came the sound of shouting and hooves pounding down on the wood floor.

Otto whispered to Asper, "Cluny brought reinforcements?"

"I don't think so."

The noise grew louder. We all just stared up at the ceiling. Then something pounded down the steps. The cellar door burst open, and in charged Bull the mule, pulling Turk like a toy on a string. Bull brayed and started kicking and bucking everything in the room. Turk released the rope bridle and rolled to Asper's feet. Bull jumped around the room several times. He smashed the table of crossbows then knocked Abbey, face-down, to the ground. While she lay there, he kicked over the caldron and the hot steaming fluid ran across the floor and under her face. She lurched up while screaming in rage.

Turk lowered his hands from around his head and shouted, "Sorry boss. A pack of crows was out there pecking at him, and it drove him mad. I thought it would be safer in here."

He jumped to his feet, saw Abbey and ran after Bull who was exiting the cellar, back up the stairs. Just as he turned the corner, Turk screamed, "Sorry Lady. You still look lovely in profile!"

Abbey started shaking all over in a fit of rage. She looked at all of us with hatred and through her gritted teeth said, "I'll get you all for this. Then I'll go and kill that stump of a king, too!"

She put her fingers in her mouth and took a deep breath.

Asper said, "Just hold on a minute."

She ignored him and blew a strong whistle call. Straight away, the room filled with flying ravens, all screaming and circling. I still couldn't move, but I closed my eyes tight for fear of them being pecked out.

Abbey let out another scream of pain, and they attacked. It was over in seconds. The ravens had killed Abbey. Then like some grim black cloud, they flew off.

Asper and Otto helped me get loose. I asked, "Why did they kill her?"

Asper, in his quiet way, answered, "Because Lourdes Abbey should have paid more attention to the type of servants she employed. Ravens are known to turn against the injured of their own kind."

We dragged her body out of the cellar and loaded it onto the wagon. We hitched up Bull and gratefully rode out of the Chateau. In passing, I mentioned the painted words on the side of the wagon to our guide, Turk. He looked shocked and then laughed while shaking his head and said, "That explains it. Majorca, in the peasant dialect roughly translates - of the ravens."

We returned to Castle Churningfoss as heroes. In addition, we each received a double portion when the King found out what Sheriff Cluny had done. All in all, it wasn't a bad way to get into a legend.

About the authors:

Robert Lee Frazier lives in Hagerstown Maryland where he works hard at keeping his published author alter ego a secret. However, you can follow his authorial trials, and tribulations at www.robertleefrazier.com.

David A. Hill is a freelance writer, artist, and RPG designer. His science fantasy poetry and short fiction were published in *Scifaikuest* and *Lore* magazines. He is currently finishing a mythic fantasy novel featuring a raven and a museum curator saving the world from dragons, giants, and really big maggots.

Ruth's Choice

by Jamie Lackey

Ruth watched Mahlon's chest rise and fall and held his limp hand to her lips. He'd been a good husband to her. Always kind, always gentle. He made her smile and listened when she spoke. He'd given her hope for a happy future. But even as he slipped away, she knew that he wasn't the one she'd really miss.

His chest rose, fell, and didn't rise again.

Oprah squeezed her shoulder. Ruth's sister-in-law was already shrouded in mourning robes. Her husband, Mahlon's brother, had died a few days ago of the same wasting disease.

"Naomi will leave now, won't she?" Ruth asked.

Oprah shrugged. "Probably. She doesn't have any reason to stay."

Ruth buried her face in her husband's still chest and wept.

* * * * *

Ruth stuffed all of her dearest possessions into a bag. Oprah looked up from her mending and frowned at her. "What are you doing?"

"Packing," Ruth said. "I'm going to go with her."

"Are you crazy? We don't even know where she comes from."

"We know that it's not here," Ruth said.

"How do you know she even wants you to go?" Oprah asked.

"I don't." Ruth hesitated over the bracelet her mother had given her on her wedding day. It had been in her family for generations.

"You'll never see your parents or brothers again!" Oprah said.

Ruth shrugged and shoved the bracelet into her bag. She'd been happy to escape her father's house. She didn't think she could stand going back.

"You—you don't think she expects us to go with her?" Oprah asked, clutching her mending to her chest at the idea.

Ruth didn't. But Oprah's horror at the idea rankled. "We are members of her family. By all rights, our lives are in her hands."

"I won't go."

"Why not?" Ruth asked. "Look at her. She's healthy and beautiful and strong. My mother is years younger than Naomi, but she looks older. She's bent and broken. My father beats her, you know. Naomi would never stand for something like that."

Oprah shook her head. "How would she have stopped it? She belonged to her husband, just as we belonged to ours."

"Mahlon never made me feel like property," Ruth said.

"If our husbands had been stronger, we might still have them."

Anger surged in Ruth's belly. Her palm itched with the desire to slap Oprah across the face. "Kindness is not weakness."

Oprah shrugged. "Dead is dead."

* * * * *

They laid Mahlon to rest beside his brother and their father in the dry, rocky earth. Ruth wept as her husband vanished into the ground.

Naomi stood silently beside her through the funeral. Her cheeks were dry, but the sadness in her eyes tugged at Ruth's heart.

Naomi had come here with a husband and two healthy sons. Now they were gone. She looked lonely, standing above their graves. Ruth took Naomi's hand and twined her fingers through her mother-in-law's. She vowed that Naomi would never be alone as long as she drew breath.

Naomi squeezed her hand and managed a small smile, and Ruth's heart lifted.

* * * * *

Naomi shook Ruth awake. Her strong, smooth face was a mask in the moonlight. "It's time," she said, her accent like honey smoothing her words. "I must go."

Ruth clung to her. "Take me with you."

Naomi squeezed Ruth's shoulders. "Are you sure?"

Ruth nodded.

"You know that you'll never be able to come back?"

Ruth nodded again. "There's nothing for me here. I won't go back to my father's house. I have no desire to follow in my mother's footsteps."

Naomi hugged her. "I'm glad. I worried about you, going back there. And I would have missed you."

Ruth's stomach fluttered. Naomi hadn't refused her—she'd even welcomed her. Ruth pulled on her clothes—a traveling outfit, not her mourning robes—and grabbed her bag.

Naomi woke Oprah. She pressed a gentle kiss to her forehead. "I must go now, Daughter."

Tears glittered on Oprah's cheeks, and her voice shook, but her words were dutiful. "Shall I come with you?"

Naomi shook her head. "No. Stay, be with your family. You have my blessing."

Oprah wiped her eyes and smiled. "I wish you the best." Her eyes flicked to Ruth. "And you as well, Sister."

Ruth gripped her bag and forced a smile. She was ready to go.

Naomi led her through the outskirts of their village, then into the rocky fields. They passed by the graveyard. Ruth stumbled, and Naomi caught her elbow. "We're almost there," her mother-in-law whispered.

Naomi turned and vanished into a cave.

Ruth froze. "You're from under the earth?" she asked.

Naomi laughed. "No. But we kept our ship here." She took Ruth's hand. Her skin was warm and dry, and the touch sent a shiver along Ruth's spine. "Come on."

The cave ended a few steps in, but Naomi laid her hand on the stone and said a few words in a strange language. The rock parted. Something inside glowed gently. Naomi's face was beautiful in the strange, otherworldly light. "It's still not too late to go back," she said.

Ruth shook her head and gripped Naomi's hand. "I—I just want to be with you. Wherever you go."

Naomi's other hand brushed tears from Ruth's cheek.

Ruth seized the moment. She needed Naomi to understand. She leaned forward and kissed her. Naomi's lips were warm, and far softer than Mahlon's. She tasted like spiced wine.

Ruth pulled away and waited. Would Naomi still let her go with her? Or would she force her to stay behind?

Naomi smiled and pulled Ruth forward. "Come on. I want to show you the stars."

The ship gleamed in the faint light. It was smooth, streamlined, and silver, like a huge fish. A ramp lowered as they approached.

"This is it," Naomi said. "Your last chance to turn back."

Ruth took a deep breath, then followed Naomi inside without looking back.

About the author:

Jamie Lackey lives in Pittsburgh with her husband and their cat. Her work has appeared in *The Living Dead 2* and *Daily Science fiction,* and she has stories forthcoming from *Beneath Ceaseless Skies* and *One Buck Horror.* She reads submissions for *Clarkesworld Magazine.*

The Big Card Game

by Paul Peppers

The moon hung in a clear sky, so big and bright that I could almost reach out and touch it. Because it was bright enough to see, momma had not insisted we come home immediately. Any other time she wouldn't have minded if I stayed out a little late, but since my little brother "the brat" was with me it was a different story. It was like pulling nails to get her to say yes.

I felt my bulging pockets with satisfaction. I had totally trashed my smart aleck cousins at poker. I didn't feel a bit guilty about it either. After all, I won fair and square. Anyway, neither of them, Bill or Hank, would have passed up the chance to put my lunch money in their pockets. I offered to loan Hank some money too. I told him I would loan him enough for lunches; for a tiny amount of interest. Is it my fault that he refused? He didn't even thank me.

Maybe I'll be a professional gambler when I get out of high school, or a movie star, maybe a famous singer. I was dazzled by the endless possibilities.

"Bubby . . . ."

Like I said, my brother "the brat' was with me. He is an insufferable tag-along, but mom wouldn't let me go unless I brought him with me.

"It's important for you to spend time with your little brother," she'd said.

Yeah right! What she really meant was: It was important for her *not* to spend time with him.

"Bubby!"

"What?" I snapped.

"Cow," he said. "Moocow!"

"Quiet, squirt."

Not that I hated the little *bra*—Tyler, or anything, but I had a pretty sweet deal worked out with mom and dad before he showed up to ruin it all.

Even though it was a full moon I was still a little spooked. Maybe because it was a full moon. Ghosts, werewoves and vampires all prefer a full moon, after all. Our neighbor, old man Cooper, once told us about some dumb kid that stepped on a snake, and before they could get him to the hospital, he died. Cooper said that it was one of the drawbacks of living this far out in the country. There was another kid that tried to fish with some baby snakes. He got bit and died too.

"Stay close, squirt," I told the brat so he wouldn't get scared and start crying or anything.

There was also a write-up in the paper a while back about Bigfoot. Some people said they saw him, which was just plain dumb.

They should have known it wasn't Bigfoot, if for no other reason than the fact that *nothing* ever happens around here. Turned out it was an old hermit in a fur coat. The newspaper said the coat was Russian sable and worth a ton of money. But that's probably not true. Dad said that you can't believe everything you read in the papers. The police never did find out where the old man got the fur coat, though.

Tyler griped my hand tightly. "It's scary out here Bubby," he said in a hushed voice. My name is Bobby, but he's called me Bubby since he was able to talk.

"It's ok squirt, I'm here," I said. It was such a quiet night that every little sound seemed loud, and the poor kid's imagination was working overtime.

The pasture fence followed the dirt road, and the trees were cut back on both sides. Nothing could sneak up on us, even if it wanted to.

A cow loomed before us, startling me. It was so still that I hadn't noticed it, at first. I don't know how I missed the thing because its patches of black and white stood out plainly in the moonlight.

"Is it a bull, Bubby," Tyler asked fearfully. Maybe he had seen a bullfight on TV or something.

"It's just an old cow," I said.

"Really, Bubby?"

"Yes, it doesn't have any horns, for one thing." As I was speaking the animal turned and looked back at us. "And it also has a vagina," I said.

"Oh," Tyler said.

"You don't even know what a vagina is, do you?" I asked.

"Yes I do!"

Any other time I would have tried to teach the little brat something, but at that moment the cow walked away a few steps, stopped and looked back at us again.

The animal had huge, intelligent black eyes, and for some reason my attention was drawn to it.

"It wants us to follow it, Bubby."

"No way," I said. "That's silly."

Taking a few more steps, the cow looked back at us for some seconds then jerked its head in an unmistakable gesture.

No way, I thought.

"Yes it does!" exclaimed Tyler.

The cow looked at us with those large bovine eyes before taking a few more steps. It looked back, evidently waiting for us.

"Son of a biscuit eater," I exclaimed. "It does want us to follow."

"Let's see what it wants, Bubby."

"Hold on squirt." How could I explain to the brat that cows are not the same as people? Probably all he knew about them was that when the dial on his toy pointed to the cow it said, "M*oo*. The cow says, *mooooo.*"

The animal pinned us under its hundred-watt bovine stare for a while and winked. I mean blinked. It couldn't have winked. Duh! It's a darned cow, and it blinked.

At least it's not a werewolf or anything. "Maybe it's a were cow," I said aloud, and the last bit of tension fell away from me. I couldn't help laughing. "Sure, squirt, let's see what it wants."

The fence was of the one-wire electric type. I set Tyler on the other side then stepped over myself.

"Moo," said Tyler. "Moocow!"

The cow wasn't the least bit spooked by us, which was strange. She waited patiently as we crossed the fence to follow and then continued walking slightly ahead of us.

This is crazy. Where are we going? It was so strange that it couldn't really be happening, so I took the leap and followed. I resisted the urge to pinch myself because I was afraid it wouldn't do any good, and if I didn't wake up, what then?

"Owl!" exclaimed Tyler. "I'm telling mom."

"Oops, my bad." Well, I thought grimly. What now?

We followed for a while, during which time it seemed to me that reality had taken a night off. The cow swished its tail and looked at us, from time to time, with those big black eyes. It looked like the animal was attempting to reassure us.

"I'm sleepy, Bubby," Tyler, said.

"Me too squirt. You ready to go home?" The poor kid was dead on his feet. Scooping him up in one arm, I turned, planning to return to the road, when the cow walked to a huge oak stump and sat down next to it. It didn't lie down, it sat down. I had never seen a cow sit down before, and I walked over to look, despite myself.

A series of large stones surrounded the big stump, and the whole setup looked like nothing so much as a table and chairs. "*Whatever,*" I said. So many weird things were happening that by this point one more wasn't much of a surprise. Picking a seat across from the *mystery* cow, I dropped my weight onto it to rest for a minute. I still held Tyler. The little rat was sleeping, and he weighed a ton. It had been a long day, and it seemed like it would never end. Shoot! Momma is probably worried to death over us, I thought. We've got to get home.

I started to rise. She will be furious when—*if*—she found out that we'd trekked through the pasture at night. I starting up to leave when a raccoon climbed onto the oak stump, causing me to freeze in place, not knowing what course of action to take. Should I stay still? Should I run? I remembered hearing that you were supposed to lie down and play dead if you came on a bear, but what do you do if you meet a raccoon?

Tyler must have sensed my nervousness because he awoke long enough to mumble, "raccoon!" before going back to sleep.

I had never heard of a raccoon coming near people unless it was rabid. I was getting ready to run when the smiling raccoon—*I swear he was smiling*—held up a worn deck of playing cards in one little hand.

"Oh," I said in relief, and dropped back onto my seat. "You just want to play cards . . . ." I can't imagine why I felt relieved at this realization, but I did. The fact that the little animal had brought its own deck of playing cards was pretty scary, all by itself. Why I should have trusted a creature that was born with a built in burglar mask I can't say, but the black eyes seemed to twinkle, and the raccoon's manner was so casual and friendly that I was put at ease. With his little hands—hands that appeared incredibly human-like— the raccoon took the cards out of the box and began to adroitly shuffle them.

Anything, *I mean anything*, could have happened at this point, and I would not have been surprised. Pink rocket ships could have landed, disgorging green aliens, and it would have seemed commonplace.

Well, needless to say I learned a lot of things that night. We cut for high card for a while, until the bear and the fox arrived, then switched to black jack. The raccoon wasn't the least interested in the money I'd won from my cousins; it was of no use to them whatever. It wasn't like they could go to the store and buy anything.

I also realized during the card game that I could communicate with the raccoon and the rest of the card players. They didn't talk or use sign language. It was nothing so crude. They communicated with me through imagery. It was a method of communication that people already knew, they said, but had put aside when they developed a spoken language. It was a kind of empathy that far preceded the spoken word. After I got the hang of communication, they wanted to play some Texas hold 'em.

Something else I learned was how much the cow wanted my ball cap. The big lummox won it from me by throwing the ace of diamonds. Now I'm not a sore loser or anything, but if you have never heard a cow laugh you have been spared a terrible sound. Its hooting laughter echoed horribly across the pasture. And the bear . . . . Who would have thought a bear didn't like going *bare foot*? I soon realized that with nothing else to occupy their time, 'the crew' had learned to play poker like experts.

I would be lucky to get away with the shirt on my back, an item the fox seemed to be looking at with relish. After a while my luck kicked in. Thank god it did because if it hadn't I wouldn't have had a pair of drawers to wear home. I began to run the table.

The bear growled irritably and folded in disgust. He stomped off toward the woods in his new boots. The cow sensed my luck and peered at me knowingly from under the brim of the ball cap. She also folded. The coon looked at me through his outlaw mask, and he called the hand. My straight won the pot.

That's why I couldn't later tell the police how I learned where the body was. But, the mystery of the sable fur coat and the old hermit was finally solved. Though why the woman had died in the Georgia woods was never answered.

Epilogue

"Why are you moving the TV over there," mom asked.

"I can see the screen better with it in front of the window, mom," I told her.

"Oh," she said.

And I didn't say, *never welsh on a bet* . . . .

About the author:

Paul Peppers is a diesel mechanic working in Cartersville Georgia. He has an Associate of Applied Science Degree from Coosa Valley Technical College and is fifty-three years old. Paul's published stories include, *The Storekeepers Town* and *A Change Of Heart* at thewesternonline.com; *Southern Feelings* online at drunkmonkeys.onimpression.com; *Swimming Lessons* online at *Larks Fiction Magazine; Poppas House* at *One Bookshelf.*

VISIT THE LOCONEAL BLOG AT

www.loconeal.com

Breaking News
Forthcoming Releases
Links to Author Sites
Loconeal Events